Okey

C.A. VALENTINE

Dokey

A NOVEL

Sensei

Copyright © 2020, by Chad Anthony Valentine
All rights reserved

This is a work of fiction. Names, characters, places, and incidents either are the product of the author's imagination or are used fictitiously. Any resemblance to actual persons, living or dead, events, or locales, is entirely coincidental.

Edited by Jasmin Kirkbride

Cover design and layout by Geoffrey Bunting Graphic Design

www.cavalentine.com

For Rena, my loving wife. And for my family, without whom this book would have never been completed.

To the reader, whoever, wherever, whenever you may be. This novel is a product of several years of alternating hard work and degenerate procrastination. Long after the fire of my life has faded into nothingness, you will always be able to find me here, resting in the margins of my own creation.

Okey Dokey Sensei

CHAPTER ONE

A Review of Performance

"Your manager has a lot to say about you," Mr. Reed said.

Martin shifted uncomfortably in his chair. He kept his hands stiff at his sides and resisted the urge to wipe the beads of sweat that now lined his forehead.

"Is that right?" Martin managed with a gulp. There was a rock in his throat, and it was all he could do to keep from choking on his own words.

In front of him, Mr. Reed sifted through a file of papers that Martin couldn't quite read. He had not been allowed to know what was written on the performance review, but he knew beyond doubt that its black letters contained not a single word of praise.

"It seems you had some trouble here in your first few weeks," Mr. Reed said without looking up. "Can you tell me in your words a bit more about what happened?"

Martin nodded briefly. "It wasn't intentional. The information I had about the class was incorrect."

Mr. Reed looked up, his eyes penetrating. "Don't give me a summary, tell me exactly what happened."

Martin moved his hands into his lap and began cracking his knuckles one by one as he spoke. "The file I received about the class." *Crack*. "It didn't say anything about them using a different book to the one the other classes use." *Crack.* "I took the book and the lesson materials that the other classes were using." *Crack crack crack.* "It wasn't until I was a few minutes into the class that one of the students corrected me and told me that they were using a different book."

"Stop that," Mr. Reed said.

"Huh?"

"Your knuckles. *Stop popping them.* Your manager has a note about that here too. She writes that you crack your knuckles in every meeting and that she has to tell you to stop every time. I can see now that this is not exaggerated."

Martin balled his hands into fists, suddenly ashamed of what he was doing. "I–I'm sorry. It's just a bad habit."

"I don't care what it is. Stop." Mr. Reed leaned back in his chair and crossed his right leg over his left. "I shouldn't have to tell you by now, Martin, but that class you teach isn't part of our usual contracts. They are a private company that hires us out to come to their offices specifically to teach their employees. They pay a very high price for our services. They pay for the taxi you take there. They pay for all the classes that you could be teaching in the time that you miss during your travel to and from their office. And they expect a certain level of professionalism. No, that's incorrect. They *demand* it. Do you understand?"

"Yes, sir."

"And now I understand that they are going to be terminating their contract with us at the end of this month. Why do you think that is?"

Martin's mind dashed for an answer, but all he found were excuses. They were all he could offer, so he gave them despite his better judgment.

"But how could I have avoided this situation? No one told me that they were doing anything different to what was on the usual schedule." His voice was weak and he hunched over himself, staring at his shoelaces.

"I didn't come all the way from Tokyo to hear you rehash excuses that you gave two months ago. I was hoping to hear you just take responsibility, to acknowledge that it was due to your own lack of preparedness and good judgment that we lost an account worth almost a third of your school's combined student body. I'm disappointed."

Martin said nothing. There was nothing more to say. His whole body was tight, and he felt the walls of the room close in around him.

After a few moments, Mr. Reed leaned forward and picked up the piece of paper sitting at the top of the pile. "Well, I guess there's nothing more to be said about it." He sighed deeply. "Not from the reports I'm reading right now, anyway."

Martin looked up with confusion. "What do you mean?"

"The rest of this review from your manager is pretty outstanding, and the reports from the other teachers here seem to concur with the manager's judgment."

Martin straightened his back and unfurled his hands. "Mr. Reed?"

"That's right," Mr. Reed said. "Professionalism, four stars. Dress and appearance, four stars. Rapport with students, four stars. Rapport with staff, four stars. Attendance and punctuality, five stars. Material knowledge, three stars. These are quite high marks for an instructor who has only been with our company for two months, Martin. To be frank, I don't know how you were able to recover from such a devastating first two weeks on the job, let alone last two months."

Martin gave a faint smile of relief. *At least I'm not going to be fired. At least that.*

"There is one point of contention, though." Mr. Reed started again. "Sales and sales support are only one star. You do know that you are supposed to be *selling* to your students, not just teaching them, correct?"

"Yes, sir."

"The company can help you improve this aspect of your performance, at least. I will send you some of the materials I have on hand about how to conduct sales more efficiently. You will read them during your office hours, of course."

"Yes, sir. I will, of course, it's just, well..." Martin stammered.

"Well, what?"

"I just, I don't see the point in selling them additional materials when they already get what they need when they sign up for the classes. I just think that—"

Without warning, Mr. Reed slammed his fist down on the table, sending the documents in Martin's file flying.

"Enough of this nonsense," he shouted.

Martin froze.

"What do you think you're doing here? Making friends? Is that why you came here, Martin? To make some pals and maybe meet a nice cute girl in one of your classes? Well, let me tell you something. This is a business. The business of education. These students, they aren't your friends. Have you got that? They're customers. They're dollar signs. They're here to buy, and we're here to sell. If you have a problem with that, Martin, then I can arrange to have you replaced. Is that clear?"

Martin moved his hands together again nervously. He didn't have the right answer. He didn't have any answer. *Don't crack your knuckles. Just nod and look down. Just... nod.*

However, as his mind went one way, his body went the other, and before he could even feel what was happening, his fingers stiffened, and with one fluid movement, he cracked all the fingers on his right hand in unison with a satisfying *crunch*.

Mr. Reed winced and sucked the air through his teeth. "I strongly suggest, Mr. Stilwell, that you seriously evaluate what it is you hope to accomplish here with us in the next ten months. Now if I'm not mistaken you have a train to catch and your evening classes still to teach."

"Yes, sir."

Martin stood up slowly and gave Mr. Reed a brief bow. "Thank you, Mr. Reed," he said. "I'll try not to disappoint you."

"See that you don't." He turned his chair around in silence, and Martin took that as his cue to leave. He clutched his briefcase in his hands and, stomach heavy with regret, he hurried toward the door and turned the knob.

"You don't belong here, Martin," Mr. Reed said, his chair still facing the wall. "And you never will."

*

Kanazawa's school was large—the largest of the six in the region—but still a runt school compared to the ones in Osaka or Tokyo. Despite its overall size, it still had the same dull blue carpet and off-white walls as the school Martin taught at. The same campaign posters hung in every room; the same lobby had the same glass table. The only thing noticeably different in the whole building was the number of classrooms—everything else, from top to bottom, was uniform with the office in Toyama.

The other five teachers who had joined him for performance reviews had long gone, leaving the lobby empty, save Kanazawa's assistant manager who noisily complained as she stuffed small packets of tissues five-at-a-time into plastic bags. Martin approached the front desk and cleared his throat.

"I'll be going now," he said.

"Ahh, Martin!" She rose from the small mound of tissues at her feet. "How did it go? The others looked pretty happy before they left. Yours must have been good too!"

"I guess. There was a quite a bit of trouble, but my manager gave me some decent reviews."

"She did? *She* did?"

"Yeah, that was my reaction too," Martin said with a half-smile. He removed his hand from his pocket and checked his watch. "I'd better get going, though. I have to get back to Toyama soon."

"Martin." The assistant manager leaned forward and folded her hands on the counter. "Don't think any more about what the manager put on your review than you have to. I know it isn't my place to say, but..."

"But what?"

"Well." She fidgeted, searching for the right words. "It's just, I think she has a reason for doing what she does, you know?"

Martin shook his head. "I don't quite follow."

"Look, we all heard about your big mistake. Normally a person would be fired for losing such a big account, but..."

Martin felt suddenly uncomfortable. *Does everyone know?* He sighed.

"I'm sorry." Martin cut in. "But I really have to go. Excuse me."

"Hang in there, Martin!" the assistant manager shouted as he hurried out the door.

But Martin ignored her. He quickened his pace to a swift jog down the street towards the station.

It was a freezing January morning, and the layers he wore under his best black suit were barely enough to keep the shallow warmth of his body from escaping. Weeks of constant snow had left the landscape stark white. If it had been any other day, he would have stopped to admire the beauty of his surroundings, but right now he had a train to catch.

Kanazawa was the capital and largest city in the prefecture of Ishikawa, the middle of three prefectures that made up the Hokuriku region. To the southwest was prefecture of Fukui, and to the east was the prefecture of Toyama, where Martin had made his home. While Japan as a whole might be quite famous for its convenient public transportation, that convenience seemed to stop at the borders of Hokuriku. Trains came once an hour, and most of them were only two or three cars long. There was no proper express line, either. Just local trains that stopped at every station, no matter how insignificant.

It was this measure of inconvenience that dictated Martin's day-to-day schedule. If he chose to go somewhere, he had to know exactly what train left at what time. A missed train was a missed hour. He thought about this as he took his seat on the 11:30 A.M. local, bound for Toyama. It was a stuffy, older car: the seats were an obnoxious orange and the interior, which must once have been a crisp, clean white, had chipped and yellowed.

The seats around him filled quickly with similarly dressed men and women, but there was room for everyone, and no one was forced to stand. Martin had been fortunate that he could avoid rush hour. There were few things he disliked more than competing for space to breathe every morning on his way to work.

The loudspeaker crackled above him and the conductor announced their imminent departure. It was the voice of a middle-aged man, his words made mostly unintelligible by relentless static.

Toyama City was eight stops away from Kanazawa, and four stops away from Martin's apartment in the small town of Takaoka.

On a normal morning, it took fifteen minutes for him to walk from his home to Takaoka Station. After that, it took exactly twenty minutes for the train to reach Toyama City. Three minutes for him to climb the stairs, cross the overpass, climb down another set of stairs and walk through the tunnel to reach the turnstiles. Seven more minutes from the gate to his office down the street. All told, it took him precisely forty-five minutes to get to work, a little more in the winter when trudging through slush and ice bogged him down.

Inconvenience aside, the train was never late. It departed at exactly at 9:47 A.M. and reached Toyama at exactly 10:07 A.M. every day. The clockwork of it astounded Martin. Even now, slightly over halfway to Toyama city, he felt an air of confidence knowing that this would never change.

That's right. At least in this country I couldn't be late to a day of work if I tried. Provided I make it onto the train, that is.

As if the thought of it had cursed him, the train came screeching to a sudden halt, throwing the passengers violently forward and causing an unprepared Martin to smash his head into the metal back of the seat in front of him.

"Ladies and gentlemen," the voice from the loudspeaker crackled. "There appears to be damage to the track ahead. We are terribly sorry for the inconvenience. Please stay inside the car as we work on the problem."

Martin rubbed his hand over his forehead, feeling warm blood where his head had hit the bar. He quickly retrieved some tissue from his backpack and held it against the wound. All around him, businessmen in suits had already taken out their phones and were furiously apologizing with bowed heads. A group of middle-schoolers helped up one of their friends who had fallen, and the cabin began to buzz with conversation.

"What happened?"

"Are you OK?"

"What could have caused damage to the tracks?"

"It has to be something else. You don't think we hit someone, do you?"

Amid the flurry of questions, Martin found himself staring out the window. As if by some greater will, clouds had once again massed overhead, darkening the late morning sky. His heart sank into his stomach. He was going to be late. It was inevitable. Even if the train started up again just this minute, there was no avoiding it. There was nothing left to do but call in. He took his phone out from his coat and stared at it. It was twelve o'clock exactly.

Martin hated the idea of calling Manager. She had a name. Ueda or Owada or something of the sort, but she preferred to be called by her title— "Manager"—and nothing more. She had a first name too, supposedly, though she had never deigned to give it and Martin had never dared to ask. He had her number entered only under "M" in his contacts and slowly moved down the list of names to her entry. His finger hovered over it for a few seconds.

Maybe it would be better not to call just yet. The train could start up again any second. It could pick up speed to get there on time. *I could just run straight to the office once we get there and make up for the lost time.* Martin nodded in agreement with himself. Certain that benevolent intervention was bound to come, he slid his phone back into his coat.

But 12:00 P.M. turned into 12:01 P.M., and it seemed that without even a moment's notice 12:02 barged its way in. Martin sat perfectly still, staring at the other passengers on the train. Most of them were still on their phones, offering profuse apologies for their unexpected tardiness. Some of them pressed their faces against the windows, trying desperately to see ahead to what had caused the delay. This continued for some time, until Martin's phone started buzzing. It was 12:16 now, and the train still hadn't moved an inch. He was officially one minute late to being fifteen minutes early for work. He stared at the screen of his phone which only read the letter "M" and let it ring four times before picking up.

"Where are you?" a voice thick as sap asked. Despite the annoyance in her tone, Martin knew she was smiling. She was always smiling.

"The train stopped suddenly," he squeaked. "There seems to have been an accident, Manager."

"Why didn't you call me sooner?" she hissed. Despite her local heritage, her Japanese was rigid and unaccented. He had never heard her speak English, and was unaware if she even could.

He loosened his tie and tried to breathe normally. "I'm very sorry, I was just trying to call you right now, actually." Martin had never been a good liar. Especially on the phone. He hated phones. He hated calling people and getting called. There seemed to be something invasive about the whole ordeal, and if possible, he would avoid it like the plague.

"Why didn't you ride an earlier train? You should have expected this. What am I going to tell your first class? Do you realize how this makes you look? How it makes me look? How it makes *the company look*?"

There they were, the words Martin hated to hear above all else. *The company*. Manager spoke with the reverence one would give to a priest or to God himself when she said those words. The company was Rome and as far as Martin knew Manager was its Caesar. Everything a man did was a reflection of his company. Any shame he took reflected on the company, and any notable deeds were credited to it in some way as well. It was an inescapable part of life here.

A REVIEW OF PERFORMANCE

There were three teachers at the school who were Martin's senior. The youngest, and the one Martin got along with the most, was Chris. Chris had once gotten in trouble for unknowingly appearing in a magazine advertisement for a local bar. He had recalled to Martin the experience of being summoned to the regional headquarters in Tokyo, where he was forced to bow his head in shame to upper management and listen to their endless prattling about duty and company before sending him back to Toyama with his tail between his legs.

Now, it was Martin's turn. By being caught on this unfortunate train, he had shamed the company, and just like every other businessperson sitting around him, he found himself head bowed and spitting profuse apologies over the phone, promising that he would do his best to get the train moving again.

Pray and beg as he might, though, the train did not move. 12:20, 12:25, 12:30—the old Seiko he wore on his wrist ticked away without a care for Martin and his dilemma.

As expected, Manager called every five minutes demanding an update and giving him a fresh reminder of his incompetence. Martin's fear turned to stone around his heart and his apologies became a mechanical trigger at every split-second opening in Manager's chiding.

"You can't do anything right. Why do you even bother?" she finally said before abruptly hanging up after the third call.

Martin turned off his phone and stared back out the window. The train ran west to east parallel to the main highway that lead in and out of the city. In the distance were a mix of empty rice patties and the occasional shack, but directly across the highway was a run-down convenience store. Its parking lot was nearly empty, save for an old red Toyota pick-up parked awkwardly across two spaces.

Martin looked around for the owner of the truck, but saw no one inside the store and no one standing outside. *Has someone left it there overnight?* He rubbed his thumb against his index finger, but before he could pay it much thought, the voice of the conductor crackled over the intercom. "Thank you for riding the JR Hokuriku line. We apologize for the delay. We will be departing shortly. We are deeply sorry for any inconvenience this has caused."

Martin briefly returned his eyes to the inside of the car, where strangers had begun talking with relief at how they would finally be moving again. "Unbelievable." He heard. "How can a respectable line like this have had damage to the tracks without anyone noticing? Don't they inspect these things?" Several people nodded in agreement. Martin kept his right hand on his forehead. Another person said, "Well, there's nothing to be done about it." To which, once again, everyone nodded their heads in agreement. "It is what it is," other voices chimed in, and soon Martin found himself thinking the same.

I am where I am and there's nowhere else I can be. He wrapped his fatalism around him like a warm blanket, then closed his eyes as the train groaned back to life.

CHAPTER TWO

The Proper Apology

As Martin had expected, Manager was waiting for him on the platform as the train arrived. Her form was more than generously rotund. Rolls of fat merged with other rolls, working together in a futile attempt to burst their way out of her all too tight-fitting clothes. Martin often felt that he had much in common with the buttons on her blouse: pressured to the point of rupture—and with nowhere to go should it leave orbit except the cold hard ground. Manager was an oddity in a place where the obese were nearly as foreign as the foreigners themselves. The afternoon wind blew her jet-black hair across her face, and her brand-name heels and purse attracted jealous glances from the other commuters.

Martin hurried towards where she stood, but she turned around before he could reach her and started walking ahead of him.

"Unbelievable," she said. "Embarrassing. Aren't you embarrassed?" She huffed and shook with every step.

"I apologize. The train suddenly came to a stop and–"

"That's enough. You can't blame the train. It's your fault for not being here on time." She snorted as she quickened her pace.

"Yes, Manager, I'm sorry." Martin cowered.

"Don't you see how kind I am? I had to leave Colby in charge at the office just to come pick you up because I was so worried.

I called the train line and asked what had happened and came to meet you here, and you haven't even thanked me!"

"Thank you, Manager, I appreciate—"

"Be quiet! Don't interrupt me!" she snapped.

Martin's cheeks reddened. *There's nothing to be done about it. There's nothing to be done.* Martin accepted his lashings and got in the car. His face was ablaze with embarrassment, but he said nothing. *I am where I am and there is nowhere else I can be.*

The ride to the office passed in a short, oppressive silence. Manager parked in the front space just outside the main entrance.

"I expect that you will apologize to everyone else in the office. It's the least you can do. We'll talk about it at the meeting."

"Yes, Manager." Martin quivered.

He entered the office, removing his coat and scarf. Colby sat at the front desk and gave Martin half a smile. Martin opened his mouth to apologize, but Colby spoke first.

"We'll talk about it later. Just get in there and prep for your next class. Your students are already in there studying." Martin nodded and did as he was told. He hung his coat on the rack next to his desk in the teacher's room and pulled his chair over to the bookshelf against the back wall. The teaching materials for the lowest level classes had been placed along the top shelf, just out of his reach. He stepped up on his chair and ran his finger over each text before landing on the one he was looking for, then climbed back down and pushed his chair back to his desk. A degrading routine, but one he put up with. The classroom was the only respite he had from Manager's ire, and he savored it.

The office in which he worked had served as a school for over two decades. The whole country was dotted with such private language schools. Some of them catered to children, others to businessmen. Martin had chosen to work for a company that mainly taught adults—high-school-age and above, and worked a fixed yet unusual Tuesday to Saturday schedule. When he had first joined, Martin had thought it would be a small school without much of a student base, but he soon found it was a bustling academy with over two hundred students separated into nine different levels of English ability. And more came in every month. That was Manager's doing, of course. If nothing else, she could sell.

Martin overheard her shrill voice in the adjacent room as she talked to Colby. Martin pressed his ear against the wall. He knew that she was talking about him. He didn't want to hear that voice, and he didn't want to hear anything she had to say, but he listened all the same.

"This is just as much your fault as it is his. You should have called him this morning and told him to leave early! Aren't you the head teacher here?"

"Let me handle him, Manager, I think I can communicate to him about how he has caused you so much stress. He was wrong to do that." Colby said with the skill of a lion-tamer.

Colby always knew the right buttons to push and wires to cut. The bomb could be diffused as long as he was around. Colby had been with the company and in this office for nearly four years. The powers that be had even discussed the possibility of promoting him to Assistant Manager, but he had refused twice. It was an honor, really. In the history of the company there had not been a single foreign Manager or Assistant Manager. He would have been fantastic at the job, of that there was no doubt. But becoming the number two for Manager would mean that there was nothing he could do to escape her. His seat would be at the front desk right next to hers, his every movement watched and critiqued. There had been three Assistant Managers in the past four years, according to Colby, and none of them had lasted longer than four months.

Colby himself was tall, clean cut, and serious. His kept a lint roller in his desk and used it between every class. Today, he had worn a dark brown suit with a light blue collared shirt. Martin strained to remember the last person he'd seen wearing a brown suit (outside of a movie set in the 1970s) but not a soul came to mind. He was six years older than Martin, and though he had barely reached the age of thirty, most students mistook him for a man in his forties. Colby was also the only staff member who was presently married. Martin had seen a picture of his wife, a slender Japanese woman with shoulder-length hair dyed a chestnut brown. Her name was Yuka, and Colby often talked fondly of her. When Martin had very first arrived in Toyama, Colby had been the one to meet him and show him around.

After the hustle and bustle of moving into his new apartment, Colby took Martin out to a quiet restaurant located along the Matsu River.

"I have two jobs here," he had said with his eyes locked on Martin. "The first is to teach you how to do your job. They gave you a foundation in training back at HQ but believe me when I say that foundation isn't good enough."

Martin had looked back at him intently. "And the second?"

Colby had stirred in his chair and wrapped his hand around a fresh beer. "The second is to be your shield from Manager."

Martin had studied Colby's face. *Shield me? Why would I need a shield from her?* If only he had known.

"She is very... peculiar." Colby had chosen his words carefully. "In your classroom you have your own kingdom. And you can run it however you wish so long as you abide by the rules of the company and get through the lesson. But the school itself is *her* kingdom. And the Queen demands perfection."

As he passed Colby's desk, Martin shook his head, disappointed at the recollection of his own foolish optimism.

*

The students themselves came from all walks of life. A great number of them were young businessmen who had suddenly found themselves needing to travel abroad for their work. They were always polite and tried hard enough in class, but none of them ever put in more than was needed for a lesson and their improvement was never fantastic.

The next biggest group were high school students whose parents were determined to see them into the best universities through their English scores. Often, these students would start in their first year of high school and—for the ones that put in the effort—would find themselves in the second or third highest level classes by their final year. Of course, there were others who hated being there more than they hated being in high school itself and would do anything to avoid the work required to improve.

The group of students that Martin disliked the most, however, were the housewives. Martin had never been married. He'd never dated a woman long enough to even consider the prospect. When his mind turned to the idea, he always imagined a different face with a different personality, the latest in a series of ideals his mind had come up with. But he never imagined himself getting sick of marriage. He never imagined himself as these women were: washed up on the beaches of some middle-aged salary man's troubled life. Unloved, unwanted, and, for most of them, seemingly unsexed as well. They were a cackle of clucking hens that lived for nothing more than spending their husbands' money and complaining about said husbands' inadequacies.

The one thing Martin did partly enjoy about them, was there infinite ability to gossip about the poor, hopeless, single women around them. And above all the poorest, most helpless, and absolutely most single woman around was Manager.

"I wonder if she's seeing anyone now?" one would hum.

"No, no, impossible! At her age? Who would have her now?" another would say.

Martin could only guess at Manager's true age. He assumed that she was no older than forty. She had no visible wrinkles on her face and dressed in the manner of a younger woman.

"I heard she was engaged once. The fiancé ran out on her the day before the wedding!" a third housewife once said, to an uproar of objections and laughter.

Martin should have been happy to hear gossip about a person he disliked so much, but in his own mouth their gab tasted bitter, and he preferred to avoid the topic altogether.

*

After the last of the students had left for the day, Manager called everybody into one of the classrooms for an emergency meeting. As she was about to start, the phone in the lobby began to ring. Not one to lose time, she hurriedly shoved her clipboard into Colby's hands and told him to begin without her.

"OK then, let's get started," he said, flipping through the pages of Manager's notes. "The situation this month is tight, as usual. We were expecting to bring in seventeen new students but so far only four have showed up for interviews. We have seven students up for renewal next month and Manager requests we take extra care of them to ensure that they all renew."

"As if we don't already," Stacy cut in. "Why does she have to put it like that? You *know* that we always give all of our students good attention." She rolled her eyes and crossed her legs.

Stacy was an intimidating woman, but not in the same vein as Manager. She had been in the office for two years and was second to Colby on the food chain. She had long legs and long auburn hair with piercing green eyes that glared through a pair of black-rimmed glasses. She always wore tight-fitting skirts and tops, much to the distraction of the male student population. She was beautiful in every way that a woman could desire to be beautiful—and she knew it.

"But we have to give them *better* good attention, Stacy," Chris said. "How many students of yours renewed last month? What was that percentage? Sixty? Sixty-five? Maybe you should put those giant breasts of yours to better use and attract us some more clientele."

"Shut up, Chris," she snapped back. "I only lose students who graduate or move away. Unlike you."

"What are you talking about? I believe all of my students renewed last month, if you could check that for me!" Chris pointed at Colby.

"It's true." Colby laughed. "But then again it's easy to get one hundred percent when you only teach three students all day."

"Yeah, why don't you try working for a day in your life?" Stacy added.

Martin laughed along with the banter, but it was quickly interrupted by Manager's entrance. Their faces hardened and Colby stood up. "We were just going over the numbers for this month on renewals and new students." He handed the clipboard back to Manager with a bow of his head and took his seat.

"I expect there will be no problems then," she said, moving her eyes over her notes as she wedged herself into her desk. "Now,

I believe you all know about what happened this afternoon?" She raised her eyebrows at Martin.

"I was late for work this morning and I know it caused you all a great deal of trouble." Martin stood up. "There was an incident on the train, and I couldn't make it here on time. Fortunately, all of you were able to cover for me while I was stuck. I just want to say thanks and–"

"No," Manager said behind a smile.

"I'm sorry?" Martin tilted his head in confusion. The rest of the teachers were looking down at their desks. No one said a word.

"You're wrong. Try again." Manager folded her hands together.

"But I just apologized, Manager, I don't know what else I should say."

"You lied."

Martin let out a shocked gasp. "Uh…" He fumbled for words but couldn't find anything to say.

Manager's smile grew and she stood up and walked to the front of the room. "It is the responsibility of all employees to get to work on time. Chris, why was Martin late?"

Chris looked at Martin with apologetic eyes and answered, "He was late because he was inconsiderate. He didn't take the proper time to look at the train information when he woke up this morning. He did this because he is selfish and was not thinking of the rest of us."

"Like you," she added, turning her nose to Chris.

"Like me," Chris agreed. Words were coming out of his mouth, but Martin could see in his eyes that Chris was no longer there. Stacy looked at Colby, and Colby began to stand.

"Don't get up. If you had done your job properly then we wouldn't be here having this conversation, would we, Colby."

"Right, Manager."

"Well, I guess I could contact the head office about this incident." Manager moved towards Martin. "Or we can make sure this never happens again. But how can we make sure of this? Martin, what do you think?"

His mind raced for the right answer. The answer she wanted to hear. But once again all that came out were excuses. "I'm sorry Manager but there's really no controlling something like this. I'm sure you understand," Martin said desperately.

"I'm afraid I don't. Colby, in your four years have I ever been late for work?"

"No, Manager."

She reached in her pocket and pulled out a key attached to a short, green lanyard. "This is the key to our building, Martin. You will open at nine every morning from now on."

"But Manager, the trains!" Chris protested. "You can't expect him to get here that early every morning. It's unreasonable."

In a flash of anger, she spun around and pressed her face to within inches of his. "You want to help, then? I do think it's time we tested how you deal with having a younger teacher under your wing, don't you? Very well. Tuesday, Thursday, and Saturday will be Martin's responsibility. Wednesday and Friday will be yours. If either of you are ever late, if you should lose the key or if you for some reason fail to open this office at exactly nine o'clock every morning, you're *both* fired."

Neither teacher gave a response, choosing instead to submit through their silence.

"The two of you are pathetic," she said, picking up her clipboard from her desk. "This meeting is over. What do we say, now?"

"Thank you for all your hard work, Manager." The four teachers answered in unison. She nodded, then pointed at Martin, signaling him to follow. They walked down the hall and into her office behind the reception area.

She shuffled through a few documents on her desk, scanning them one by one. Martin did his best to avoid eye contact, looking from object to object in the room, waiting for her to speak first. The office itself was no larger than a walk-in closet. Manager's desk was an assortment of files, folders, and folios. On the wall behind her was a large painting done in a Western style, of what appeared to be a woman walking with her back to the viewer. The picture was black and white, apart from the woman's scarf and the umbrella that she held overhead, which were both a devilish crimson. Martin admired it for a time. The more he looked at it, the more details appeared to him. The artist had masterfully captured the reflection of the woman walking along the rain-soaked sidewalk. The trees on either side of her were sparsely leafed. The way she held her umbrella, tilted to the left, exposed the right side of her body to the rain. Her hair on that side looked visibly wet and tangled, and Martin couldn't help but wonder if that was the way she had wanted it.

After several minutes of silence, his hands instinctively began to move together. As he was about to crack his first knuckle, she glared at him.

"Don't," she ordered.

"Sorry." He put his hands back at his sides.

"I was talking to some of Colby's students today," she began, licking a finger and flipping through a new set of papers. "It's so refreshing talking to the younger students, don't you agree?"

Martin nodded.

"They can be so precious. Did you know, Martin, that they like to give nicknames to their teachers here?" She raised an eyebrow and looked up at Martin. "They call Colby 'Lion-Sensei.'

He used to have a big beard, you see. I suppose they thought it was cool."

Martin nodded again.

"Do you know what they call you, Martin?"

"No."

"Nothing. They don't call you anything, Martin."

Martin put his hands together again and pulled on his right middle finger, giving it a pop. It was his only form of reply at this point, one which the Manager seemed to ignore.

"I want you to understand that you occupy a space here somewhere between an afterthought and a mild annoyance. But I take pity on you, Martin. I'm a fair person. I want everyone under me to succeed."

There was something about the way she smiled when she talked: insincere, but confidently insincere. She may have believed every word that came out of her mouth, which made it hard for Martin to tell whether she was lying to him or lying to herself.

"Here is the key." She stretched out her hand, dropping it on the floor in front of him.

He picked it up without a complaint.

"Just remember, Martin. One slip up. Just one, and I'll have both you *and* your good friend Chris on the next train out of here."

"Thank you, Manager," he said. They were the only words left that would make their way out. He gave her a small bow and let himself out of the office. It was half past nine, and Martin could hear the faint sound of passing traffic outside.

CHAPTER THREE

If I Only Had a Thousand Yen...

For many nights after that, Martin was unable to think of anything other than returning home. The other teachers encouraged him to stay, of course.

"Don't worry about Manager," Colby said. "There are certain things you are never going to be able to control in life, and your boss is one of them. You shouldn't let her have that much power over you."

Martin felt the truth of Colby's words, but became increasingly unsure whether he could live through the incessant brow-beating for much longer.

His apartment was on the second floor of a small building that housed about twenty identical rooms to his own. The heavy front door opened onto a small entryway that in turn led into a narrow hall about ten feet long. At the end of the hall was a small alcove on the left that housed a mini-fridge and a stove-top with one burner. Martin had set a toaster-oven on top of the fridge, and above that were two cabinets full of plates, bowls, and a variety of cooking materials that Martin had never bothered to use.

Just before the kitchen, the hallway branched to the left where the bathroom and washing machine were. This part of the apartment had no heat, which made night trips to the bathroom torturous. Martin glanced over at a pile of clothes in front of the washer. He had run out of detergent three days ago and was down to his last pair of clean underwear.

After the kitchen was another door—this one lighter and made of wood—that led into the bedroom. Martin flipped on the lights and turned on the heater. The room lacked a proper bed, just a thin Japanese style futon that Martin had set in the middle of the room. There was a television that he mostly kept on for background noise against the wall on the left, and against the wall on the right was a small table and two chairs that Martin had completely covered in plastic soda bottles and empty snack bags.

The smell of the room must have been offensive, but Martin had got used to it. There was no one to cook or clean for, yet even if there had been, he was not the type of man to frown at filth. He was living the bachelor's life: he had an old Nintendo Gameboy he kept at the top of his bed for entertainment and a fridge full of nothing but snacks and ice cream. He kept almost no personal items in the room. There were no pictures on the walls. No decorations of any kind. No sports equipment or anything to show that he had any kind of hobby. The only thing in the room he used with any frequency was his laptop computer, his only lifeline to the world outside this frozen backwater.

After the run in with Manager, he developed a nightly ritual of *almost* making flight arrangements back to the States. Getting off at Takaoka Station, he stopped at the closest convenience store to purchase a ready-made dinner—fried chicken and rice was his favorite—and a beer. When he got home, he popped his sodium-rich meal into the microwave and watched as fatty meat bubbled and burst. Impatient, he pressed the stop button before the last seconds wound down and snatched it up with a thin napkin. Prize in hand, he slid through his bedroom door and took a seat against the wall under the window. There was no easy route home for Martin. The most reasonable way was to catch a flight from Toyama airport back to Tokyo and then get a direct flight back to the States, but this always seemed to be the most expensive option. The cheaper alternative had been either to fly from Toyama to Korea or China, then from there back to California. But this process involved almost forty hours of travel time and Martin was unwilling to put up with the hassle.

One night, after scarfing his fried chicken and chasing it down with a mild lager, Martin found an incredibly reasonable flight from Osaka back to California. It was everything he wanted. A good price. Conveniently timed. He could take the train to Osaka in the early morning and hop right on the flight without ever telling a soul. He could run out like a thief in the night, and pretend this experience had never happened. At home, he could start afresh. Go to grad school, hide out in academia until the recession passed. The more he thought about it, the more it seemed like the best idea he'd ever had.

Martin rolled out of bed to find his wallet. This was it, he decided in a moment of euphoria. No more Manager. No more opening the school early and getting out late. No more of this freezing country bumpkin town. Martin approached his desk and began searching for his wallet.

"I can leave!" he said out loud. "What's she going to do about it? Nothing!"

Martin began laughing hysterically as he shoved old bags with empty plastic lunch trays aside. *Where is my wallet?* Martin's hands began frantically moving under the pile of trash that had become his desk. *Wait, how would it get under all of this if I just got home?*

For the next fifteen minutes Martin tore through every nook and cranny in his room to no avail. He checked his pockets, opened his closet and frisked his suit. He went so far as to check the refrigerator, sink, and laundry machine before finally collapsing on the floor against the wall. *It's not here. It's not here. It's not here.* Martin's shirt was drenched in sweat and his breathing was labored. His mind raced through the actions he had taken in the past hour, before coming to a single conclusion. *The store!*

In a flash, Martin was up, grabbing his coat from the rack and sliding on his shoes. The night air was freezing but Martin hardly noticed. It had to be there.

The convenience store where he shopped was two blocks back towards the station. By the time he got there it was nearly midnight, and completely devoid of life. Takaoka was a town that slept early. There hadn't been a single lit window on the way down and even the store's night staff had retreated into the back room. Martin paced through each of the aisles with his eyes glued to the floor, but found only naked tiles staring back at him. *I had to have had it here. I bought dinner with it.* Empty handed, Martin walked to the counter and cleared his throat. His face was covered in sweat and his stomach felt like it was being stabbed from the inside.

"Excuse me," Martin called toward the back room.

"Yeeeees?" a sleepy voice answered. A young man suddenly shot up from behind the counter. "Do you want something?" Martin stared at the boy, taken aback by his odd demeanor. His face was blanketed in large pimples. He was nearly as short as Martin, with slicked black hair and eyes that seemed to be looking in two different directions at once. He spoke with a heavy Toyama drawl which Martin still hadn't quite acquired an ear for.

"I, uh..." Martin started. "I lost my wallet. I was just here maybe an hour ago and I thought I might have dropped it."

The boy nodded slowly, as if he was struggling to comprehend each word as it came out of Martin's mouth. "I see..." the boy whispered.

Martin stared at him waiting for him to continue. *He must have some kind of condition.* When no response came, Martin tried again. "Have you seen my wallet?"

"I have a wallet."

"Yeah... uh, but do you have *my* wallet?"

"Why would I have your wallet?" The boy suddenly cackled through crooked, yellow teeth. "You're funny!"

Martin was losing his patience. "It's a brown wallet. Leather. Has about a thousand yen inside."

"Only a thousand?"

Martin's annoyance began to grow visible. "Is there someone *else* here I can speak to?"

"No."

"No one?"

"Nope."

Martin looked down and put his hands on the counter. "Look, I just need a little help here. I'm trying to book a flight home to America, you see." Martin thought of the open webpage on his computer. Someone else could be looking at that flight right now. It could be filling up. Martin was becoming desperate. *"Please,"* he begged.

The boy's smile straightened out and he nodded. "I'll look for it. Please wait." He disappeared into the back. Martin tapped his fingers on the counter impatiently. The sound of shuffling papers punctuated by the occasional grunt was all he could hear.

After a few moments, the boy came back to the counter. "No wallet," he said flatly. "You sure it's here?"

Martin took a step back and put a hand on his forehead. He wasn't sure if he believed the kid, but he couldn't just barge into the back and look for it himself. Defeated, he thanked the youth and headed for the door, out into the dimly lit winter night. The blissful thought of escape had been swallowed whole by a dejected dullness in his heart. No wallet, no money, no credit card or ID. Nothing.

"You looking for your wallet out here?" The boy's voice came from behind him. Martin half-turned towards him. "No, no I'm not," Martin said, looking at the boy's name tag. "Shimodoi?"

"Oh, you can read!" Shimodoi smiled wryly.

"It's an unusual name."

"You're an unusual foreigner."

Martin laughed. There was nothing to do but laugh. The whole situation was absurd. His he was as lost as his wallet. There was nothing to do now but go back to his flat.

"You should check the trash. If I only had a thousand yen, the trash is the first place I'd put my wallet too."

"Thanks. Thanks a lot."

"I'll tell my boss, OK? You come tell me if you find it!" Shimodoi gave a slight bow and produced a can of beer from his pocket. "For your memory!" He laughed nasally and went back inside.

Martin turned back and started walking. He passed all the houses without lights and crossed the street without cars, through the boulevard walkway and back to his apartment next to the small rice paddy still covered in snow. The only light on the whole street came from his window. Martin ascended the stairs to the second floor and entered his room, locking the door behind him.

The heater had been left on and a gentle warmth emanated from his room down the hall. He stripped down to his underwear and T-shirt and crawled back into his bed. The clock in the corner of his laptop read 12:04 P.M. The web page was still open, and he stared at Flight 71 back to Los Angeles with wanting eyes. When he refreshed the page, a new screen popped up.

We're sorry. The flight you requested is no longer available. Please click below to find similar flights.

Martin sighed and shut off the computer. There was no escape. No money, and now no flight to book even if he had money to book it with. *It's just a bad dream. I'll wake up from it tomorrow.*

*

He awoke to thin rays of early morning sunlight penetrating his frosted glass window. It was still a full hour before his alarm was meant to ring, but despite the unfortunate events of the previous night, Martin found himself feeling strangely renewed.

"There's nothing to be done," he said aloud. He stared unmoving at his popcorn ceiling.

Then, as if remembering something long forgotten, he threw all of his weight forward and peeled off his blanket. He turned toward the corner of the room and slogged to the trash bin. He gave his eyes a second to adjust, then peered downward. There, peeking out from under a clear plastic bottle, a brown, leather wallet looked back up at him.

"If I only had a thousand yen, the trash is the first place I'd put my wallet too." He heard Shimodoi's voice in his head.

Joke's on you, Shimodoi. This whole apartment is trash.

CHAPTER FOUR

The Rooster's Call

The evening after his wallet fiasco was resolved, Martin thought he had better return to the store and let Shimodoi know. After all, Shimodoi had said that he would inform his manager, and Martin believed it only polite to tell him directly that the issue had been settled.

He rode the 9:45 P.M. train back from Toyama, arriving in Takaoka just after ten. It was a spectacularly clear evening. Stars punctuated the sky and the crescent moon shone down from directly above. Martin found himself in better spirits as he walked home. Manager had been unusually docile for the past couple of days and he had been graced the good fortune of only exchanging morning greetings and evening farewells with her. He had made plans for Friday night to go out to a small movie theater in downtown with Chris and was gleefully looking forward to it.

The lights of the convenience store where Shimodoi worked were visible from the train as it pulled into Takaoka Station. Just as before, the parking lot was empty, and the shop itself was vacant. He reached for the door handle with a gloved hand and flung it open only to be hit by a burst of freezing cold air.

"Ugh!" He covered his mouth. *Who would have the air conditioner on in the middle of winter?*

"Hello?" Martin called. "Shimodoi? Are you here?" He walked towards the counter and poked his head around the register.

All at once there was a great rustling and crashing of plastic and metal from the back room.

"Oh no!" He heard Shimodoi exclaim. "Oh no, oh no, oh no!"

Martin peered over the front desk and tried to get a view of the damage. Cans of soda had spilled out from the back room into the area behind the counter, and Martin caught a glimpse of more mess that had been made further in. Cans, jars, plastic toys and all manner of goods covered the floor so thoroughly that there was barely room to set one's feet.

"Shimodoi?" Martin called again. But this time a head popped through the doorway.

"Ten Yen!" He smiled. "What are you doing here?"

Martin glared back at him. "It wasn't ten yen. It was a thousand yen. And look–" he reached into his pocket and produced the wallet in question "–here it is!"

"Oh, great! You found it! Uh, sorry but we have a minimum purchase limit at this store. Two-thousand yen, you know." Shimodoi pulled off his glasses and stuck an intrusive finger in his nose.

"How can you have a minimum purchase at a convenience store? That's not convenient," Martin said.

"It's for the courtesy of letting an ugly foreigner like you shop here." Shimodoi burst into his nasal laughter so fiercely that fresh green snot flew from his nose.

"You're disgusting"

"Hey! I have a girlfriend! She's way cuter than anything you ever get in your life!" Shimodoi stood erect with such a serious face it made Martin laugh out loud.

"Why is it so cold in here, Shimodoi?" Martin asked, realizing his nose had gone numb.

"Ah," Shimodoi started, bending over to pick up the cans on the floor. "Well, I guess I could tell you, but you have to keep a secret!"

Martin's curiosity piqued. "I promise."

"There's a chicken in the vents."

"Blow off, Shimodoi."

"Hey! Watch your mouth! You kiss your mother with that mouth?" Shimodoi's face reddened. "It's true, why don't you go on the ladder and see for yourself! Look, it even attacked me!" He rolled up a sleeve, showing a long scratch that went down his forearm.

"Damn, it really got you good, huh." Martin admired Shimodoi's battle wound for a moment before returning to the problem at hand. "How did a chicken get in the vents? How did a chicken even get into the store? Are you sure it's a chicken? Have you ever seen a chicken?"

"Of course I've seen a chicken! I just saw one up there! You don't believe me? You climb on that ladder and look!"

Without taking even one moment to think, Martin opened the panel in the counter and crossed into the back.

"Help, help! A foreigner is robbing me! Cowboy has a gun!" Shimodoi stuck his hands up in the air and dropped the cans he was carrying all over the floor.

"You're an idiot." Martin said, sliding his feet through the debris. "So, if there's a chicken up there, why did you turn up the AC?"

"Don't you know? Chickens hate the cold. They always stay in warm places."

Martin had no idea whether that was true or not, but he decided to go along with it. He stepped onto the ladder and began to climb. There was a small vent in the ceiling that was hanging open. Frigid air blew from it straight into Martin's face. "Jesus. Shimodoi turn this thing off. It's freezing."

Shimodoi slid towards the opposite wall and pressed the power button, and Martin felt the icy ventilation slowly subside. "Thanks," he said.

He took his final step up the ladder and, sticking his head through the opening, he peered down the dark shaft.

Sure enough, not three feet in front of his eyes, there it stood. But it was not some fat white-feathered farm chicken, as Martin had expected to find. Before him stood the most brilliant black-feathered rooster he had ever seen. A long, crimson wattle hung from its neck and an equally impressive comb stood like a great crown atop its head. It stared ferociously at Martin with beady, unmoving eyes.

"Do you see it?" Shimodoi's voice came from below.

Martin hesitated. He suddenly remembered the long scratch on Shimodoi's arm and, not wanting to provoke the rooster, slowly backed his head down through the hole and turned towards Shimodoi.

"It's about three feet down the vent," Martin whispered. "Maybe you can use a broom or something to scare it into running out. Maybe it'll run outside." Martin gestured towards the broom in the corner.

Shimodoi slid through the cans and retrieved the broom. "OK! I'll scare the chicken!" he said enthusiastically.

"Wait, wait hold on, let me make sure it's still in the same place." Martin turned and pushed his head back through the opening, but before he had a chance to react, there it was. Not two inches from his face. It stood firm, beak pressed against Martin's numb nose. Its sable, beady eyes locked on him. There was no escaping it. The rooster was either going to poke Martin's eyes out or scratch his face until he fell from the ladder onto the bed of cans underneath him.

But all the thoughts he had of the pain he was about to suffer were interrupted by the sudden banging of wood against the thin metal of the vents.

"Chicken! Chicken!" Shimodoi yelled as he thrust the broom upward.

Martin tried to lower himself, but the rooster let out a mighty caw that made his body shudder so violently his grip failed, and he began to fall. He let out a pained cry, but before any sense of panic could overtake him, he felt a sharp pain in the back of his head, followed by nothingness.

※

She can't leave. A whisper intruded his unconscious mind. Martin's body was numb. He opened his eyes and saw a different world before him. An endless field of untamed grass. Trees swaying in the distance, and in front of him, the mouth of a large cave.

You have to take it off. She can't leave, the whisper said again.

"Who can't leave?" he asked.

She doesn't belong here, another voice whispered. *She can't leave.*

"Hello?" he called, but the whispers grew in number, repeating the same three lines until it was all he could hear.

She can't leave. She doesn't belong here. You have to take it off.

"You have to take it off!" Martin yelled—but now, Shimodoi was kneeling by his side holding a hot towel to his head.

"I'm not taking off anything for you, you pervert!" Shimodoi removed the towel from Martin's face. "That chicken got you good! Just like me!" he said proudly.

Martin groaned. "What happened? Where'd it go?"

"The chicken? It ran out the back door. Jumped right out of the vent onto your ugly face and gave you something to remember him by."

Shimodoi stood and grabbed Martin by the hand, helping him to his feet.

"Well, at least it's out of here." Martin winced.

Shimodoi took Martin by the arm and helped him to the sink so he could wash his face. "Here." He motioned towards a pile of bandages sitting on a table next to the sink.

Martin looked up in the mirror and stared into the long cut along the side of his right eye. "Thanks," he said. "But man, how am I ever going to explain this one to my boss?" He thought of Manager staring down at him and the gash on his face, demanding an explanation.

"Just tell him that you cut yourself shaving!" Shimodoi offered.

"It's a her. And who the hell shaves along the outside of their eyes?"

"Hairy foreigners like you."

Martin couldn't help but laugh despite the pain. It certainly was more believable than being mauled by a rooster in the ventilation system of a convenience store. Martin brushed himself off and turned to the mess of cans that had broken his fall to the floor.

"Need a hand with these?" he asked.

Shimodoi looked around and shrugged. "If you want. No one else comes here after eight at night except for you."

Martin nodded. "I've got nothing better to do." he said, picking up the broom Shimodoi had used.

They spent the better part of an hour cleaning. Shimodoi was a foul-mouthed pimply-faced teenager, but he had the gift of gab.

Before he knew it, Martin had made his first real friend outside of work in Takaoka.

"Do you have a nickname?" Martin asked as he swept the floor.

"Everyone just calls me Shimodoi," he said.

"All right then, Shimodoi it is. And I'm—"

"You're Ten Yen, I already know that," Shimodoi interrupted.

"I'm Martin."

"Martin Ten Yen."

"It was a thousand yen."

"Who wants to take the time to say Martin Thousand Yen? Ten Yen's better. Ten Yen's useful." Shimodoi nodded enthusiastically.

"Isn't a thousand yen more useful than ten yen?"

"You ever try to put thousand yen in a vending machine? It eats it right up! Gobble gobble gobble, like your chicken!" Shimodoi's voice burst out in clucks and cock-a-doodle-doo's, imitating the call of their recent visitor.

"That's true. But who cares if the machine eats your ten yen coin? There's fifty more hanging around in my pocket weighing half a ton. Everyone would care if they lost the thousand yen note," Martin said as he set the broom aside.

"You lost, Ten Yen?"

Martin thought on the question, recalling the plane ticket he had failed to book. "I guess not. I am where I am and there's nowhere else I can be."

"What the hell does that mean?" Shimodoi asked, looking up at Martin.

"In a word, I guess it means that people can't be lost. You arrive at the culmination of all of your decisions and... well, there you are."

"Hm..." Shimodoi turned back towards the front desk and nodded several times. From behind the counter, Martin looked down each aisle at the array of snacks and sweets. The back wall was lined with beer and other sodas. He eyed a Budweiser behind the glass and started to think of home again.

"You want a drink?" Shimodoi asked, reading his mind. "Go ahead, grab something, might as well have it on the house for helping me clean up. Get me one too."

"Aren't you a little young for drinking?"

"Aren't you a little old to be hanging around vulnerable teenage boys?" Shimodoi retaliated.

Martin retrieved two cans out of the back and popped them open.

"Cheers," they said, taking seats on the counter-top.

Martin inhaled a gulp from the can and let out a deep exhale. American beers weren't commonly sold in restaurants or bars around here. Most places just had Asahi and Kirin, both fine beers in Martin's opinion, but they lacked that familiar bland smoothness that American lagers had.

He took a moment to look back at the room they had just cleaned. A small urge began to come over him to clean his own living space, but he quickly dismissed it. *I'll clean it tomorrow.*

He and Shimodoi spent the next few minutes in silence drinking their beers and clearing their throats occasionally to fill the void of conversation. Martin looked around at the dairy products. Milks lined the bottom of the wall, with a variety of cheeses above that. Next to the cheeses was a large empty space, followed by a selection of frozen goods.

"What goes over there?" Martin said, finally breaking the silence and pointing to the empty shelves.

"Eggs." Shimodoi pushed his glasses back on his nose. "New shipment comes in at 4:00 A.M. They're usually gone within a few hours, though. Selling like crazy. You'd think the whole world had just stopped farming eggs the way those things go."

As if by Pavlovian reflex, Martin suddenly developed an unquenching hunger for eggs. Scrambled, fried, boiled—anything would be fine. He hadn't been cooking since he had moved here, and the only eggs he'd consumed at all were the ones included from time to time in the pre-packaged lunches he bought from the store.

Then, immediately becoming aware of the time, Martin slid his hand out from his pocket and looked at his watch. It was 1:30 A.M. "I have to get home. I've got work in the morning," Martin said, swallowing the last of his beer.

Shimodoi looked at the clock on the wall and let out a long yawn.

"Be careful, Ten Yen," he said, looking down at the laces of his shoes. "Chicken's smarter than you think, might be waiting outside for you in the parking lot."

"I hope it's not planning to mug me, then. I only have ten yen to give it and it might not be satisfied."

"You're right, chicken don't want penniless ugly foreigner. He come back when you worth his time," Shimodoi said.

"Thanks again for the beer." Martin reached his hand over and slapped Shimodoi's shoulder.

There were no roosters waiting for him outside in the parking lot, nor along the sidewalk on his way back home. The night was quiet, and the windows of the houses were dim. As he approached his own apartment door, he heard the sound of an engine starting, and watched as a red Toyota truck pulled out from his parking lot and drove back the way Martin had come.

CHAPTER FIVE

Trial and Error

It was just as he thought the next day. One look at Martin's face was all it took to send Manager into a rampage.

"What did you do? What happened to you? Why do you look like that? Did you go to the hospital? You can't do your job in this state! You can't do anything!"

Martin stood and took what was coming to him with a hitherto undiscovered grace.

"I'm sorry, Manager, it was my fault." Martin squeezed out an apology between Manager's incessant tirade.

"You stupid, filthy–" Manager stopped, staring down at Martin.

"I was careless shaving this morning. It's my fault for not coming to work with the proper appearance. It disrespects you and the company, and it is the fault of my own stupidity."

Manager nodded her head in agreement. It was the first time Martin had appeased her, and he felt a swelling of pride in his chest despite the humiliation. A greater pride came when he realized he had successfully lied through his teeth to her without even breaking a sweat. Colby stood at his side in equal awe at the fact he had stopped Manager in her tracks.

"Yes, yes." Manager's mood was changing, and Martin saw his opportunity to finish the job.

He turned to Colby, head bowed. "And I'm sorry to you as well, Colby. I have disrespected you and the other teachers by showing up in such a sorry state."

Colby was speechless.

Manager's smile returned to her face. "I'm glad you can admit these things about yourself, Martin. There, doesn't it feel so much better to just say the truth out loud?" Her voice had become poisonously jovial. "Get ready for your classes, now, and remember to apologize to your students for your appearance."

"Yes, ma'am." With a bow, Martin backed out of the room and let out a great sigh of relief. He had found his method of survival.

Martin did exactly as Manager had instructed and properly apologized to every student he taught that day. At three o'clock he found himself sharing a lunch hour with Chris, and they decided to head down the street to a small Indian curry shop.

"I heard what you did," Chris said as soon as they had closed the office door behind them. "Talk about bending over and taking the big one with a smile on your face the whole time. Don't tell me you're starting to like it."

Chris had always been the most approachable of the staff at his office. An old-fashioned man's man type. He was often seen in the lobby talking to the students of other teachers, and on many occasions even planned outings with the older students—usually to local bars or clubs. Martin often wondered what life would have been like here for Chris had it not been for Manager. He was ruggedly handsome, popular, and charismatic. He had his rough edges, of course, but Martin admired him.

But today there was a heavy weight around his shoulders and the whole office could see it. Even as they walked down the street, he kept his head down and his pace slow.

"Did she get to you today?" Martin asked.

"Nah... I mean, when *doesn't* she get to me, know what I mean?" Chris reached up and tightened his scarf around his neck. "You ever just wonder what it'd be like if we'd been placed in any other school? Hell. You hear about those Kanazawa teachers? They've got that brand new Manager. I saw her at the regional meeting over there last month. I went to lunch with the whole staff and it was all smiles and jokes."

Martin stayed silent. He knew about the other schools and other Managers. On some level, he understood that for every school with a better Manager there was probably another school with a Manager just as bad if not worse than their own. He could say nothing of the sort to Chris, however, so he kept his silence and continued listening.

"I tell you, Martin, I don't even know what I'm doing here sometimes. Maybe I should just put in for a transfer."

"They'll never let you go and you know it," Martin countered, alarmed at the prospect of change.

Chris's foot found a rock on the sidewalk and he kicked it furiously down the way. "You want to know something else?" Chris said with half a grin. "They're sending us a new AM."

"AM?"

"Assistant Manager, my friend. Second one since I got here. Probably fifth since that old coot Colby has been here. If you think you've seen some shit now, just wait until you see the hell she gives the new girl."

"How do you know it's a girl?"

"It's *always* a girl. I only heard this, but apparently the Manager won't take a man for an AM. The big-wigs offered it to Colby, of course, but I think they knew he'd refuse. Anyway, they tried to send her one once and apparently she went down there personally and started a shit-storm right in front of her AM-to-be that was so bad he walked right out of the office and they never heard from him again."

"Jesus Christ."

"Jesus isn't saving anyone from that bitch." Chris laughed. "I should just say that to her face one day. *Bitch*."

"Just let it go," Martin said. He skipped over a crack in the sidewalk as they approached the door and opened it for a group of customers on their way out. Everyone in his life he had ever met until this point had always had a boss to complain about. *I should spit in her face. I should cut his brakes so he dies in a car accident. I should punch them right in the stomach.* They all had ideas of what they *should* do, but never once had he known someone to do it. It was all just blowing off steam and Martin knew it. But when Chris spoke there was a seriousness in his voice that unnerved him.

One morning he would wake up and open the newspaper and there it would be. A giant headline reading, *Local woman dies mysteriously in car crash*, and a picture of Manager stretching across the front page. He would read about police investigations and interviews all the while going to work every day and seeing a smiling, laughing Chris. And no one would ever be the wiser.

"A woman like that has got to have a bunch of enemies, you know," Martin said, snapping back to reality. "She probably knows that everyone hates her. Come on, even the students complain about her and they only have to deal with her when they need to renew their contracts."

Chris smiled. "Guess so. Yeah. You're right."

"Just know that everyone's on your side whenever she's on a tirade. No one agrees with anything she says." Martin tried to act cheerful.

Little by little as they ate and drank, the life seemed to come back to Chris's face. Martin tried to swing the topic off of work and onto other things. Girls, vacation, the Japanese National soccer team. The busty waitress who worked at the French bakery two doors down. Before he knew it, Chris's anger had gone out like the tides and his normal joviality returned.

"You got a girl?" Chris asked suddenly, his mouth busy chewing on a piece of bread.

"Sure do. Met her back in California. Not much of a looker but she's been following me around ever since."

Chris nodded slowly and let out a soft "uh-huh" like grunt. "So, her name Handrea?"

"Yep. Met her on Palm Sunday." Martin lowered his head in pitiable regret. Chris half choked on his bread with laughter.

In fact, Martin had never been in what a normal person might call a requited relationship. In high school he had been the object of affection for a rather awkwardly tall girl one grade above him. They shared the same Math class and had often made small talk in the hall before the teacher arrived. Martin was completely oblivious to her advances. He always greeted her with a smile and laughed at her jokes because he sincerely thought them funny, but it seemed she had taken that as a sign that he was interested.

He stirred in his seat, remembering the day that she had asked him out.

"Maybe we could go bowling this weekend. You know, if you wanted. You could bring a friend if you wanted." She let out a faint giggle to mask her shyness. Martin had actually loved bowling and had agreed to it instantly without even considering the possibility that he was being asked on a date. It wasn't until he had told his older brother later that day that he learned the truth.

"So, you're going on a date then," his brother had said with a snort. "Ha. You going to take her out to dinner too? Maybe get a little something-something in the car? You better clean those seats afterwards. I have to use that car too."

"It's not a date!" Martin insisted. He had never been so sure of himself as he was about this. "She just asked me to go bowling, no one goes bowling on a date!"

But as the words left his mouth it slowly began to dawn on him. The blushing, the giggling. The complete and utter joy that she expressed when he agreed.

"Oh God..." Martin sunk into his chair his realization having come full circle.

"Ha ha!" His brother laughed. "And you were too stupid to even notice! You're hopeless, man!"

When that Saturday finally came, Martin drove himself to the gym in his jeans and T-shirt. He turned off his old flip phone, then got on the treadmill and ran. He ran and ran until his clothes were completely soaked through with sweat and his legs started to shake, unable to bear the strain of anymore steps.

He turned his phone back on a few hours later to see seven missed calls and a plethora of text messages, which he summarily deleted without reading. He and the girl never spoke to each other again, much to Martin's relief. He had successfully stood a girl up, a fact that had weighed on him as the years went by. He sometimes thought of her on days when he had too much time and too little to do with himself. Despite her awkwardness, she'd had a pretty face and a sincerity about her that many other girls lacked. Her sense of humor was great, and her jokes were always just uncomfortable enough to be funny.

There was a pang of regret when Martin thought of this now with Chris, but he swallowed it down and pushed it out of his mind.

"There's something else I've got to ask you," Chris said, leaning back in his chair. "What really happened to your face? Only an idiot would actually cut himself shaving next to his own eye."

"Believe me the real story is just as unbelievable." Martin frowned. He thought of the rooster and the dreamlike cave. The wind in the tall grass and the trees in the distance.

"Well?" Chris said after a moment too long of silence.

Martin took a deep breath. "OK, OK," he said. "But don't laugh."

He told Chris about the store clerk, Shimodoi, and about the rooster in the vent that had successfully outwitted and out-scratched them both. Finally, he told him about falling off the ladder and hitting his head on the floor. Chris sat silently, absorbing each word without interrupting and nodding slowly.

"Pretty crazy, huh?" Martin said.

Chris put a hand on his glass of water, his index finger slowly traced the rim. "Crazy, but not unreasonable, I suppose," he said thoughtfully. "You know, I've heard that there's been all sorts of trouble around here recently about the egg business."

Martin's ears perked up, remembering his conversation with Shimodoi the night before. "Yeah, the store clerk I was with mentioned something about that too. He said that there was a shortage of eggs, that they had been selling like hotcakes."

"Right, right!" Chris agreed. "But what could cause all this trouble? Chickens don't just stop laying eggs, do they? What, did they suddenly become sterile?"

"Maybe they're *eggs*-hausted," Martin mused.

"Maybe they're not getting enough *eggs*-ercise," Chris fired back.

"Maybe they're b-*egg*-ing for attention."

"That one was lame."

"Really? I thought it was *egg*-cellent!"

The two men let out hearty laughs and stood up.

"This one's on me," Chris said as they walked towards the register.

Outside the sun had come clear through the clouds, and they walked back to the office with smiles on their faces.

CHAPTER SIX

Stories of Gods

The weeks passed by with some semblance of stability after that day. Manager, seemingly pleased with her part in Martin's new view on life, became rather subdued and even agreeable on some days. The frigid February weather gave way to a slow but steady March thaw, much to Martin's relief. He'd had his fill of white fields and frozen roads and was ready for a change.

On the second Friday of the month, Colby invited the other teachers over to his house for a dinner party with him and his wife. Chris declined due to some previous engagement, but Martin agreed to join with some enthusiasm, as did Stacy.

It turned out, Colby was the only one of them who lived in a proper house—it had been a gift from his wife's parents on their wedding day, and it was incredible: three blocks from a small station on Toyama's light rail loop-line stood their castle of a home. A tall wall of bricks surrounded the property with a large metal gate that jealously guarded a wide-open yard. The house itself was two stories tall with light blue paint covering the walls and bright light flooding through a bay window. Martin was immediately envious.

"You going to stand out here all night?" Stacy said, turning back towards Martin. In her hand she held a floral-pattern umbrella that matched an equally flowery bag which she kept at her side. She wore a long white coat and long white jeans that hugged her curves and accentuated all of her seductive features. As much as Martin had felt like a stranger in this country, he knew that Stacy must feel far more outcast than Martin ever did. She stood several inches taller than even the tallest of their male students. Her skin was a pale white that other girls frequently fawned over and commented on. Whenever the school put out its monthly advertisements, she was always on the front cover with a brilliant smile and just the faintest hint of her large cleavage.

Yet, despite all these features, most members of the opposite sex were terrified to approach her. She walked with an air of aristocracy, and her outward confidence was in fact all-too masculine for the regular Japanese male. Martin hadn't spent much time with her out of the office, but he could see why other men shied away from her.

"It's quite a home," Martin said, coming to Stacy's side.

"Better than the holes we live in by far, huh?" Stacy replied as she ascended the front steps, tapping the end of her umbrella on the concrete.

Martin gave the door a timid knock. From inside, he heard a woman's voice calling out followed by a pitter-patter of footsteps and the twisting of the locks. After a moment the door swung open, revealing a red-faced Colby wearing a pink apron, a spatula gripped tightly in his hand.

"Come in, come in," he said, standing to the side to let his new guests pass. Martin went in after Stacy and began to take off his shoes before inspecting his surroundings. The entry gave way to a long hallway that stretched into a darkened room. A sliding door opened on his left revealing a spacious living room that came alive with the clattering of pots and pans and the smell of breads, meats, sauces and spices. The aroma filled Martin's nose, setting off a deep rumble in his stomach.

In the kitchen, Colby's wife toiled ceaselessly in front of the stove, raising her head as her guests came in through the door. She smiled warmly and invited them to sit down at the table. It was the first time Martin had seen her in person. She stood at around the same height as him. Her hair was done in a bob that had been died a shade of brown he could only describe as rust-like. She had small, brown eyes and a wide face dotted by a stout nose. Her neck was too long and her legs were too short, but she had an inviting warmth around her that Martin immediately appreciated.

"Pour them some wine!" she insisted, scrunching her face at Colby.

"Yes, dear." Colby complied. "We've got a nice wine here for you to try, actually. Stacy, I know how much you'll like it. How about you Martin? Care for a glass?"

"I've never really drank much wine," he confessed.

"Hm. Well this one isn't full bodied, so it should be all right. It's from Argentina, actually. It's called Tilia," Colby said, expertly pouring the bottle's dark red contents into Martin's glass. "Give it a try."

"Not yet!" Mrs. Colby's voice rang out from behind the stove. "We have to have a proper toast!"

"Yes, dear." Colby complied again.

Mrs. Colby came out from behind the counter and introduced herself to Martin.

"I'm Yuka!" she said, thrusting her hand out to greet Martin. "Nice to meet you!"

Martin returned her smile and introduced himself briefly. "You have a beautiful house," he added, looking around the room.

The living room walls were lined with bookshelves whose contents were full of decorations, pictures, and an assortment of other items—none of which were actual books. Atop the center bookshelf along the wall stood a cross of gold with two copies of the Bible surrounding it. One in English and one in Japanese.

"I didn't know you were a Christian," Martin said, extending a finger to the pair of Bibles on the wall. "I didn't even know there were any churches up here."

"I am, and there are," Colby said. "It's actually not so hard to find Catholic churches around these parts. The parishioners are mostly Brazilian or Russian, though. Not many Japanese. In fact, most of the time mass is held in Portuguese."

"You understand Portuguese?" Martin inquired.

"Not a word," Colby said. "But the word of God can be understood without using the language of man."

Colby's wife took her seat next to her husband and they joined hands. "We like to pray before meals, if that's all right with you," she said, extending her other hand across the table to join with Stacy's. Martin himself joined hands with Stacy and Colby, and they lowered their heads. "Go ahead, dear," Yuka said, giving Colby a nudge.

"Bless, O Lord, this food we are about to eat; and we pray to You, O God, that it may be good for our body and soul; and if there be any poor creature hungry or thirsty walking along the road, send them into us that we can share the food with them, just as You share your gifts with all of us. Amen."

"Amen," the rest of them said in unison.

"Try the wine," Yuka said, her own glass already in hand. Martin raised his cup to his nose. It had a light, fruity scent that he found quite pleasant. With a tilt of his wrist he gulped and let the flavor rush through his mouth and down his throat. It was delicious.

"I've never tasted such a nice wine," Martin said happily. "It's almost like drinking juice!"

"Don't drink too much," Stacy cautioned. "I'm not carrying your flubbery butt back to the station."

Martin ate ravenously. Before anyone else was even half way through their own meals he collected another round of stir-fried vegetables and meat for himself and began scarfing.

"This chicken is amazing," he said with a mouth half-full.

"It better be. The price was through the roof. What was it, dear? Seven hundred yen?"

"Seven hundred and fifty," Yuka answered. "And if you think that's expensive try getting eggs these days. It's almost a thousand yen for a half-dozen!"

Martin thought of the empty rack where the eggs should have sat in Shimodoi's shop. *I wonder if it's still empty.* He refreshed his wine cup. With every sip, Martin began to think more and more about Shimodoi and the runaway rooster that had assaulted the both of them. "You know, I saw a rooster not long ago," he started, curious to see if perhaps this had been a common occurrence.

"Oh? Where?" Colby asked, raising an eyebrow.

"It was in a convenience store... actually, it was in an air duct. I helped the staff there get it out of the building and it ran away."

"Is that how your face got messed up?" Colby inquired.

"He was just born that ugly," Stacy interrupted. Her face had become as red as the wine they were drinking and she was clearly enjoying herself.

"Easy there, killer," Colby said, motioning to Stacy. Yuka let out a hoot and she and Stacy both laughed.

"You know, I always thought it was a bad omen to come across a rooster," Colby said with a more serious tone.

"Like a black cat crossing your path?"

"No, that's just a superstition. But roosters are dangerous." Colby leaned in towards Martin. "Before the rooster crows you will deny three times that you even know me."

"But I do know you."

"It's from the Bible."

"Oh." Martin rubbed the back of his neck, embarrassed.

"Jesus said this to Peter before he was crucified," Colby continued.

"What did Peter say?"

"Well, of course he said that he would do no such thing, but he did. I guess to me the crowing of a rooster is the sign of betrayal."

"Hm…" Martin pondered this for a moment. The rooster from the air ducts had been frightening, and it clearly wasn't something to be underestimated. Despite this, he couldn't help but admire the bird. Its sheer black feathers were almost regal, and it clearly wasn't afraid of creatures several times its size.

"That's not how Japanese view roosters, though," Yuka said, lowering her fork back to the table. "In Japan I think they are much brighter animals."

"How so?" Martin asked.

"Long ago, there was a Goddess named Amaterasu. She was the Goddess of the Sun, but she had a bad relationship with one of the other Gods. Her brother, I think it was. Anyway, he played some kind of trick on her that made her so furious that she retreated inside a cave, taking all the sunlight with her."

"What happened then?" Martin asked. His body had become hot with wine and sweat began beading on his forehead.

"The other Gods realized how much they needed her. The world was dark and they despaired. So, they arranged to have a great gathering outside the cave where she had retreated. They made such a ruckus that she couldn't resist the temptation to come out and see what was happening outside."

"What does the rooster have to do with that?"

"Well, the rooster is associated with all the ruckus they were making that caused her to come out and the sun to rise again. Whether there was actually a rooster there that caused her to come out... I'm not too sure. But anyway, it's a good sign."

Martin thought about the cave in his dream. It had been dark. Too dark to see what was inside, or how deep it went. *It was just a dream anyway. There's nothing to be gained by dwelling on dreams.* He took another sip of wine.

"You know, there's a bar that serves this wine, Martin. Maybe you should check it out sometime if you like it," Colby said, changing the subject.

"I do," Martin responded. "What's the bar called?"

"Sora," Stacy answered. "You'll probably find Chris there on any given Saturday."

"Or Friday," Colby added.

"Or any day that Manager has been in a mood." Stacy laughed.

"It's actually not too far from the office. In the downtown area near the station. It's kind of on the outskirts of the red-light district, if you can call it that," Colby explained, his wife's ears perking up at the mention of a red-light district.

"Oh, you know about that place, do you?" she asked, glaring at her husband.

Colby shrugged and rolled his eyes. "Everyone knows. Besides, it's a nice bar."

"What's the bartender's name?" Martin asked, sensing the sudden rise in tension between the hosts.

"There's two of them actually. Brothers from Brazil. The older one's name is Sami. He's tall and pretty well-built. The tattoos on his arm scare off half the local population over the age of forty. He's often behind the bar but he's not really in charge of it. His younger brother, Tuba, is the one who runs things and generates all the business. He's a lot shorter and thinner. Always wears a fedora and gets along well with everyone." Colby picked up his knife and began cutting into a large baked potato. "Chris sometimes helps out at the bar there when they need it."

"Isn't that against the law?" Martin said, surprised.

"It's not exactly illegal in terms of his working visa, but it's against company policy. He would lose his job over it if Manager found out," Stacy said somberly. "He knows the risks."

Martin had seen the street where this bar was located every day on the walk to and from the office and Toyama station. For the past couple months, it had been snowed in and he hadn't bothered to stray from the main road. But now the snows were all but gone and he realized that the world had suddenly opened up to him.

It was near 10:30 P.M. when conversation at the table finally began to slow. Martin's full stomach pressed hard against his belt, and he wanted nothing more than to throw off his pants and lie down for the night. He stared at the empty bottle of wine at the table thoughtlessly until Colby spoke again.

"It's been a pleasure having you both over here for dinner. We should do it again sometime."

"Not at my apartment," Stacy said, resting her arms on the table.

"Well, you're both welcome here anytime. It's nice to have time with coworkers that isn't in the proximity of *her*." Colby's brow furrowed.

"Ugh. Don't even start. God only knows what she does on her weekends." Stacy bit her lower lip, considering the thought.

"Kidnaps children and eats them?" Martin said.

"Wouldn't surprise me. She probably turns into Hannibal Lecter and feeds them to people she knows." Stacy burst out laughing.

"You're sick," Colby said. "Don't listen to this troublemaker, Martin. Just keep doing what you're doing. It's going to get hard again starting in April, but you'll be fine."

"What happens in April?" Martin asked curiously.

"It's our biggest season. First, the school year starts in earnest, so all the concerned parents who want their kids to get ahead in English take them to schools like ours and sign them up. That means a lot of new faces. A lot of prospective student meetings. You'll have to judge their level of English and place them in an appropriate class." Colby folded his arms across his chest. "Look, don't worry about it for now. It's still a month off and I'm sure you don't want to spend your weekend with that on your mind. Take some time and have fun."

Martin nodded. "I'll do just that."

CHAPTER SEVEN

Eiko

The following Saturday, Martin thought to visit Shimodoi at his shop on the way home, but fatigue from a long day's work got the better of him, so he passed the store up and went straight to his apartment.

He had managed to stay under the radar for most of the week. In fact, the Manager had seemed preoccupied with something else during their staff meetings. Martin had overheard her on the phone with what he assumed was one of the upper brass in the company by the way she spoke, but he couldn't pick up enough of the conversation to understand its contents.

He slept clear through his alarm the next morning and awoke only when the urge to use the bathroom forced him out of his covers. When he returned to his room, his phone was vibrating on the table.

"Hey, Martin." A voice crackled from the other end.

"Chris? Why are you calling me this early? Did something happen?"

"Uh, no," Chris answered. "Can't a friend just call a friend in the morning to see what's going on?"

"Well I guess he could. But why would he want to?"

"Come on man, haven't you ever had a friend that you called sometimes to check up on?"

"No."

"Why do I even talk to you?"

"You called me."

"Oh yeah."

A brief moment of silence interrupted their morning banter before Chris cleared his throat and summarily let out a stream of "Um"s and "Uh"s and other sounds that were unintelligible. Martin clutched the phone between his ear and his shoulder and reached over to grab the remote control off his television.

"Are you drunk?" Martin asked, flipping through the channels.

"Shut up, man, I'm trying to do something."

"Well if you're busy over there trying to do something why the hell did you call me in the first place?"

"Look, uh, can you just come over to my place in an hour or two?"

Martin checked the time on his clock. "I guess. What do you want?"

"I'll tell you when you get here. I'll even throw in a lunch for you. Please?"

Something in the way Chris asked raised an eyebrow. *"Please?" When was the last time this guy ever said "please" for anything?*

"All right. The next train to Toyama doesn't leave for another half an hour though. I can probably get to your place at around eleven. That cool?"

"Yeah, yeah. Oh wait, wait! Can you bring some shaving cream with you?"

"What?"

"Just buy some at the store at the train station when you get here. Come on."

"This isn't going to end with me naked and tied to a chair in your room is it?" Martin asked.

"Christ, you're sick. Just bring it."

The call ended with a *click.* Martin turned his phone over in his hands and bit his lip, then looked over at the girl doing the weather on the television.

"What do you think about this?" he asked. But the low hum of his heater was the only response.

*

He boarded the 10:30 A.M. train at Takaoka station and rode it into Toyama City. Beyond the turnstiles of the south gate was a lone Seven-Eleven that carried just what Chris had asked for. Martin imagined that Chris wouldn't be picky about the brand, and after a few seconds scanning the shelves, he grabbed the cheapest one and took it to the front counter.

Martin had been to this store several times in the past. In the early days before he had drawn up the courage to actually enter a restaurant by himself and order food, he often came here and bought one of their pre-made lunch boxes, after which he would hide in a corner of the station waiting room and eat while watching old sumo match re-runs on their big screen TV. The clerks at this particular shop all seemed to be terrified of Martin, and avoided eye contact even when taking his cash or handing him his bag. Martin found the whole process left a sour taste in his mouth. He wished for the more casual back-and-forth that Shimodoi offered him, but he knew that was unlikely to happen anywhere else in the entire prefecture.

The girl behind the counter this time was one he had never seen before. She had a young, bright face with light makeup that stood in stark contrast to the other withered crones that usually darkened the atmosphere. She had a slim figure, and her hair was shoulder-length and dyed an obnoxiously bright orange.

Martin guessed she was college-aged—maybe two or three years his junior. She looked straight at him through a pair of glossy brown eyes.

"Just this, please," Martin said, putting the can of shaving cream down on the counter in front of him. She stared straight at him but made no move to take it.

Martin cleared his throat and gave the can a push towards the girl, but there was no response. *Is this girl all right?* he thought, beginning to blush nervously.

"Are you American?" she asked in a clear Toyama accent.

"Uh, yeah," Martin replied, letting out a slight giggle and pushing the can closer to the girl. *God, not one of these conversations again.*

"Can you use chopst–"

"Yes. I can also eat raw fish and read *kanji*," Martin cut her off.

"Wow!" she said. "How did you know what I was going to ask? Are you psychic?"

Martin pushed the can of shaving cream even further across the counter until it was practically in the girl's hands.

"Oh!" she exclaimed. "I'm sorry!"

"Thanks." Martin forced a smile.

The girl rang up the shaving cream and threw it almost carelessly in a plastic bag. "That will be five hundred yen." She said with a nod.

"Here you go." Martin slid a five-hundred-yen coin across the counter with one hand and grabbed the bag with the other. "I don't need the receipt."

He stuffed his wallet back into the pocket of his jeans and strode out of the shop. *What a strange girl.* He made a left at the door and started for the east, but no sooner had he exited the station than a high-pitched squeal rang from behind him.

"Customer! Customer! Customer!" she called. Martin picked up his pace in a discreet attempt to flee, but the girl was persistent. "Customer!" she called again. Martin broke into a half jog. Footsteps matched his speed behind him. He could feel the eyes of onlookers upon him as the girl continued to chase him on the sidewalk. *Oh, Christ, she's probably nuts. What the hell does she–*

Then it came. "Hey! American!" she screamed at the top of her lungs.

Martin stopped dead in his tracks, half the population of the surrounding block stopping with him. *This is it. She's one of the crazy ones. She's going to knife me right in the spine and saw my legs off with dental floss.*

But all that came were three heavy taps on his shoulder. Martin turned around.

The girl's face was all business. "You forgot your receipt," she muttered, holding out her hand.

"I didn't want my receipt."

"You should always keep your receipts!" She huffed. "Don't you know anything about finances? What are you going to do if the government asks for your records? What are you going to say when they ask about that five hundred yen that doesn't add up, huh?"

Martin had absolutely no retort. *She's nuts.* He kept telling himself. *Just nod and agree and get her on her way so these people stop looking. Stop looking! Damn it!*

"Well? Aren't you going to take it?"

Martin took the receipt in his hand. "T–Thanks," he said with an awkward bow of his head. "But I don't really need–"

The girl glared at him, shutting him right up again.

"I'm Eiko," she said, folding her arms across her small chest.

She stood an inch or two shorter than Martin, but spoke with the authority of a colossus.

"Hey, aren't you going to introduce yourself? God, I'm a girl, you know. You're supposed to be introducing yourself to me. You're supposed to be the one chasing me and giving me *my* receipt! Don't you know anything?"

Martin didn't know whether to apologize or introduce himself or take off running anymore.

"Forget it!" She puffed. "Just give me the receipt back!" She shot a hand out for Martin's, but Martin backed off in time, leaving her grasping at air.

"It's mine," he said, crumpling the receipt in his hand.

"Just a minute ago you we're saying you didn't even want it! So give it back!"

"No."

Jesus Christ, what am I doing? Just give her the damn paper so she'll go away. But it was too late. Martin was no longer acting under the power of logical thought.

He parried attempt after attempt on the receipt in his hands, until the whole ordeal had attracted quite a crowd to their location.

"Give it!" she cried again and again. But Martin danced around her every attempt at seizing the half-mangled piece of paper in his hand.

"Just a minute ago you were trying to give it to me!"

"Yeah, well, that was before I found out that you're an asshole!" The girl looked up, her face full of fire. "I'll get it back from you!" she declared with a lunge.

She flew through the air, her hands outstretched at Martin's chest, but somewhere along the way she tumbled.

"Hey!" Martin shouted. In a flash he moved forward into the path of her falling body and caught her in his arms on the way down.

Their faces were inches apart. Martin could feel the warmth of her breath on his face. For several seconds neither of them moved. Comments from the crowd all around them filled Martin's ears.

"What's that American doing to that poor girl?" said one voice.

"Is he attacking her?" said another.

"Someone call the cops!"

"You pervert!"

Martin wanted to cry. *No! You've got it all wrong! She's the one who came after me!*

"Eiko. Hey, Eiko!" he whispered. "Come on, get up! Everyone's looking!"

But there was no response. She stared unblinkingly into his eyes, her body limp in Martin's arms. Sweat poured from his forehead. He had no moves left to make.

That's when he saw it. From the corner of his eye, a flash of brown leather moved lightning-quick towards him, but before he had time to react it struck him on the side of the head. Martin staggered, nearly dropping Eiko in the confusion.

"Get off her, you sick deviant!" his assailant shouted. Martin looked up, dazed. It was a small, old woman. She grasped the strap of her bag and wound up again for another attack.

"I didn't do anything!" Martin shouted. He put his arms over his head in a feeble attempt at defense, but the elderly lady was already upon him.

"Deviant! Deviant!" she shouted. And before he knew it, a horde of elderly ladies had joined in on the assault, their joints grinding with every swing of their bags.

Martin cowered and took the shower of blows with a look of unmitigated self-loathing on his face. *March the eighteenth. Assaulted by a store clerk on the way to exchange shaving favors for food with another man. Saved said clerk from falling to the ground and in turn have become the target of assault by an unruly group of elderly purse-toting women. Wish tomorrow would come soon.*

Several minutes later, the crowd dispersed. Eiko was gone. His five-hundred yen can of shaving cream had vanished. A bruised and beaten Martin stood up without the slightest ounce of dignity, and began searching for another convenience store.

*

"Good God, Martin. What happened to you?"

Martin leaned against the door of Chris's apartment, his head hung with that special shame that comes with being emasculated by half a dozen elderly women armed with handbags and bitter cruelty. His face was red with small cuts, and the light blue of his T-shirt was covered with stains.

"It wasn't easy," Martin said, pushing his way into Chris's apartment. "They got me good."

"Who?"

Martin gave no attempt to answer. The shame was too great in his heart, and he limped along through the hallway in silence.

For the most part, Chris's apartment was a carbon copy of Martin's. Both of the homes were owned by the company, and were part of the same apartment building project that had been set up in the early 80s. There were minor differences between the rooms: Chris had a loft bed with a ladder, Martin had a loft bed with a small set of hollowed out steps that also functioned as storage. Chris's closet had regular doors, Martin's closet had sliding doors. But they both had the same hallway, the same pathetic kitchen, the same frosted windows and the same heavy, cream-colored drapes.

Chris's apartment was impeccably clean. Books were shelved, loose cords were tied and bundled together, and he kept all his coins separated in jars that ran harmoniously along the top shelf next to his bed. An earthquake hazard if there ever was one, but beautifully aesthetic nonetheless.

Martin sat at the table and leaned his head back against the wall. *This is it. From now on in this city I'm going to just be that guy who sexually assaulted a store worker in front of the station.*

"So, do you want a beer then?" Chris asked, opening his fridge.

"It's still morning."

"It's eight o'clock somewhere in the world." Chris extended an icy cold brew in Martin's direction. "Liquid courage, my friend. Imbibe early and often."

Martin took the beer from Chris and pressed it against his aching forehead.

"It's for drinking, you know."

"I'll get to that part."

Chris took a seat on the opposite end of the table and popped open his own beer, taking a few moments to breathe before up-ending its contents into his mouth.

"How many of those have you had so far this morning?" Martin asked.

"What, are you my mother?"

Something in Chris's tone was more hostile than usual. Martin looked across the table, scanning his face.

"You seem nervous."

"A girl like this comes along once in a lifetime, Martin. Let me tell you."

"A girl like what?"

Chris played with his empty beer can on the table, avoiding the question. "It's nothing a guy like you would understand," Chris said after a few moments.

"What's that supposed to mean?"

"She's *pure*," Chris answered. He threw his head back and stared up at the ceiling. "Pure in the way a woman should be."

"Who?"

Martin waited for him to continue, but Chris had become lost in his own maze of thoughts, and only continued staring up at the pores in his ceiling.

"I brought you the shaving cream." Martin said, changing the subject. "But what are you planning on using it for?"

"For shaving. What the hell else would I need it for?"

Martin raised an eyebrow. "You're a big boy, you know, you don't have to go out of your way for me to help you—"

"I need you to shave me," Chris interrupted.

Martin observed him coolly and waited for some form of follow up, but none came.

"I'm not helping you shave your junk."

"No, you sick little man." Chris stood up and took off his shirt in one swift motion, revealing a forest of brown hair across his chest. Martin could not help but stare in disbelief. Chris said nothing, and after the break in conversation became too much for Martin to bear, he stood up and said the only thing that was on his mind.

"Must be tough in the summer."

"Most people who see this chest have more of a reaction than commenting on my seasonal discomfort." Chris stuck his chest out with pride. "Pretty cool, huh?"

"Yeah, if you're a logger whose best bet for intercourse is Sasquatch."

Chris pointed an aggressive finger at Martin with the words, "Don't push it," written all over his face.

"I still don't get why you wanted me to come all this way out here and deliver you shaving cream. And I don't think any amount of shaving cream is going to help that mess," Martin said.

"I want you to shave me," Chris replied matter-of-factly.

Without a second thought, Martin was already turned around and headed for the door.

"Come on, man!" Chris pleaded. "I need you to get the spaces I can't reach!"

"No way. No, no, and no again. I'll do you the respect of forgetting this ever happened but for the love of God!" Martin turned back around to face Chris. "And can you at least put your shirt back on?"

"You don't got to touch anything up front," Chris said.

"What the hell does that mean? Why don't you just–" Martin stopped mid-sentence and watched in awe as Chris turned around.

The rugged wilderness that was his front gave way to a perfect ring of hair around the bottom of his neck. An apron of body hair so unsightly Martin couldn't help but pity him. He had always thought of Chris as a good-looking guy, handsome even. But what stood before him was nothing short of a genetic tragedy.

"Now do you see what the problem is?" Chris asked. "The only thing I can do is some cursory manscaping now and then. But this time I want to go all out. I want it all off."

"Manscaping?"

"Yeah, it's like landscaping. But for men."

"Uh huh." Martin leaned against the wall, his body still in pain from the morning's attack.

"Look," Chris said, sliding his shirt back over his head. "I just don't want this girl to think I'm some kind of disgusting man-beast."

"Who is this girl?" Martin insisted.

"I met her last night at the bar. Gave her my number. Her name's Fukiko."

"That's not a real name."

"That absolutely is a real name. And I'm going to see her again tonight."

"Aren't you getting completely ahead of yourself? In what reality are you living in that you end up in a position with her tonight that requires that your shirt come off?"

"I don't want to live in a reality where my shirt doesn't come off with that beautiful woman," Chris said. But Martin could barely hear him now. His head had ascended far beyond the clouds, and it was clear that his brain was no longer receiving oxygen.

"Just help me this once, Martin. I promise it'll be worth your while."

"Worth my while how?" Martin replied.

"I'll let you in on a little secret. But only if you promise to help me out here and keep hush-hush about it."

Martin closed his eyes and took a deep breath. *He's a friend. I should help him. I know I should help him. But good lord, the hair!* He folded his arms together and gave a slight nod.

"Really?" Chris asked.

"This never happened. This whole day never happened. I swear, if somehow, somewhere, someway it ever gets out that I helped you shave your damn man-muff –"

"It won't. I promise."

"OK, OK." Martin took a cautious step forward. "And what is this secret of yours anyway. Can't be that big."

Chris took a big step towards Martin and, with a big smile, put a hand on his shoulder and gave it a squeeze.

"I've been thinking of a plan for us," Chris said. "Something that's going to make all of our lives better. Better for a long time."

Martin looked into Chris's eyes and waited.

"You won't have to worry any more, Martin. Just leave it to me."

"Leave what to you?" Martin asked.

Chris looked straight back at Martin and licked his lips.

"I've got this friend," Chris said. "Well not really my friend, but a friend of the friend, works for the General Union down in Osaka. You ever heard of them? They're a labor union that does a lot of work for foreigners. That's what he said, anyway. My friend. Not the GU guy. I'm thinking we can put in a proper complaint. Something to make her feel the heat for once."

Martin said nothing.

"I'm still in the contemplative phase," Chris continued. "But I'll let you know when things start moving forward. Until then, just hang tight. We'll get her."

CHAPTER EIGHT

Brothers of The Sky

They took lunch together at a mid-sized sushi bar a block north of Chris's apartment, but Martin found himself without much appetite. After four plates he put his chopsticks aside and waited for Chris to finish his meal. The lunch rush was in full swing now, and while Chris ate, Martin traded eye contact with the other patrons. As his gaze passed from person to person, he thought on Chris's plans. There was nothing he had been able to say in response, so he listened with hollow optimism until the subject finally changed.

Fifteen plates and two beers later, Chris paid the bill in thanks, and the two exchanged goodbyes. The walk back to Toyama Station was short, but a prickling fear that he might bump into Eiko again persuaded him to circle around to the north entrance. He arrived just as the train pulled into the station and found himself back at home at a quarter to three.

He set his wallet and phone down on his bed, but instead of taking off his jacket, he slowly made his way over to the windows and slid them open with a grunt. Outside was a small rice field that had up until recently been completely covered in snow, and a parking lot beyond whose spaces had never been occupied. He looked down at the brackish water that had pooled in the paddy.

It stretched out a good fifty feet to the east, abruptly coming to an end at a rickety old house with no windows. It was a pathetic paddy, and Martin wondered why someone would even bother maintaining such a thing. The rest of the world outside his bedroom window was perfect. The trees lining the road had the first hints of green on their limbs, and a group of high school boys rode their bicycles at a leisurely pace north towards Takaoka Station.

All this stood in blunt contrast to the world that existed on the inside of his window. The mountain of trash on his desk had nearly doubled, becoming so large that Martin no longer dared to set anything upon it for fear that an avalanche of papers and plastics might drown his entire apartment. Martin took a deep breath as he surveyed the peaks and crevasses that had once been his desk.

"It's time to clean," he declared to the garbage heap. He turned the television on and flipped through a few channels before landing on an afternoon cartoon series, then removed his jacket and set to work.

The cupboard in his entryway housed a treasure trove of trash bags. He had found soon after arriving that the handling of garbage was quite different than he was accustomed to. Each type of waste had to be separated then put into the correctly colored bag, and each colored bag had a certain day of the week to be collected. Burnables went into blue bags, which was easy to remember though nonsensical to Martin. The next color on the list was pink, for aluminum cans. Plastic bottles had to be stripped of their labels and caps (which went into the blue trash) and put in a yellow bag. But the yellow bag could also be used for other non-burnable trash every Tuesday.

That was how it had been explained to Martin by Manager when he had first arrived, though he had failed to empty the trash from his room since. It was one of the first things he had complained about to Chris during their initial meeting.

"The trash here is so confusing," he said one day after their last classes.

"Yeah. I just put it all in the same bag and throw it out at two in the morning so no one sees me and complains," Chris said.

Martin had thought it a bad thing to do, but after a few minutes of starting into his cupboard of assorted trash bags, he reached for the opaquest blue ones and tossed the others aside.

"To hell with it!" he said, closing the cupboard door and returning to his room.

Martin carefully opened and set the bag on the side of his desk, and with a sweeping motion of his arm he pushed the mountain slowly over the edge into the eagerly awaiting bag below. One by one items trickled off the edge of the table until the mountain shuddered unexpectedly, sending a landslide of filth crashing to the floor in every direction.

"God damn it!" he yelled, kicking a box of cereal off his foot. He huffed in frustration, then looked back at the table. A sticky sheen reflected off its surface, but it was a table once again.

The rest of the day was filled with similar occurrences, but by the time dusk came, a sweaty and worn Martin stood victoriously over no less than seven bulging blue bags of rubbish. Even the sink and toilet had not escaped his quest for cleanliness. His sheets had been washed of their yellow-stained hue and he had even arranged the shoes and clothes in his closet by color and purpose. He felt the cool breeze come from the window and breathed a sigh of relief. The battle was over.

After tidying up the last corners, he stripped himself naked and entered the shower, letting the hot water melt away the grime that covered his entire body. He brushed his teeth and combed his hair, all before realizing that the sun had been replaced by streetlamps and the occasional twinkling of headlights in the distance. He sat at his desk until the sky had lost the last of its navy hues, then listened as tiny droplets of spring rain tapped against the roof.

His vigor renewed, Martin opened his closet and removed a light blue pair of jeans and a green fleece jacket, then checked himself one more time in the mirror before setting out towards Takaoka Station.

*

The bar was located exactly where Colby had said. Four blocks from the station, after the gaudy neon lights and aggressive inhabitants of the red light district. It sat at the edge of an old arcade whose tenants had long since up and quit for better prospects. Doors and windows had been boarded up, and before long he could no longer hear the rambunctious calls of prostitutes or the blaring music of nightclubs. As he continued down the road, he became increasingly alert to the silent world that now surrounded him. He heard no passing cars, no stray animals. Even the monotonous hum of electricity was suddenly absent.

The bar itself sat on the second floor of the arcade. He would have missed it if not for an oddly placed red umbrella sitting proudly against the glow of a softly lit stairwell. It was a brilliantly crimson thing with an elegant wooden handle that begged him to admire it, but his own trepidation forced him quickly up the stairs, out of the soundless void he had entered. At the top was a thick wooden door, with the Japanese character *sora* (sky) carved into it.

Martin started towards the door only to have it swing open before his very eyes. The staircase, which had been enveloped in silence, was suddenly transformed by the deafening blare of electronica and a rainbow of lights and lasers that danced along walls. In an instant a hand stretched out before him and grabbed his jacket, pulling him inside.

"You son of a bitch!" a voice from the rainbow of lights screamed. Martin felt the grip of hands reaching around his neck.

"Hey, hey!" another voice shouted. "That's someone else. Let him go."

"Well then who is he?" Martin felt the man's hot breath on his face, though he could not make out his features. His hands were so large that they reached around the entirety of Martin's throat, pinning him mercilessly against the bar.

"Well he isn't going be a customer now that you've gone roughed him up now, is he? Let go of him for the love of—"

Feeling the hands around his neck loosen, he gasped and coughed for air, sliding from the bar to his knees on the floor.

"What the hell is this?" Martin managed to ask. He looked around and saw the whites of eyes all around him, though he could make out nothing more than that.

"I'm sorry about my brother. We thought you were someone else. We just kicked someone out of here not thirty seconds ago. Thought they were trying to get back in."

"There wasn't anyone outside," Martin responded, slowly rising to his feet. "Not anyone that I could see."

"Hm. Well, there's nothing to worry about now. I'm Tuba. Who're you?"

The face of a man formed in front of Martin. The man had remarkably slender features, and stood only three or four inches taller than Martin. He wore a black and gold striped fedora with a collared grey shirt, and spoke English with an alluring Brazilian accent.

Martin folded his arms across his chest. "I'm Martin. I heard about this place from a coworker of mine and thought I'd check it out. I was—"

"You're Chris's boy!" Tuba shouted, punching Martin in the arm.

"Ow. What is it with you people?" Martin fumed.

"Oh, uh, sorry. Why didn't you say who you were sooner?"

"Because I was being choked to death by a behemoth?"

"Ha!" Tuba put his hand on his chest. "Sami got you good, huh? Damn, Sami, at least apologize to the boy. You took out Chris's coworker, man! Come on now say somethin'!"

"I didn't mean nothin' by it." Another voice said from behind the bar. Martin turned around to see what he presumed to be the other brother. The features of his face were identical to Tuba's in every way, but he stood over six and a half feet tall and his visible body rippled with muscles. His arms were covered in tattoos, the most prominent of which was a wild boar charging across a veiny bicep.

The music which had quieted somewhat returned to a deafening volume and Martin found his indoor-voice no longer sufficient to keep up conversation.

"Drinks are on us for the night," Tuba shouted, coming behind the bar aside his brother. "What'll it be?"

"Just give me whatever's on tap," Martin shouted back. He took a seat at the stool in front of him and looked around. The other patrons, who had seemed featureless to him only moments ago, were now easily recognized. Two girls in revealing red dresses sat at the far end of the bar, one of them laughing hysterically while the other took a puff of a half-finished cigarette. Smoke hung heavy in the air, and Martin scrunched his nose tightly in displeasure.

The second-floor establishment was comprised of one room. To his left it opened up into a small dance floor encircled by high tables for standing patrons. Black walls were completely covered in pictures and words written in a variety of languages and colors. Most of the guests congregated on the dance floor, engaging in undiscernible conversations.

Tuba and Sami both stood behind the bar. Sami's back was turned towards a laptop computer from which he adjusted the music, and Tuba had just finished pouring a beer from the tap. It was a perfect pour, with only half an inch of head that foamed just above the edge of the glass.

"Now you just let me take care of this for you. I know how you Americans like it." Tuba slid the beer across the bar into Martin's open hand. Martin brought the frosted glass to his lips and let its frigid contents flow unimpeded down his throat.

"These Japanese all like seven-to-three. They love the head, ya know," Tuba said, another glass already under the tap. His brother grunted in perverted laughter from behind him.

"Yeah, they *love* it, don't they Tuba."

"Shut up, Sami." Tuba turned and slapped him on the back of the head. "Ask anyone in here and they'll all tell you the same shit. 'But the head is so delicious! It adds to the taste of the beer!'" Tuba mocked their local accents. "It's just air, right? But that's how they are. Trying to convince them of that is like walking down to Hiroshima and tellin' them, 'Thank God for this bomb, ending the war and saving lives!'" He bellowed a laugh.

Martin shifted uncomfortably in his seat and said nothing.

"It's all good, though. Drinking and dancing is what brings us all together, right? Even in our little chicken coop," Tuba pointed up at one of the speakers. "The rooster crows, and the hens dance."

Martin took another sip of his beer. The track had changed to a slow techno remix of Michael Jackson's "Thriller", settling the atmosphere and making conversation at a normal tone of voice more manageable.

"So, what brings you to our lovely corner of the world then?" Tuba asked. It was a question that Martin had answered at least a hundred times from his students, and though he had a polite and rehearsed response, the truth of the matter was that he had no answer. It had been neither a spur of the moment impulse nor the result of a particularly long and thought out process. Like many others his age, he had come to find that decisions made ponderously or promptly were of equal hazard, and the decision to leave home and family had been no different. He felt no particular pressure from them or any of his friends to leave, nor had he felt any particular inkling to stay with the rest of his childhood. His life was being pushed by the shallowest of currents, so shallow that for most of his life he had wondered if he was even moving at all.

"It's just where I was assigned. It's not like I had a particular reason to come to Toyama. I guess that's the same answer you get from most teachers out here," Martin said. "What about you? How'd you end up running a bar here?"

"Well, I was born here," Tuba raised his own glass and clanked it against Martin's.

"So, are you half Japanese then?"

"No, no, no." He let out another laugh. "My mom and dad were both born in Brazil. But like a lot of other Brazilians they came over here in the 80s when the economy was good. There's a lot of us around, you know. You ever been to Brazil?"

Martin shook his head.

"You should go!" Tuba brought out a set of three shot glasses and filled them with Grey Goose. "Get yourself a nice Brazilian girl with a big ol' keister to wrap your face in on a cold night."

Martin laughed. "Is that what you do with it?"

"Man, that's how you get things started. But never mind that. Maybe you don't even like girls."

"I like girls"

"You like girls?"

"I like girls. Do you like girls?"

"I'm just sayin', you know, it's OK if you don't. I mean there's somethin' for everyone on this earth, right? And yes, I like girls, shit!" Tuba threw his arms up in the air. "Don't worry Martin, we'll help you out." He slid one of the shots to Martin and passed another to Sami.

"Help me out with what? I just met you like seven minutes ago."

"Man, there's only one reason people come to a place like this. It's 'cause they need a little help. And I, my friend, happen to be the most helpful person in town."

"Is that why Chris comes here so much?" Martin asked. Tuba raised a finger and looked him square in the face.

"Now that man needs help that I can't provide. I've seen a lot of people come and go in this bar. People who sat right where you're sitting now. People who worked in the same company you work for now working under the same Manager you work under now."

Martin shut his eyes and saw Manager's face staring back at him. "She's not like any boss I've ever had." Martin chose his words carefully. Just the thought of her seemed to summon a shadow that loomed over him, scrutinizing his every motion.

"Yeah, I've heard that before." Tuba pressed his thin lips together. "Some answers you've gotta find all by yourself in this world. Colby found his answers with his beautiful little wife. I'm the one who introduced them, you know." Martin did not know. "Chris is still looking for his answers. Looking in all the wrong places, but looking. And you?"

"I don't even know what the question is." Martin tapped his fingers against the shot glass.

"Well, I'll tell you that it starts with a 'why,'" Tuba said, leaning forward. "Now here's how I can help you. The right question to ask is never 'who', or 'what', or 'when', or 'where', or even how. But 'why.' 'Why' is always the right question to ask. If you don't know the 'why' of something, then you don't know anything worth knowing at all." Martin looked up at Tuba, whose face was only inches away.

"And believe me, my friend." Tuba paused, licking his teeth. "That your 'why' is gonna come lookin' for you real, real soon."

CHAPTER NINE

Rice isn't a Popular Target for Bombs

The first class on Tuesday morning was always reserved as a private lesson with an elderly lady named Yoshiko. A traditional and demure woman who had married into a wealthy family from somewhere in southern Toyama. She dressed only in traditional Japanese garb, and spoke with an eloquence befitting a governess. A true raconteur, Martin never felt a moment of pressure to come up with topics or carry a conversation. She did all the work for him.

"I was just a child when the city was bombed," she said, closing her textbook. Martin enjoyed this about her. She never felt restricted by a curriculum or rushed to get through a chapter. Some days she was happy to skip the contents of a lesson entirely and simply talk. Good enough English practice for her as far as Martin was concerned.

"My family lived on a farm well away from the hustle and bustle of downtown. My mother had just put me to bed when the bombers came. I ran outside to our front porch, and found the whole city ablaze in the distance." She spoke with an unusual smile on the face, as if the memory itself was a treasure she had just dug up from the sands of some faraway beach. "I thought it was a festival. What is war and fire and death to a child? I remember smiling and laughing and clapping my hands together. It was exciting."

"You didn't run away?" Martin asked.

"There was nowhere to run. We had no bomb shelter, there was nothing around us but rice. And rice isn't a popular target for bombs." She covered her mouth with her hand and let out a small laugh. "I look back now and think of all the people who died in the bombing. It must have been a nightmare, I know. But all I could think about was how beautiful the fire looked against the night sky. I wanted to reach out and touch it."

Martin listened silently, nodding his head as she spoke. War was a foreign concept to him. He had seen the World Trade Center crumble on TV back in High School. He watched the clips of the invasion of Afghanistan and later Iraq, but war only ever existed to him through a camera lens.

"After the bombing, a lot changed for us. It wasn't long after that night that..." She stopped and shook her head. "Well, let's just leave it at that."

"It's fortunate that you were so far away," Martin said, folding his hands on the table. Yoshiko was always a bright way to start his day, even when they discussed such dark topics. They spent the rest of the hour talking about the more recent past, and how she now lived up in the mountains with her husband and their butler.

When their hour was up, he walked her to the front door and exchanged farewells, then watched as a black Rolls Royce spirited her away.

At three in the afternoon, Martin and Chris found themselves sharing the same lunch hour. They made the short walk up the road to their usual curry shop, and took a seat at a table near the front window. Chris talked about the girl Fukiko he had met the previous weekend. To his displeasure, the night had ended prematurely, and his manscaping efforts had gone unrewarded.

As they finished up another late lunch, Martin took the bill in hand and offered to pay. "This time it's on me," he said and, before Chris had an opportunity to protest, Martin was up and at the register.

They had stayed quite long and half-jogged back to the office, where they were immediately called in by Manager. "Your students for the next hours both canceled. Colby and Stacy are going to lunch now, but we need to have a meeting. Get in my office." The two teachers exchanged anxious glances, then fell in behind her.

The picture of the woman with the red umbrella was still hanging on her wall. There were no places to sit in front of her desk, so Martin and Chris stood shoulder to shoulder, eyes locked on the woman in the painting. Manager exhaled heavily and looked both of them over, taking her time before she spoke.

"We're getting a new Assistant Manager," she said. "We're going to be very busy soon."

She opened one of the drawers on her desk and retrieved an unopened pack of Camel cigarettes. She took her time opening the package, then tossed the plastic wrapper aside and pulled one out. She lit up with a deep inhale, then leaned back into her chair and crossed her legs. It was the first time Martin had seen her smoke. She had never smelled of tobacco. In fact, she seemed to prefer the same peach-scented perfume that some of the college-age girls liked to use. The room quickly filled with a wretched combination of odors, turning his stomach.

"Do you smoke?" Manager said, offering the package to Martin.

"No, ma'am," Martin replied flatly. "I quit three years ago."

"Oh?" Manager said without the faintest hint of interest. "That's a shame."

Manager turned to Chris. "The Assistant Manager is coming here after the weekend. Which means she will be opening the office from now on. Give me the key."

"I don't have it, Manager. Martin opened today."

She took another puff of smoke and blew it at Martin. "Well?" She smiled. "What are you waiting for?"

Martin dug through his coat pockets but found them empty. "I'm sorry, Manager, I believe I left it on my desk."

"On your desk."

"Yes, Manager."

"So why aren't you getting it right now?" She pointed towards the teachers' office.

Martin stuttered for a moment, then quickly composed himself and hurried out. Since Chris and Martin had taken over opening the school, they had always put the key on their desks for the other to take at the end of each day. He checked Chris's workspace first. No key.

Where is it? He moved over to his own desk and began lifting up all his books and papers. When there was nowhere else to look, he threw open all of his drawers and pulled out their contents. Still, there was no key.

"Martin?" A cold voice called from Manager's office.

In an instant he had been defeated. The thin shell of confidence he had built shattered into pieces around him, leaving him naked and defenseless. Losing the key was the same as losing his job. He walked back into the Manager's office head bowed, barely able to contain the panic in his heart. "I'm sorry Manager. I can't seem to find it."

Manager looked at him and exhaled the last bit of smoke from her cigarette, then put it out in a waiting ashtray. Desperate, he turned to Chris, but Chris's eyes only stared unblinkingly forward.

"It must be here. I opened this morning, so it can't be anywhere else but here. Please, let me find it. I know I can find it," he begged.

"Well, Martin. This is quite serious," Manager said, coming to her feet. "Fortunately for you, you have no more classes today. Just your office hours, which you can use to search for that missing key."

Martin's head sank lower. Office hours for a teacher were gold. Though the majority of his day was spent teaching, his office hours were used for grading papers, reviewing texts, and getting special instruction from the other teachers on how to improve the quality of his lessons. All of his preparation time had been bundled up into a clean-cut four hours per week, and he was about to lose three of them.

"There's nothing else to be done about it. You'd best start looking." Manager dismissed Martin with a flick of her hand and a twisted smile. He turned once more to Chris, who stood like a castle of sand, with nothing left to do but wait for the waves to wash him away. Abandoned, Martin left the miasma of smoke and peaches, then closed the door behind him.

Over the next few hours, Martin searched. He searched in the classrooms and the study room. He searched in the lobby and behind the front desk. His panic gradually reduced itself to empty withdrawal. *I'm finished*, he thought as he went through his desk for the third time. There was nowhere he hadn't already looked, and at this point his body was simply going through the motions, hoping that by some grace of God he would stumble upon it.

But there was no key. Chris didn't have it. Colby and Stacy had full schedules and weren't even around to ask. He had no explanation to give, no excuse to offer, and no words came out of his mouth when Manager called him back into the office that evening.

There was no yelling. There were no raised voices or arguments. Manager sat with her trademark smile and spoke in a controlled, almost polite manner.

"This is a grave mistake," she said. "I of course will have to inform the main office of this. They may ask for your immediate resignation."

Martin was silent.

"Maybe I can do you a favor though. You know, everyone here likes you so much, Martin. Colby talks frequently about how he is impressed with your progress. Stacy doesn't complain about you at all and you seem to have gotten close to Chris as well. I don't want you to leave Martin. I hope you believe me."

Martin no longer knew what to believe. He had retraced his steps throughout the morning perfectly. There was no explanation he could think of—and as it was his responsibility for the day, the blame fell squarely on his shoulders.

Manager stood up from her chair and began to speak in a sickly-tender tone. "I suppose there is another way. I don't have to tell the main office anything you know. Perhaps there is something you can do for me instead?"

Martin swallowed hard and looked up at her.

"As I said, we have a new staff member coming," Manager started, coming to Martin's side. "Assistant Managers are always a problem. They can't do anything right." She looked at him. "Much like yourself."

"I see," he said.

"All they do is cause trouble. Trouble for me. Trouble for the school. Trouble for the teachers. We have to avoid trouble, don't you agree?" Her voice was barely more than a whisper, as she circled around Martin and returned once again to his front. The lines of her face hardened as she stared into Martin's eyes. "Watch her for me, won't you? Let me know if you see her doing anything... unacceptable."

Martin furrowed his brow in confusion. "Manager?" he asked in a small voice.

"That's all. It's not much of a favor, really. You don't even have to do anything special or work any extra hours. It's all rather nice of me, don't you think?"

"Yes, ma'am," Martin whispered.

"Go home, Martin. It's been a long day."

"Yes, Manager. Thank you, Manager," he said. But as Martin turned away, he felt a hand seize his arm, squeezing his bicep with torturous strength.

"Martin." Manager's eyes pierced any resistance he might have offered. "She *will* do something unacceptable. Do we understand each other?"

"Yes, ma'am." Martin's body went limp. "We understand each other perfectly."

CHAPTER TEN

The Shepherd of Chickens

In his dreams, the rooster appeared. Its body had grown to human-sized proportions. They stood together in the dark, the sound of rain their only companion. The same cave stood before them, black and lifeless. Martin stepped towards it only to be stopped by a flash of lightning striking the earth in front of him. The rooster lowered its beak at him. More lightning streaked across the sky and in brief moments of refulgence he realized that they were not alone. A great congregation of hens stood motionless at the edge of the woods that surrounded them. Their numbers were beyond counting. Some stood tall with long, white feathers. Some stout with pinions of deep orange.

Only the rooster was black. Rain dripped from its wings to the cold earth below, but it seemed to take no discomfort in this. Martin returned to his place alongside the rooster and stared into the cave. *There's nothing to see. It's too dark.*

A voice responded in his mind. It was the same voice as before. *You have to take it off. She can't leave. She doesn't belong here.*

Martin closed his eyes. *Who is she?* he asked the rooster. *What do I have to take off? I don't understand.*

But the sound of rain was his only answer. Another flash of lightning and the thunder that immediately followed shook him from his sleep. He was back in his apartment, staring up at the ceiling.

His sheets were soaked. He often perspired in his sleep, but now it felt like he could swim in his own sweat. He got up slowly and ran his hand along the wall, searching for the switch to the overhead light. When he found it, he gave it a flick and covered his eyes.

"Ugh," he grunted. He ripped off the sheets from his bed and carried them to his washer, then stripped naked. It was nearly three o'clock. Taking a shower now was sure to wake him up completely, but there wasn't any way around it.

He washed himself from head to toe, soaping himself up twice over before finally standing in the stream of hot water and letting himself fully awaken. After a few minutes, he shut the water off and grabbed his towel, then made his way back to the bedroom and closed the door. Outside, an engine sputtered and choked, and a pair of voices from the dark argued among themselves. Martin cracked his window slightly open to a rush of freezing cold air and listened.

"Come *on*!" the voice of a little girl insisted. A shadow moved in the darkness. "We won't make the delivery!" Her voice was high-pitched but serious.

"Now, now," said the other voice from the dark. It was gruff and masculine. "You know we get there every time and no one ever comes. No one ever comes."

"Someone will come this time! They've got to! They'll realize we've got the best stuff in town!" the little girl replied angrily.

"They'll come, they'll come." The man's voice sounded more distant.

"OK! Try it now!" the little girl yelled out. The engine roared and the little girl cheered alongside it. "It's just down the road, let's go!" Martin watched as the lights of their truck drove into the distance and made a right at the corner. *What are they doing at this hour? And just down the road? Are they selling something?* Martin kept staring out the window into the darkness. Curiosity getting the better of him, he took a pair of fresh clothes from the drawer and threw on his winter coat.

Before long he was jogging down the road following the path the truck had taken. *They went towards Shimodoi's shop*, Martin realized, quickening his pace. The ground was wet and fresh rain had melted slush into small streams that coursed down the gutter, reflecting the gentle glow from streetlights hanging overhead. The air was brisk, and each step was invigorating.

He noticed the red truck immediately, parked across two spaces sitting right in front of the convenience store where Shimodoi worked. The little girl was standing with her faced pressed against the glass. She wore long blue jeans and a pink coat, with her long black hair in pigtails. The man stood behind her leaning against the tailgate of the truck, flicking the ashes of a newly-lit cigarette onto the ground.

"I want some candy," the girl said, pointing at the rack of chocolate behind the glass.

"You know we ain't got the money for it. Ain't got no money at all."

"Hmph!" The little girl put her hands on her hips and walked back towards the truck. She threw open the door with as much force a child of her age could muster and crawled in, leaving her companion alone outside. Martin snuck forward and turned his attention to the man. He had a distended belly and a double chin, both of which protruded sharply from the rest of his body. He had puffy cheeks and big lips, all crowned by an unkempt mane of black and grey. He wore an old tan pea coat and dark blue jeans, and tiny boots that covered tiny feet.

Martin approached the store quietly, looking inside to see if Shimodoi was anywhere to be found. *He's probably in the back, watching TV or taking a nap.* Martin's heartbeat quickened, and he started to think it might be better to return home. Before he could make a decision, however, the man flicked his cigarette to the ground and turned his direction. The pair made brief eye contact, but instead of turning away, a panicked Martin lowered his head and proceeded quickly through the front doors.

Just play it cool. You aren't stalking them. You're just a concerned citizen. Find something in the store to buy and go back home.

"Shimodoi? Shimodoi?" Martin called, but there was no answer. He stopped at the register. The door to the back room was closed. *Of course he's not here.* Martin walked to the end of the store, till he came to an empty space where the eggs ought to be. *They really must be as popular as Shimodoi says.* Martin squatted down and pretended to shop for nothing in particular.

"Need eggs?"

The immense voice of the man he had followed boomed from behind Martin, giving him such a fright that he jumped with a yelp and fell backwards onto the floor.

"Jesus Christ!" Martin scrambled to his feet. "You shouldn't scare people like that!"

"Scare people like what? I just asked you a question. I did, I did."

"How did you even get in here? I didn't hear the door open," Martin said, straightening up.

"Need eggs?" the man asked again. His Japanese was heavily accented, but his words rhymed almost musically as he spoke them. Martin stood silently for a moment sizing the man up. He was larger than Martin by at least fifty pounds and he stood about five inches taller. He breathed from his mouth in prolonged heavy breaths, as if the act itself was a burden to his being.

"I don't really cook," Martin said, folding his arms across his chest.

"Don't gotta cook 'em, just gotta eat 'em," the stranger replied.

"I... I guess not," Martin stuttered as he stretched his mind for more excuses. "But you can't really eat raw eggs from just anyone, right? They have to be approved by the health department."

"Eggs are good. I checked 'em all myself. I did, I did."

"Checked them how?"

"With my hands, how else do you check an egg?"

"So how do you tell if there's a bad egg? What does it feel like?"

"No bad eggs. Bad chickens sometimes but the eggs are OK."

"Bad chickens? You mean the meat is bad?"

"You eat chicken meat?"

"What else do you do with chickens? And if there are no bad eggs then what's the point of checking them in the first place?" Martin said indignantly.

The strange man paused for a moment, thinking the question over. His heavy eyes began to shut and his head slumped back. For a moment, it looked like he was about to fall asleep where he stood, when he suddenly shot back upright and started coughing violently.

"Are you all right?" Martin asked, taking a step towards the man. *He smells terrible. This guy must be one sandwich short of a picnic.*

The man hunched over and thrust an oversized hand into his coat pocket, then fumbled around for a moment before producing a single large brown egg. A smile cut through his rounded face and he held it out in front of him with a childish pride.

"Now this is an egg! It is, it is! Come on, hold it!" the man insisted.

"I don't really need to hold it. It's just an egg, right? They all feel the same."

"You'll see, you'll see!"

Hesitant, Martin stepped forward and reached for the egg. He hovered his hand over it for a moment and eyed the strange man warily. He suddenly thought of those prank packs of chewing gum that snapped down like a mousetrap when you tried to pull a piece out. Martin's older brother had tricked him once when they were young with such a contraption, and he had become quite cautious about taking things from the hands of others. But something about this egg was irresistible to him, and before he could give it another thought, his hand pressed down on the egg's smooth shell. Martin's stomach growled the moment he touched it.

"Ha!" The man gave a short nod to Martin, and quickly returned the egg to his pocket.

"Ha, what?" Martin said perplexed. "It's just a normal egg."

"But you want it now, don't you?"

Martin stopped, putting a hand on his stomach. The man was right. Martin's mouth started to water and suddenly all he could think about was devouring the egg he had held.

"How much?" Martin asked, bringing his wallet out from his jacket. "And how many of these do you have?"

The man gave no answer. The enthusiasm in his face was replaced by something else, an emotion Martin had never seen before. He grabbed Martin's hand, forcing him forward until they stood only an inch apart. "We gotta check you first." His deep voice rumbled from the back of his throat, and again he produced the egg from his pocket, this time slamming it into Martin's palm.

In an instant, a white-hot pain shot up the entirety of Martin's arm. Caught between the two men's palms, the egg neither cracked nor broke, but burned. Martin squirmed and struggled to wrench himself free of the man's vice-like grip, but it was no use.

"Let me go!" he shouted, but the man stood his ground. His eyes closed, and the veins on his forehead started to bulge. A profound fear welled up deep within Martin. With his left arm he punched and with his legs he kicked, but to no avail. The soft body of the other man had turned to stone.

Martin winced in pain. He could feel the flesh of his hand melting away, and his heart was ready to burst forth from his chest. He tried shouting for help, but his throat had dried and barely a whisper escaped. *I've got to get out of here. Why did I come here? I've got to run!*

But his limbs would no longer heed him. Like a raft caught in a whirlpool, he felt himself being sucked in. After one last gasp for air, a final eruption of agony coursed through his body, enshrouding everything around him in darkness.

Somebody help me. Anybody.

For a long stretch of time, the only response to his plea was silence. He was conscious—or at least aware of his consciousness. Something in him was beginning to change. The person who was Martin was gradually being replaced, and before he could do anything about it, he felt the bars of a new mind shut down around his own. Feelings from this foreign mind rushed through his heart. A dire loneliness. An unrelenting guilt. Madness, and a tormented thirst for revenge.

The weight of these emotions pinned him against the edge of his own sanity, and just as it was becoming too much to bear, he heard a voice. An unaccompanied alto, singing words he did not understand.

Nen, nen korori yo. Okorori yo
Boya wa yoi ko da, nen nen shina.

As if responding to the alto, a distant horn blew, reciting the same notes the voice had sung.

It lasted less than twenty seconds, but as the notes of the horn played, the despair he was feeling faded, replaced instead by solemn peace.

Emboldened, Martin pushed against the bars of his own mind and took control of the body he inhabited. He took his time, opening his eyes first to observe the world around him. He stood inside a colorless cave. The earth below was wet and uneven, and the air was oppressively stagnant. After a few minutes getting used to his new form, he took a handful of steps in the direction of the distant horn. But movement in this body was difficult. The legs he now used were longer and lighter than his own, and something unendurably heavy weighed down on his right arm.

"What is this?" he asked in another voice. Martin brought his left hand to his right, but where there should have been an arm, there instead was the unmistakable feeling of wood. He ran his hand up and down splintered coils that wrapped around themselves until he touched something else. Fabric, taught and smooth.

No sooner had his fingers run over the fabric, then the stinging madness of his host's mind returned. The appendage that was his right arm tightened, sending lightning bolts of pain up through his shoulder.

"Get off me!" he shouted. He took hold of one of the wooden coils and pulled with all his might.

"Get off! Get off, get off, get off!" he screamed.

The brief control he had exerted over this body vanished. It writhed and flailed, suddenly aware of his presence. He could only feel his hand, tightly gripping the wooden parasite that held him hostage.

"Ow! Let me go!" a familiar voice said. Martin squeezed harder.

"Are you drunk!? Well two can play this game, Yankee Doodle!"

A bony hand struck his cheek with enough force to knock him back into reality. Hot blood rushed through his body, and he shot up from the ground and turned to face his opponent. It was Shimodoi.

"What the hell, man! Do you usually beat people up who are lying unconscious on the floor!?" Martin stood over Shimodoi ready to pummel him.

"What the hell? That's my line! You giant white potato! You almost broke my wrist!"

Shimodoi stuck out his arm, the print of Martin's hand still fresh upon it. Martin backed down, ashamed. "Sorry, I didn't realize what was going on. Are you all right?"

"Better than you, Ten Yen. You're all white like a ghost. Maybe I call an exorcist to get your crazy ass out of my store."

Martin looked around. He was back in the store, within his own body. The strange man had gone, and the parking lot was empty.

"What time is it?" Martin asked, kicking his legs out and stretching his arms.

"It's 3:45 in the morning," Shimodoi said, coming to his feet. "I came out here ten minutes ago and saw Ten Yen sprawled out across the floor like a polar bear."

"There wasn't anyone else here? I was talking with a man. He was here with a little girl and I think they were trying to sell eggs."

Shimodoi scratched the bottom of his pimply chin and narrowed his eyes. "You met Yuji!"

"Who's Yuji?"

"Are you stupid? You just described him to me, I just told you the name."

"OK, yeah, thanks. So, tell me *more* about Yuji," Martin asked.

"Some old farmer who lives up near Tateyama. He used to have a giant poultry farm, but I heard they ran into some trouble and went out of business." Shimodoi turned and walked towards the drink aisle.

"What happened?"

"I'm not sure. I heard on the news that he disappeared. Caused a big commotion. But if you saw him, then maybe he's trying to start things up again? Though even if he tried, I doubt anyone would buy his eggs. People around here have a habit of trying to forget painful memories." Shimodoi removed a pair of beers from the cooler and tossed one at Martin.

"I'll pay you for this one," Martin said, reaching for his wallet.

"We don't accept your foreign monopoly money here. And we get charity tax breaks for serving the dumb and ugly, which means we get double for giving things out to you."

"You're a real charmer, Shimodoi."

"I know." He snorted.

Martin tapped the top of his beer a few times with his fingernail before finally deciding to open it.

"Did he say anything to you?" Shimodoi asked, hopping on top of the counter alongside Martin.

"He asked me if I wanted eggs." Martin scratched his head. "He tried to give me one but then he went all crazy and knocked me out, I guess. I had this weird dream, then the next thing I knew you were giving me five across the face."

"What, you mean he hit you?" Shimodoi asked, surprised.

"Well no... he showed me an egg and put it in my hand. Then he held it in my hand and—"

"You passed out from holding hands with a man? Oh, Ten Yen, now I see!" Shimodoi choked with laughter and put his hands over his chest. "Don't do it, Ten Yen, I'm just a boy!"

"Shut up, Shimodoi."

He laughed until he had tears coming out of his eyes. "Dumb, ugly, and a sexual deviant! Hey! Maybe I ask if we get triple charity for giving you free stuff! Ha!"

Martin took a sip of his beer and waited for Shimodoi to get a hold of himself. In a few hours, he would have to be awake again and off to work. Manager had relieved him of his key-holding duties, but he was now bound to a much darker type of work. He thought of Chris standing next to him in the office, and how he had remained silent through the whole ordeal. *Maybe it's just a rite of passage for us. She makes us get rid of the Assistant Managers so she doesn't have to deal with them. Maybe Chris had to do the same thing before. Maybe the others did, too.*

Shimodoi continued his obnoxious horse's laugh, tears streaming down his red cheeks. *This kid is ridiculous.* Martin looked down in the palm of his hand, where Yuji had held the egg.

"Hey, Shimodoi," he started, looking over at his young companion.

Shimodoi snorted a few more times and wiped the tears from his cheeks. Fresh snot was coming out of his nose and he wiped it conspicuously on the sleeve of his shirt.

"What do they do with all the chickens when a poultry farm goes out of business suddenly like that?"

Shimodoi took off his glasses and rubbed his eyes. "I don't know, Ten Yen. Why don't you go and find out?"

Martin took another sip of beer and hopped off the counter. "Maybe I will," he said. "Maybe I will."

*

By the time he got back home it was just past four. Martin ascended his stairs and removed his key from his pocket. He unlocked the door with a jiggle and slid inside, taking off his jacket and throwing it on the floor he had worked so hard to clean the previous weekend. Without turning the lights on, he kicked off his shoes and started walking down the short hall towards his room, when a slender glow caught his attention. A straight line of white light shone out from the refrigerator in the hall.

"Now how did I leave you open without noticing? Don't tell me the door is broken." He gave the door a firm shove, only to have it ever so slightly pop open again. *Damn thing must be busted.* Martin pressed on the door with his foot, trying to lock it in position, but something from inside pushed back at him. *Did I forget something in there?*

With a flick of his wrist Martin opened the door to something wholly unfamiliar. Large brown eggs arranged perfectly in columns and rows from the very back to the very front, from the very bottom to the very top. Hundreds of eggs stood like a phalanx ready to burst forth. On the inside of the door was taped a single sheet of white paper that read, *No bad eggs. Just bad chickens. Make sure to eat every day.*

Martin plucked the note up and flipped it over, finding a small business card taped to the back. Written in plain black text was a name and address. *Tateyama Eggs. Yuji Sakasegawa. 18-7-82, Tateyama.* Martin turned the card over. The back was bordered in pink and red hearts that had clearly been drawn by a child, and simply read, *Come visit us again soon!*

Martin sank to the floor and stared into the open fridge. "Well," he said, admiring the perfection with which the eggs had been inserted. "At least I won't have to worry about going hungry for the next six months."

He propped a chair from his room against the fridge to keep it closed, then climbed back into bed and fell fast asleep.

CHAPTER ELEVEN

A New Student

A few hours of sleep and one short train ride later, Martin was back in the office. He exchanged groggy greetings with the other staff and made his way to his desk, where he plopped his bag down at his side and collapsed into his waiting chair.

"Good morning." Chris waved as he slid through the doorway. Martin grunted in response.

"Ah ha. I see you slept about as well as I thought. How did it go yesterday?"

"How'd what go."

"With Manager, man. How was it?"

"Oh that." Martin leaned back in his chair and stretched out his arms as far as they would go and yawned. "It went OK, I suppose."

Chris slapped a hand down on his desk, and Martin jumped forward. "I thought you were a goner! So, what's the punishment, then?"

Martin turned his mind back to his conversation with Manager. "Watch her for me," she had whispered in his ear. The hairs on the back of his neck stood up, sending shivers down his spine.

"I just got to put in some extra hours, take on an extra lesson or two," he lied.

Chris offered no push-back, accepting Martin's words at face value. "Well that's great!" He seemed genuinely relieved, and Martin managed a small smile despite himself.

Manager pushed herself into the staff room at half-past ten with a clipboard in one hand and a folder stuffed to the brim with papers in the other. She slammed the folder down on Chris's desk and pulled up a chair at the front of the room.

"Listen," she declared. Everyone turned their heads. "We've got six prospective students coming in today, so I don't have any time to deal with all of you and your incompetence." She pulled out what looked like a candy bar from her breast pocket and started peeling off the wrapper.

"Four of them are yours, Stacy. Skip the formalities and just get enough of an idea of their English level so I can place them somewhere. Our lower level classes are getting full, so if someone seems like they are even the slightest bit mediocre, push them until they believe they're better than they are so I can close them."

"Yes, Manager."

Manager took an enormous bite out of her candy bar and continued talking. "Colby, I've given you the other two." She chewed between every word, and Martin could only watch in absolute disgust as her mouth became a cesspool of chocolate and peanuts.

"Any queshchuns?" she gobbed, sucking the chocolate out of the spaces between her teeth. The four teachers shook their heads.

"Well, then. Get to work." She dropped the candy wrapper on Chris's desk and picked up her folder before waddling out the way she came. Martin looked over at the wrapper and nodded.

"Milky Way?"

"Snickers." Chris picked up the wrapper. "The kind with extra nuts."

A NEW STUDENT

The office was abuzz with activity all day. For the most part, Manager spent about an hour with each prospective student. Colby and Stacy wove placement assessments between their own classes, leaving Martin and Chris to take turns covering the lobby and make sure everything ran smoothly.

The pair of them greeted each student as they came in. Martin had the better command of Japanese, so he put himself behind the front desk and answered any phone calls while Chris stayed in the lobby interacting with everyone he could. The placement assessments took around ten minutes total, which left zero time for the teachers to do anything but move from one thing to another.

For his part, Martin was happy to be relegated to phone duty. The phone hardly rang, and when it did it was almost certainly someone calling to talk to Manager. Martin took detailed messages, leaving them on Post-It notes for her to see when she got back. "Your handwriting is disgusting," she commented after the fourth consultation. Martin nodded and apologized.

At four o'clock, however, the wheels came unhinged. Martin's lunch hour had just started, and he decided to grab a sandwich from the supermarket and eat it at his desk. He was halfway through a three-hundred-yen turkey and Swiss cheese when the door flung open.

"Martin!" Manager snapped. "What do you think you're doing!?"

"Eating a turkey and Swiss." Martin looked down at his half-eaten sandwich. "It's good."

Manager's face took on a tomato-like glow. She marched straight up to Martin until she stood directly over him.

"One of the appointments had to come early. The others are all teaching lessons. You need to do an assessment," she barked.

"But my sandwich..." Martin looked down.

"Enough about your sandwich!"

With one gelatinous motion, she snatched the half-eaten turkey and Swiss from his desk and hurled it at the trash can, but missed high. Martin watched as his treasured lunch exploded against the wall, sending its once-delicious contents flying across the room.

Before he even had a moment to absorb what had just occurred, she grabbed him by the arm and lifted him up.

"Now listen," she spat. "You're here for the company, not some stupid, Seven-Eleven-made *sandwich*." Martin turned his head and watched a piece of tomato helplessly sag down the wall behind him.

Martin had never given a speaking assessment to a prospective client. He gulped, and wiped a sweaty palm through his hair.

"Don't mess this up," Manager said, pulling him along down the hall towards the business office. She let him go in front of the door and cleared her throat before putting on her plastic smile.

"Stay," she commanded one last time before letting herself in.

"Thank you so much for waiting so patiently!" Her voice was a full octave higher than usual. "Are you ready, then?"

"Yes." Martin heard the voice of a girl, and took a step toward the doorway.

"Let me introduce you to one of our teachers. His name is Martin…"

Martin stepped through the threshold. "Nice to mee—" He stopped dead in his tracks and looked at the girl. It was unmistakable. The short stature. The brown eyes. The orange hair—done in a ponytail today—the modest chest.

It was Eiko.

His mind went blank. He stared at her, and she stared back, unflinching.

"Martin," Manager whispered.

But Martin paid her no mind. *She's come here to finish the job. She's going to kill me.*

"Martin!" Manager raised her voice, her plastic smile was cracking, and a thin sheen of perspiration was forming around her lips.

The stalemate felt like it would continue into eternity, and may indeed have done so if not for Eiko. She stood up from her seat and slid out from behind the desk into full view. She wore a black leather jacket over a snug black shirt, and tight waist-high black jeans, which squeezed her body into an even smaller form. If Martin had any other feeling but fear in his heart, he may have found her attractive.

She took two steps forward until they stood face to face, and offered her hand. Martin gazed at it, dumbfounded.

"It's nice to meet you." She smiled.

Manager, apparently on the border of full-blown panic, picked up her heeled foot and smashed it on Martin's big toe with a crunch.

"Ow!" Martin cried. "Ow—oh!" He caught himself. "Oh! Ha ha! Nice to meet you!"

He put his hand in hers and shook.

Manager tried to giggle to lighten the mood. "Well, then! I'll let you get to it." She turned and shut the door behind her.

Don't go. Don't leave me with her. Martin couldn't believe that he was actually wanting Manager to stay. He turned back towards Eiko, whose smile evaporated with the sound of the closing door.

Martin tried to release their handshake, but Eiko only squeezed tighter.

"You." She lifted her left arm and thrust her fist straight into his gut, sending the consumed half of his turkey and Swiss back up his throat.

"Why?" Martin pleaded, falling to his knees with a wheeze.

"You big jerk!" She lifted up her purse and brought it down on the back of his head. "I lost my job because of you!"

"Ow! Stop!" Martin put his hands over his head to block the oncoming assault. "How the hell am I responsible for you losing your job?"

"Shut up!" She brought down another blow of her purse. "You caused that big scene outside of the store! It's your fault!"

"*I* caused a scene? You're the one who chased me down and attacked me in the middle of the street!"

"Shut up, shut up, shut up!"

"How did you even find me here in the first place?"

The question was enough to stop the showering of blows. Eiko took a step back, blushing. "I—It's not like it's hard to find out where one of the only ten American's in this prefecture works or anything!"

"So, you came to my work to what, beat me up? Now what? Are you going to go home?"

"Hmph!" Eiko turned back to the desk and sat in her chair. "I'm going to make you teach me English."

"You're going to what? How?" Martin stood back up, pressing his hand against the spot in his stomach she had struck him. "You don't have a job anymore so how can you afford it?"

"Ha ha!" She laughed impishly. "I don't need a single yen to get you to teach me."

"Is that so? Listen. I don't know who you think you are but if you think—" Martin was cut off by a whimper. Tears welled up in Eiko's eyes and her lips quivered. Within seconds, she was outright sobbing.

Martin reached his hand out to stop her. "Eiko, what are you doing. Stop, stop! She's going to hear you!"

And hear her she did. Within seconds Manager burst through the door.

"Martin!" she shouted. "What have you done!?"

"Oh!" Eiko wailed. "He won't take responsibility!" Martin and Manager both blinked in confusion.

Eiko brought both of her hands over her stomach. "How could you do this to me!"

"Oh my..." The Manager put a hand on her forehead, but Martin still didn't follow.

"Martin." The Manager seethed. "You got this girl pregnant?"

"Huh?"

Eiko continued to bawl. Martin looked at her, then back at the Manager. "What?"

"You said!" Eiko sniffed and snorted. "You said you would take care of us! That you would teach me English and our child and I would go back to America with you and—"

This girl. This girl. This damn girl, Martin grit his teeth as he resigned himself to defeat.

"Now I'm going to have to tell everyone! My sister! My mother! My father who works for the *Hokuriku Newspaper*!"

"No!" Manager protested. "Anything but that! There must be something we can do!"

Eiko didn't respond. Each tear on her cheek was a bullet fired in Manager's direction, and they were hitting their mark.

Martin couldn't believe what he was watching. Eiko had Manager eating out of the palm of her hand. "This doesn't have to be a scandal, Miss Nigawa! We will do anything you ask."

Eiko took a tissue out of her purse and began wiping away her tears. She looked down at Manager, who had kowtowed before her, then up at Martin with a smirk.

"Anything?" she knelt down in front of her helpless prey. "Well... in that case..."

CHAPTER TWELVE

Willy-Nilly

At 9:15 P.M., the school doors promptly closed and the four teachers retreated back into their office. Martin fell into his seat, rubbing a hand against the fresh bruise on his stomach. He had made it out alive, somehow, from that psychopathic game Eiko had played with Manager. Alive, but not unscathed.

Chris came in after him, casually flicked a piece of lettuce off his desk, and sat down.

"Well, well," he said. "You look beautiful, Martin."

Martin closed his eyes and nodded rhythmically. "Just glad to be here."

"Why is there food all over the place?" Stacy asked, looking at the floor around her desk. "Is this cheese?"

"It's Swiss cheese," Martin said, nodding. Stacy gave him a quizzical look, but Manager entered the room before she could speak further.

Manager looked as if she had just returned from a vicious battle. Her jacket was unbuttoned, her hair ragged, and not even the layers of makeup she wore could conceal the wrinkles around her mouth. Papers hung freely in the air from a clipboard she held to one side. She glared at Martin with bloodshot eyes that conveyed only the most utter disgust.

"Listen up." Her voice cracked. "I have the placement for the new students and which teacher will be taking them."

She began reading off names, classes, and teachers, adding some quick facts about each new student as she went down the list. The first two went to Colby, the next one to Stacy, the next two—a brother and sister pair—went to Chris. Martin sat on the edge of his seat after the fifth name, but Manager stayed silent.

"Five, then?" Colby asked, raising his head from the notes he had taken. "That's not bad, right?"

"Wasn't there a sixth?" Stacy asked.

Manager pressed her hand against her temple and rubbed. "Yes..." she said. "That's... good."

The other teachers exchanged troubled glances while Manager took a deep breath and looked back down at her clipboard.

"Eiko Nigawa."

Martin perked up in his seat and cleared his throat.

"What's wrong with you?" Chris whispered, turning his head back to Martin.

"Eiko Nigawa will be a private lesson. Three times a week."

"What?" Stacy folded her arms. "Does this girl just have money to burn? Three lessons a week at that rate... she's going to be paying 150,000 yen a month for that. Is this a short-term contract? Is she going on a business trip or something?"

Manager tapped her nails against the clipboard, ignoring Stacy's inquiries. "The assigned teacher will be Martin. The contract length is... indefinite."

"Wow. Good job Martin." Colby clapped his hands. "Wasn't that your first assessment? You must have really made an impression!"

"Great job, Martin!" Stacy added.

"I've never heard of an indefinite contract before. Good work, buddy!" Chris smacked Martin on the knee.

Martin did nothing to acknowledge them. He kept his eyes on Manager, who winced with each compliment. She put both hands on each side of her clipboard and began to squeeze.

Colby stood up and addressed the staff. "I think we should celebrate his success. Why don't we—"

Snap! The four teachers all jumped back as the clipboard splintered and sent slivers of wood shooting across the room. Martin could practically see steam erupting from Manager's ears.

"All of you, get out. And if I hear one more person compliment this buffoon—" she pointed a finger at Martin "—I'll see you fired!"

The three other teachers turned and stared at Martin as she slammed the door behind her, but he paid them no mind.

It can't be helped. He nodded again. *I am where I am and there's nowhere else I can be.*

*

The weather took a sudden turn for the worse about halfway through Martin's walk home. In one moment, he felt the faintest drizzle fall against his skin, and in the next, he was in the middle of a downpour. Martin jogged the rest of the way home, and arrived at his front door as streaks of lightning passed overhead.

Safe. He ripped off his suit and slung it over his chair, then stripped naked in front of the heater. Heavy drops of rain slammed against his roof, and the flashes of lightning were punctuated by wall-shaking thunderclaps. Martin stood below the heater until he was sufficiently warmed, then dressed himself in fresh underwear and sweatpants.

Despite everything that had happened during the day, his first thought was of the loss of his precious turkey and Swiss sandwich. After turning on the TV, his growling stomach pulled him towards his fridge and directed his hands to pluck a pair of eggs from the shelf along with a can of Asahi. Martin cracked the eggs into his frying pan as carefully as he could, throwing the empty shells into the wastebasket at his feet, then tapped the lid of his beer a few times before opening it. After a couple minutes, the egg whites started to bubble and pop and Martin flipped them over.

"'I do not like green eggs and ham,'" he hummed to himself, picking at the sides of the eggs with his spatula. "'I do not like them Sam I Am.'"

He overheard the familiar jingle that signaled the start of the evening news as he continued to hum along.

"'I do not like them in a house. I do not like them with a mouse.'" He flipped the eggs over one last time, then dumped them onto a waiting plate in his hand. Thunder clapped again, sending vibrations through his whole body. Martin looked up.

"'I would not, could not, in the rain.'" He stepped back into his bedroom and put the eggs and beer on the table. It wasn't the best combination, but Martin had a veritable mob of eggs in his fridge that he had to get through, and no room for anything else save the drink racks on the inner door.

He continued to hum along as he shoveled the eggs into his mouth one at a time and listened to the evening broadcast. The newscaster was a lady that looked to be in her early thirties. She sat erect and composed, and delivered the news without any noticeable judgment or excitement. She went over sports, local politics, crime, all with the same flaccid tone that Martin imagined would disinterest even dedicated listeners. He would have changed the channel, if not for a preview of the next segment—an investigative report into the Sakasegawa Farms.

Martin locked over at the business card on the table. *Could it be the same place?* He wiped his face with a napkin and pushed the plate aside. On the TV, the newscaster introduced another reporter who stood in front of a large wired gate with the sign *Tateyama Eggs* hanging over it.

"It's been exactly one year since the egg farm known as Tateyama Eggs closed its doors to the public and its mysterious owner vanished without a trace. We're here today interviewing a former worker at the farm who lost everything in the blink of an eye."

The camera changed to a news-studio interior set up with two seats opposite from each other. The reporter sat on the left, across from his interviewee. The worker's face was censored, and his voice altered to almost the pitch of a chipmunk. In order to protect his privacy, the reporter simply referred to him as, "Mr. Tanaka." Martin could not rightly tell if the worker was even a "he," but listened on.

"Tell me about what happened the last morning you came into work."

"Well," the chipmunk Tanaka started. "It was just like any other day. I was in charge of the egg collecting under Mr. Sakasegawa himself. It was my job to gather them all up and give them an inspection before moving them along for processing."

"Had Mr. Sakasegawa said anything to you that would hint that the company was in any kind of financial trouble?"

"No sir. In fact, he was in a fine mood that day. I remember. He always came to the coops to oversee us and lend a hand. That day wasn't any different."

"Tell me more about Mr. Sakasegawa."

"Well, he was a good person. He didn't rightly have any wife or kids of his own, but he lived on the farm with his niece. Little rascal of a girl. She'd follow him around wherever he went. She was with him that last day too."

"When did you realize something was off?"

Mr. Tanaka didn't answer at once. Martin sat on the edge of his seat and leaned in.

"Well,' Mr. Tanaka began again. "There had been a rumor that a woman had visited the farm about a month before. I heard that she was after the land, but the boss—Mr. Sakasegawa that is—always said no."

"Yes, we've heard about this mysterious buyer from other workers. But even after the farm closed and the land became available for purchase, no one has come forward with so much as an offer."

Mr. Tanaka agreed. "There was one other thing."

"Yes?"

"When I got to my car that night, it was quiet. I don't know if you've ever worked around ten-thousand birds before, sir, but there's not hardly anything quiet about them, no matter what time of day it is."

"Are you implying that ten thousand fowl were somehow spirited away between the end of your shift and the time you got to your car?"

"Now I don't rightly know, or else we wouldn't be having this conversation. But I'll tell you when I got there the next morning the gate was still locked up, but the coops were empty. No one man can move that many birds, sir."

"Fascinating. Why don't you tell us about—"

A flash of lightning lit up Martin's room, and thunder exploded overhead, taking the power to the TV out with it.

"Oh, come on!" Martin pleaded. The rain outside intensified.

Martin turned on his cell phone for light and looked down at his empty plate. "I guess that means you guys weren't inspected by the health board." He ran his fingers through the yolk that had accumulated at the bottom of the plate and licked them clean. After consuming every last drop, Martin started to hum again.

"'I do so like green eggs and ham. Thank you, thank you, Sam I Am.'"

CHAPTER THIRTEEN

Spring

On the last day of March, winter gave one last hurrah in a torrent of light snow before making its long-awaited exit. The city that for so long had been nothing but a blur of icy slush gave way to more pleasant colors. The trees were green and the cherry blossoms pink. The clouds parted to reveal a deep blue sky during the day, and even the occasional evening showers lost much of their wintery oomph.

After the mildly disappointing results of his eggs and beer combination, Martin began frying two eggs every morning, eating them alongside a buttered piece of toast—the bread for which he bought every Sunday at Shimodoi's shop. At first, he had been content just to fry the eggs in a pan and eat them with his toast, but his interest in that soon waned and he started experimenting with more exotic variants. He scrambled, poached, and even hard boiled when he found the extra time.

Each egg was identical in size to the last. The whites of the eggs surrounded a perfect orange yolk that burst with flavor, and it wasn't long before Martin couldn't imagine starting his days without his two eggs and toast. He kept the business card and note that had come with the eggs attached to his fridge, using a magnet left behind by the previous occupant. A well of curiosity stirred in him about the mysterious pair of egg-dealers he had met, but his duties at work had become so demanding that he found himself without time to explore the matter further.

At the office things had become exceedingly unpleasant with Manager. The arrival of the Assistant Manager had been delayed by a week due to some unrevealed circumstances, news which Manager received with a joy that Martin found unnerving. Whenever the topic of the Assistant Manager's coming was discussed, the image of Manager's unbearable grip on his arm and her words came back to haunt him: "She *will* do something unacceptable." Despite the confusion of the moment and the shock he had felt at his own carelessness in losing the key, her meaning had been crystal clear. Manager had bared her fangs, and was ready to devour the new Assistant Manager whole.

Even so, Martin had hoped that the week would last forever. Despite the above-average agitation from Manager, it was the last week he had before his lessons with Eiko officially started. He mulled over what he would do. Privately, he desired to just give such abysmal lessons that she would quit out of sheer frustration. But after seeing the way Eiko had completely toyed with Manager, he began to suspect that antagonizing her further was the wrong move.

The train rolled into Toyama Station at 10:07 A.M. He made his way up the stairs and across the walkway, down through the long tunnel to the turnstiles, through the door and into the outside world. During the winter he always found himself looking down as he walked, at the snow where his feet trod and the slick frosty muck that accumulated on the corners. At the icy crosswalks that had sent him falling flat on more than a few occasions. But with the heavy snows no more than a memory, he found himself looking up.

The streets were alive with pedestrians making their way to and from the station. Toyama City had the largest station in the prefecture, and much of downtown city life revolved around it. On the east side of the station stood Mariet, a seven-story shopping center complete with a collection of restaurants on the top floor. Martin had visited it a few times in the past, but most of the stores inside catered more to the interests of women and the elderly, and he found he had little reason to go there with any regularity. To the south was the majority of downtown Toyama, including the school at which Martin worked. There were no proper skyscrapers in the city, but the office buildings stood tall enough to create an impressive, if not somewhat humble, skyline at night.

To the southwest was the red-light district, sitting on the edge of the ghost town that was once the heart of the entire city. Martin remembered the night he had gone to Sora and how it sat riding the edge of obscurity: the empty shutter-town that encroached to its very doorstep, and the silence that engulfed the night at the bottom of staircase. It was a lighthouse turned to an urban sea—a sea without waves that carried no ships to her harbor. Martin took a deep breath and checked his watch. 10:10 A.M. Time to move.

He crossed the street with a trio of high-school-aged girls that giggled and whispered amongst each other as he looked over at them. "Always smile," they had told him during training. "Remember, you're the face of the company now. And that doesn't end when you clock out for the day. All of your actions reflect on us, so make all of your actions positive!" Martin choked down the urge to vomit at his own memories. *I'd like to see them smile at the Manager I've had to smile at.*

Without the threat of ice and sleet under his feet Martin found that his pace had naturally quickened, and he arrived at the office a few minutes earlier than usual. The school itself had a large glass door and windows across the front. Through them one could easily see the lobby and the large L-shaped front desk, which stretched from the south wall and curved eastwards, ending at the beginning of the hallway that led to the classrooms and teacher's office. The counter was absurdly high, and it completely obscured anyone who was sitting behind it, making it look deserted from the outside. The counter top was the same sky-blue as the carpet and chairs, which oddly enough hardly ever matched the color of the actual sky in Toyama.

Martin reached over to the door handle and gave it a good pull, causing a jingle of bells that had been attached to the top of the door. Before he even had one foot through the entry a dark-haired woman shot up from behind the desk.

"Yes! Good morning and welcome to our school!"

Martin nearly fell backwards from surprise.

"Jesus Christ, don't scare me like that."

The dark-haired woman raised her head in surprise, her eyes wide with fear and relief. She stood just slightly shorter than Martin. Her face was wide and square, and she had an unfortunately large forehead, the result of a receding hairline that Martin immediately pitied her for. She wore a black jacket over a tight-fitting white blouse that did nothing to conceal her generous bust. She hurried around the desk and approached Martin. Her waist was too thin for her chest, and her legs, wide around the thighs and slim around the calves, were too short for her body. She looked like she had been designed by the God of balloon animals. *Not a very powerful God.*

Her face was red and drips of perspiration ran down her cheeks, but she smiled with a perfect set of glistening white teeth that made her beautiful in her own, fretful way. Martin gave her the friendliest smile he could muster and introduced himself.

"I'm Martin, one of the teachers here. It's a pleasure to meet you." He gave a quick bow.

"I—I'm Mika. The new Assiss—Assiss—Assiss—" She stumbled over her own English. The words caught in her mouth and Martin's heart sank. *Headquarters didn't send us an Assistant Manager. They sent us food for the shark.*

"The Assistant Manager?" Martin interceded.

"*Yes!*" she half-yelled again, bowing her head. "It's a pleasure to work with you! I hope I can be a good part of your team and that I won't get in your way!"

"Calm down," Martin said. "I'm not Manager. You don't have to be so formal."

"R—Really?"

"Uh-huh."

"Thank you very much! I w—won't let you down!"

This one's hopeless. Martin smiled politely and took his leave, walking down the hall towards the teachers' office. As he approached the door, he heard muffled voices coming from within. Martin pressed his ear to the door and listened. He made out Stacy's voice clearly.

"We can't let her keep doing this, Colby. When are you ever going to get off your big ass and stand up for something around here? All you ever do is try to spray a garden hose on the fire after it's already burned out half the building!"

"And what do you want me to do?" Colby's voice answered in a strict tone that Martin had never heard before. "What do you think happened to the teacher before you, huh? Before me? Good Lord, Stacy, there are better things in life to sacrifice your job over than this."

"Like what?" Stacy retorted, her voice growing in volume.

"What do you care? She never rips on you anyway. All you

have to do is shut up and let her do her thing, and you make off without a scratch."

"Yeah well what about Chris? What about Martin? The whole 'stolen key' thing was so ridiculous, and you didn't do anything!"

"And what did *you* do about it!?" Colby's voice was laced with rage. "Let it go. Don't focus on her. Focus on your damn job! Something I wish all three of you would do more!"

Martin heard the slamming of books and quickly backed away from the door just as it burst open. Stacy sped down the hall, glistening tears streaming down her cheek.

"Where's that one off to?" Martin turned to see Chris standing at his back, an uncharacteristic grin spread across his whole face. "Come here, Martin," he said, tugging at Martin's arm.

"I really should be getting ready for my first lesson…" Martin protested weakly.

Chris led him into his classroom and shut the door.

"Dude, did you see her?"

"See who?"

"Mika, you idiot! Who else, Land-Whale the Beached?" Chris had come to be quite inventive with his nicknames for Manager.

"Very funny. Yeah, I saw her. So what?"

"So what? Man! She's a babe!"

"You're joking."

"Come on, tell me she isn't, like, the hottest chick in this prefecture."

"She is absolutely not the hottest chick in this prefecture." Martin crossed his arms over his chest, holding his ground. Chris opened his mouth to argue, but no sooner had the first words escaped his lips did the thunder of Manager's voice roar through the office.

"Shit," Chris said, opening the door. The duo ran down the hall to the front desk where Mika stood trembling before Manager.

Manager herself was dressed in a white blazer and matching white skirt that was as wide as it was long. The rolls of fat around her waist heaved with every breath she took. She stared down at Mika, her face puffy and red.

"Is this how you open the school? With dirty carpets? Did you even stop to think that you aren't the only one who works here when you got out of bed this morning?"

"I—I—I'll vacuum right away!" Mika squeaked.

"Right away? We'll have students coming through the door for their lessons in five minutes. What are they going to do when they see you?" Manager stepped forward, closing the gap between them. "'Oh, I guess they have a cleaning lady working here now.'" Manager's voice was shrill. "And they're right. We do have a cleaning lady working here now. But why is a cleaning lady wearing such a nice business suit? It's only going to get dirty."

Martin's heart was ice cold, and he wondered if this was how the others had felt when they were watching her rip into him for the first time. *She's not a friend. She's no one to me. She'll be gone before I even know where she was born or if she prefers dogs or cats. She's nothing to me*, Martin repeated in his mind.

"Get out of the way!" Manager growled, pushing Martin and Chris to the side as she led Mika down the hall. "Come on, cleaning lady, you have a lot of work to do today!"

Just like that, they were out of sight. Martin stared down the hall for a moment. "Well at least it's not me this time," Martin said turning around. But Chris was no longer there. From behind him he heard the slamming of a door, followed by the sound of silence.

*

"I'm going to kill her," Chris said, removing the last of his darts from the dartboard. "I swear to God, Martin, I'm going to put a trail of cupcakes from her house to the ocean cliffs and watch her return to her natural habitat."

"What kind of cupcakes?" Martin asked, lining up his aim at the center. The objective of their game was not to hit the bullseye in particular, but Martin found that, if one was to play darts, one might as well aim for the bullseye every time just to say, "Bullseye!" and raise one's arms in cheer.

"What kind of cupcakes? I'm here talking about rolling her off a cliff and you're worried about the damn cupcakes?"

"She doesn't like strawberry."

"Martin, why do you even know what the hell kind of cupcakes she even likes?"

"Haven't you ever looked in the trash bin in her office? She always buys those three-packs of cupcakes, the chocolate, vanilla and strawberry ones from the store across the street."

"So?"

"So, there's always a strawberry one leftover in the package in the trash."

"I didn't even know she ate cupcakes." Chris scratched his head.

"Speaking of all this, what's going on with your grand plan to 'make our lives easier?'" Martin asked, keeping his eye on the target.

"Huh? Oh. I'm still working on it. But trust me, I've got big plans."

Martin threw his first dart wide, hitting the outside ring of the seven. "Damn," he said, biting his lower lip and readying his next shot. Chris picked his beer up from the table and took half of it down in one gulp. He had been drunk since three beers ago, but that had done nothing to slow his pace.

"You notice some weird shit, man," Chris said, letting out a ferocious belch. Martin threw his second shot on the outside of the second ring. A complete miss.

"You do know that you have to actually hit the board to get points, right?" Chris snickered.

In truth, Martin respected Chris' ability to get angry to this degree. He had almost come to envy him for it. Despite the almost daily verbal lashings he had received from Manager, Martin had never come close to retorting. Once a week when he would call his mother and father back home, and they'd ask about how his work was going. The best he could manage was a mild complaint on her attitude.

"Well, hardly anyone likes their boss anyway. Just don't let it get to you," his father always said.

Martin wondered how anyone could actually achieve such thick skin, especially against a person that you're around forty hours of the week.

His last shot struck true, hitting the innermost ring, just outside the bullseye. He let out a cheer and walked towards the board to retrieve the darts. Chris shook his head in sad disbelief. "You don't even get any points for that. You might as well have thrown it wide with the last one."

"Where's the fun in that?" Martin returned to the table and hopped up on a stool next to Chris. The bar was devoid of human life aside from the pair at the dartboard. The fact that Sora was even open on a Tuesday night was something of an oddity to Martin. There was no music or light dancing along the walls. Only Sami was there when the pair arrived, but he left soon after to run some banal errand. Before he stepped out, he put on an old Japanese Samurai flick on the television, and Martin occasionally gave it a look during the brief lulls in conversation.

"That Mika though," Chris slurred, staring into his empty glass. "Now she's something."

"She's something all right. Something that was made at a circus."

"Man, I'm wasting my time talking to you, I swear."

"You know what's sad though," Martin said, twirling a finger around the rim of his glass. "She doesn't even get a welcome dinner or anything like that. All the teachers have one, but not her."

"Oh, God, we should be *thankful* that we don't have to go through one of those stupid dinners with everyone at the office. Don't you remember yours, Martin?"

It was one of the memories Martin had successfully repressed until Chris asked. All the staff had been there, of course, as well as a large number of the adult students from the school who wanted an excuse to drink and be ridiculous. The dinner itself was arranged at a mediocre Italian joint about four doors down from the office. If the bland food and hard wooden seats weren't enough, the sight of Manager rushing around the room trying to organize bingo games, rock-paper-scissor tournaments and laughing through her snake's smile sent shivers down Martin's spine.

"I mean seriously, who the hell makes grown men and women play rock-paper-scissors? Who does that?" Chris said, shrugging off the weight of his own memories.

"So why don't we do something for her sans Manager?" Martin suggested.

"Hey that's a good idea..." Chris's eyes widened. "Damn, Martin! I knew there was a reason I was keeping you around!"

"Thanks." Martin laughed. "Always good to know that I'm useful."

"So, where should we take her? We can't go to the normal places, or anywhere around the office for that matter. Manager would see us for sure."

Both men folded their arms, straining their inebriated minds as far as they could.

"We could get udon," Martin said.

"Too messy."

"Curry? The shop we always go to is nice."

"Too smelly. And too close to the office," Chris said with growing impatience.

"Well what do *you* want to do then?" Martin asked.

"I want to take her somewhere nice, you know, show her the local flavor." Martin could practically see the gears grinding in Chris's brain. He waited for a real answer.

"I've got it!" Chris said, pounding his fist onto the table. "Let's go to Mariet. They've got that Chinese place that's really good. And it's up on the seventh floor, we could get a window seat and have a great view of the city while we eat!"

"Do I get flowers too? Or just Mika."

"Let's do it, man! I'll ask the others about it and figure out a good time. Just the five of us. No suits, no students, no Manager, and no God damn bingo!" Chris's eyes were alight at the prospect.

"Well, at least it's near the station so I can catch the train back home quickly." Martin sighed. "But what if—"

"Relax, it'll be great!" Chris took out his phone and started pressing keys at a furious pace. "I'm texting the other two now. I'm telling you, Martin, this will be perfect."

Across the room the door opened and Sami came in, struggling to hold a giant silver keg between his hands.

"You guys sober enough to help me with these?" he asked, letting the keg drop through his fingers with a loud *thump*.

Martin got up and walked over to help him while an all-too-occupied Chris stared at his phone.

Martin reached down for the keg Sami had dropped and gave a mighty heave. It didn't budge, and he stepped back, bewildered.

"Geez, this thing must weigh a hundred pounds! How did you even get it up the stairs?"

Sami raised an eyebrow and placed his left hand on the keg.

"Like this," he said, effortlessly lifting the keg with a single, swift motion.

"So, uh, I guess you don't need help with these, then?"

"Nah." Sami let out a guffaw as he walked behind the bar. "I just wanted to see your pansy ass struggle with it for fun. Thanks for the laugh!" Martin watched as he set the keg down behind the counter. His muscles were carved into his arms as if they had been the great life's work of some master sculptor, and they were always on display. Martin squeezed the mushiness of his own arm and grunted in disapproval.

"Where's Tuba?" Martin asked, pulling out a stool in front of the bar.

"At home like any other normal person at eleven on a Tuesday night. You guys were lucky to catch me here. I was just about to close up shop when you and Wonder Boy over there showed up."

"Unlucky for you, I guess," Martin said apologetically.

Sami shrugged. "I had work to do anyway. Had to pick up the kegs, and it's not so bad runnin' the place with just a couple of customers."

He squatted down and removed the old keg from under the counter, replacing it with the new one. "All right boys! The tap's fresh and ready to receive your money. Tuesday night loser special, just three-hundred yen a pop!"

"You're all heart, Sami," Chris said, stumbling over himself to get to the bar. "But I'll have you know I'm quite respected around these parts. Education and the future and all that other shit."

"Oh yeah? Why don't you teach me something then?" Sami laughed again.

"I'll teach you how to pour a beer since you're so shit at it."

"And I'll teach you how to drink a beer since you're so shit at that too. Want me to put a nipple on it for you? 'Cause that's how you drink. Sucklin' from it like it's your Mama's tit."

Chris raised his hand to object but Martin could see that he was too drunk to return fire. *Ten points to Sami on that one.*

Martin drew a thousand yen note from his pocket and placed it on the bar. "We'll take two, without nipples, please," Martin said. Chris could only nod in vague agreement.

Sami poured three glasses to the brim with frosty golden nectar, putting them together in the shape of a triangle as he finished. Each man had the handle of a glass facing him, and they all put their hands at the edge of the counter.

"You ready?" Sami shifted his eyes from Chris to Martin. Chris responded with another colossal belch and pounded his chest with a closed fist. Martin took a deep breath and nodded. Sami grinned.

"On the count of three then boys. One. Two. Three!"

CHAPTER FOURTEEN

The Short Hour

The next day was Martin's first class with Eiko, and he took the time during the train ride in to review a simple lesson plan he had put together. Despite their two encounters, he had very little notion of her actual English level. On both occasions they had spoken only in Japanese, but the other young women he taught around her age had at least a grasp on the fundamentals, and he estimated her ability would be similar.

The thought of a class with Eiko distracted him well into his first lesson of the day, though he tried his best to hide his discomfort.

"Sensei?" Yoshiko asked with a hand on her cheek. "Are you feeling all right?"

Martin cleared his throat. His voice was raspy, and his mouth felt like it had been stuffed with cotton.

"I'm sorry, Yoshiko," he replied. "My voice is just a little scratchy today. Must be all the new flowers. I get the worst allergies in this country."

"Oh?" She tilted her head to one side. "Well if I didn't know better, I'd say you had the voice of a man who went out drinking all night and woke up this morning without enough time to shave!"

"Ah…" Martin couldn't help but bow his head in shame. The jig was up.

Yoshiko burst out with a hearty laugh and clapped her hands together. "Oh, Sensei! You're just as bad a liar as my husband!"

Martin tried to smile. "Sorry, Yoshiko. I didn't mean to lie to you on purpose. I was just a little embarrassed. You are my student, after all."

"Oh, come now," she said. "Men have been making the same silly lies to cover up for their drinking since long before my time. A woman can tell, you know."

"She can tell when a man has had a little too much to drink the night before?"

"Oh no, anyone can do that. But a woman can tell when a man is lying. It's her job."

"Her job?"

"Of course. Of all the things men do well—and there are only a few—lying is probably the one they do most often. They lie to make themselves happy. They lie to try to make us happy. They lie because it's easier than telling the truth even on simple matters."

Martin shifted his weight in his desk and looked at Yoshiko, puzzled. "You make it sound like we're not a very good gender."

"Oh no, no. I don't mean it in a malicious way. And I don't think most men lie maliciously either."

"I see." Martin scratched his upper lip and waited for her to continue.

"Did I ever tell you that my husband is a musician?" Yoshiko asked.

"No, I don't think so. What does he play?"

"The trombone. He played in the prefectural orchestra many years ago. Back then it was a large group that practiced very seriously. They met on Wednesday and Saturday evenings, and after that they would often go drinking together—my husband and the other members of the brass section, that is."

Martin folded his hands together and listened intently.

"So, every Wednesday and Saturday night he would come stumbling home with his trombone in one hand and his hat in the other. He'd come right through the front door, put his trombone case on the floor and his hat on top of it and say, 'Yoshiko, I'm no good. These prefectural musicians are on a different level. I don't deserve to be part of something this great.' It was the worst lie he ever told, and he told it twice a week."

"So, what did you do?" Martin asked.

"Well, one night he came home red in the face from drinking too much, and just like every night before that he put his trombone case on the ground and his hat right on top of the case and said the same thing. And after his words of self-pity and a long sigh, I walked right over to him, grabbed his hat, threw it on the ground and stepped on it!" Yoshiko covered her mouth and laughed again at the memory.

"What happened then?" Martin asked, hanging on her every word.

"I told him that he was not allowed to say that ever again. I called him a liar and a fool, and told him to sleep in the living room!" Yoshiko let out a hoot and stamped one creaky foot on the ground.

"That seems a little harsh." Martin laughed.

"A woman has to be harsh sometimes. Not because she wants to be, but because a man needs harshness in order to learn. Or else he just keeps lying, keeps sighing, and keeps being grumpy!"

"What was the lie, then? Wasn't he just telling you how he really felt? That he thought the other musicians in the band were really top-tier?"

"Nonsense!" Yoshiko waved her hand in front of her nose, as if the very words Martin had uttered stank to high heaven. "If you had asked any one of his friends, they would have all told you the same thing: he was the best. There was no one else in the band who could hold a candle to him. He wove notes together to make a tapestry of music that made the ears dance and the mind sing. But the base of the lighthouse is always the darkest."

"What does that mean?" Martin asked.

"It means that we are all as a lighthouse. We shine brightly for those far away to see, but we all stand at the base of our tower by the sea, oblivious to the light we ourselves give off."

"Did he complain about it anymore after that?"

"Not once." Yoshiko smiled again. "He doesn't play that old horn much anymore. But he could if he wanted to. Maybe you'd do us the pleasure of coming over and hearing his music sometime. Don't you have a spring vacation at the end of this month?

Martin looked up, his eyes wide. The company had three set holidays during the year, the first of which was at the end of April. Though he had made no particular plans for travel, he had been secretly counting the days until the bells of freedom would ring. It was an uninterrupted week-long break. A week without Manager. A week without wearing a suit or a tie. A week just to himself.

Martin squirmed in his seat. It was technically against company policy to meet with students privately outside of school hours. Any meetings had to be condoned by Manager, and Martin was all but certain that Manager would find no cause to allow such unmitigated socialization to occur without her personal supervision.

But before Martin could even give Yoshiko a yes or a no, she was already writing down the arrangements in her notebook. "My driver can pick you up at the station nearest your house. I could even send him directly to your home, if you'd like. Why don't you come over on a Sunday and stay for a day or two? We have a quite large piece of land and there are many things to do and see. There's a natural hot spring connected to the house that you can enjoy as well."

Martin opened his mouth to object, but stopped himself before the words reached his lips. *Forget Manager. She'll never know. And even if she did, what is she going to get angry about? Me visiting the home of a seventy-five-year-old lady?*

Martin nodded to himself several times, and after sufficiently convincing himself, he smiled at Yoshiko and said, "I'd love to."

"Wonderful!" Yoshiko clasped her hands together again. "Do you know where I live?"

"Actually no. Is it far?"

"By car it takes at least an hour," she said. "There isn't a very convenient station nearby."

"What's the name of the area?"

"Tateyama."

Martin looked up, surprised. He thought of the business card that he had kept attached to the front of his refrigerator: *Tateyama Eggs, Yuji Sakasegawa, 18-7-82 Tateyama.*

Could Yoshiko know something about him? It had been several weeks since Martin had seen or heard anything of Yuji and his young companion. He thought of the egg they held between them, and the vision that had taken over his mind.

What was it? He struggled to remember. *A cave. So many feelings. A song. What was that song?*

"Is something wrong?" Yoshiko asked, tilting her head at Martin.

"Yoshiko," he said. "Can I ask you a question?"

"Of course."

"You said your husband is a musician. Do you play music too?"

"I do!" She nodded vigorously. "I play the koto and the shamisen."

"Would you know a song if I sang it to you?" Martin tried to get the lyrics he had heard straight in his head.

"I could try. Why don't you sing it for me?"

"I just know two lines, but I can't recall it that well." He closed his eyes and focused on the notes he had heard in the cave. "*Nen, nen, korori yo. Okorori yo.*" He did his best to imitate the rhythm.

"Ah!" Yoshiko clapped her hands. "*Boya wa yoi ko da. Nen, nen shina,*" she sang.

"That's it!" Martin said. "What does it mean?"

"It's a lullaby," Yoshiko answered. "But Martin, how on earth did you ever hear that song? It's from the Edo period—hundreds of years ago!"

"Oh!" Martin's eyes darted around, looking for a reasonable lie. "I must have heard it on TV the other day."

Yoshiko raised an eyebrow, but didn't press any further. "I've played that song before. It's not a complicated piece."

"I see." Martin felt suddenly uncomfortable. "I just thought I'd ask. Anyway, tell me about Tateyama. What's it like?"

"Well, most people just think of the mountain there. Mount Tate. But it's so much more than that." Yoshiko looked around, struggling to find the right word to give voice to her thoughts. It was the first time in a while that Martin sensed her knowledge of English was insufficient to express herself easily.

"Is it a nice place?" Martin asked, breaking the silence.

Yoshiko looked up at him and smiled weakly. The wrinkles of her face all furrowed together. "I was not born in Tateyama," she started. "In fact, when I moved here, the townspeople were all quite rude to me. I didn't have any friends and I felt very alone. I hated Tateyama very much."

Yoshiko paused again, searching for the right words. "I'm sorry, Sensei, please give me a moment." She closed her eyes tightly, and slowly her neck started tilting backwards. For a moment Martin thought she had fallen asleep.

"Yoshiko?" he said quietly. No answer. Martin leaned forward.

"Yoshiko!" he called her name again, reaching his arm out to her. This time, she seemed to notice. Her whole head jerked forward and her eyes shot wide open.

"Oh!" She gasped. "I must have thought too much and fallen asleep!" Yoshiko burst into laughter. She laughed and laughed, and with every laugh her voice cracked and tears rolled from her eyes, which only made her laugh more. Martin scratched his chin in confusion.

"Are you all right?" he asked when a pause in her laughter presented itself. She held out a hand that begged him to wait a moment longer before reaching for her purse and removing a small package of tissues. Hands still shaking from laughter, she wiped her eyes and smiled back at Martin.

"There are so many frivolous things in this world," she said, wiping the last of her tears from her face and placing the tissue carefully on the desk in front of her. "Come visit me, Martin, and perhaps you'll begin to understand."

The clock on the wall struck noon, and Martin took a deep breath and stood up. "I will visit you, Yoshiko. I'm looking forward to it."

He extended his hand out to her, helping her rise from the desk, then retrieved her purse and umbrella from the floor. It was an elegant, green umbrella with a light brown wooden handle and a white ribbon that twirled around it in curves and loops. It looked like a part of nature—too beautiful and subtle to have been crafted by the crude hands of man. Martin admired it for a moment before looking through the window at the perfectly sunny day that mocked him from the outside world.

"Is it supposed to rain?" he asked, taking her by the arm and helping her to the door.

"Oh no, oh no," she said, straining with each step. "But I happen to like this umbrella very much. It's very fashionable, don't you think?" Martin had never particularly thought of umbrellas as a fashion statement, especially on sunny days. Still, it was a beautifully crafted piece, and was sure to steal the attention of anyone who laid eyes on it.

"Does it rain often in Tateyama?" he asked. She came to a sudden halt at the question and looked up at him seriously.

"Martin," she said, staring at him through foggy brown eyes. "You'll definitely need an umbrella when you come to visit. Make sure you don't forget. Do you understand?"

"Yes, ma'am."

Her gentle smile returned to her face and she nodded enthusiastically. "Good, good. Well, I must be going now. I'll see you next week?"

"See you next week, Yoshiko. Thank you very much for coming today."

She grasped the handle of her umbrella in her left hand and pressed the end of it into the floor, propping herself up like a tripod before slowly hobbling towards the door. Martin stood in the hall and watched with care as she finally made her way out to the door to the waiting car beyond. A tall, elderly man in a black suit and bow tie held the door for her.

Martin moved closer to the front to get a better view of him. He was dressed immaculately, his gray hair combed neatly. His white gloves were spotless and his shoes shone like mirrors in the daylight. The coat of his jacket even had tails. *Tails? Where do you get a coat with tails on it in this day and age?* Martin closed the door. *I guess I'll find out soon enough. Just a few weeks till spring vacation.*

*

Shortly after Yoshiko left, Manager packed a small briefcase full of notebooks and printouts, and headed out to her bi-annual meeting at the office in Kanazawa.

"Your next lesson called and cancelled," she said as she snapped her briefcase shut. "I'll be out for the rest of the day. If something happens, phone me at once."

Martin returned to the staff room and laid back in his chair, letting the realization of having the rest of his work day free of Manager wash over him. He put his feet up on his desk and stretched out until his back gave a satisfying pop.

"There need to be more days like this," Martin said aloud.

"Like what?" The sound of a voice behind him caught Martin completely unaware. In a panic, his body stiffened and the angle of his chair fell horizontal, sending him to the floor on the back of his head with his legs hovering above him.

"Ow!" he shouted, straining to straighten himself up. But the only reply to his embarrassment was the sound of Stacy's laughter, punctuated by heavy snorts that only made her laugh harder.

"How did you get in here? I didn't even hear the door open," Martin said, coming to his feet.

"Probably because you forgot to close it, you idiot!" Stacy's laughter welled up and burst again. It was uncontrollably loud, and soon enough Mika appeared behind her to investigate.

"What happened?" she asked. But before either Martin or Stacy could form an answer, Chris pushed himself through the door.

"I'm glad you're all here!" he said. Martin looked him over intently. His shirt had been ironed and the scent of cologne polluted the air around him. His hair was gelled and parted to the right, and where once prickly stubble had grown, fresh, white skin had appeared making him look years younger. *But that smile. That damn smile.*

Chris came over and put an arm around Martin's shoulder. "Well everyone, Martin and I were just talking, and we had a thought."

"Oh, you had a thought? That's a first." Stacy sat in her chair and crossed her legs.

"Don't you have a corporate lesson to be at right now? Or, you know, anywhere else but here?"

"Oh, OK. Why don't you just—" Stacy fumed, but Chris cut her off.

"Anyway! Martin really thought this one up." He looked over at Mika, standing helplessly against the tide of Chris's scheming. "Martin was saying how wonderful it would be if we had a welcome dinner for Mika here, just the four of us! What do you think?"

"Uh…" Martin tried to step away, but Chris squeezed his arm around him and held him close.

"*Four?* What about Colby?" Stacy put a hand on her hip and raised an eyebrow.

"Oh, no. Colby can't make it, he said. Too busy with the wife or something like that. It doesn't matter. Anyway, what do *you* think, Mika?" He released his grip on Martin and floated over to where she stood.

"Um… uh…" She glanced around looking for help. "But shouldn't we invite Manager? If it's a staff event I think I have to file a plan for it, and—"

"No, no, no!" Chris objected excitedly. "It's not really a *staff* party. It's just, you know, a welcome party with, uh, friends!"

"Friends?" Stacy asked suspiciously. "You have those?"

"*Actually* Stacy, I consider all of you here my friends."

Stacy smiled a crooked smile, and Martin immediately became fearful of what was happening inside her head. But Chris, taking no notice of her whatsoever, continued to focus on Mika.

"So, what do you think, Mika? Wouldn't it be nice to get to know all of your coworkers better over some drinks? Or no drinks! Do you drink?"

Martin watched the train wreck that was unfolding before him in disbelief. Mika held her hands together nervously over her chest and stared at her feet. *There's no way she's going to go for this. Does this idiot even have a plan?*

"I—I—I'd love to!" she said.

"What?" the three teachers replied in astonished unison. *Incredible. She's actually going for it.*

"Of course!" Chris answered excitedly. Martin wanted to slap the grin off his face. "And since this was really Martin's idea and not mine, maybe Martin has a good place picked out for dinner?"

Why do I have to be the one to suggest it? Martin scratched at the back of his neck, unable to grasp the intricacies of Chris's strategy.

"I've heard that Chinese place in Mariet is really good. It's near the station and all. Mika, do you like Chinese food?" Martin asked.

Mika nodded.

"Well then, it's settled! How about Saturday night? Not this one, but the one just before vacation?" Chris could barely contain his enthusiasm.

Everyone agreed, and after another minute of idle chatter, they filed out of the room one by one, leaving Martin alone again. His plans with Yoshiko were of little concern. A few days in a tucked away mountain home wasn't apt to draw any unwanted attention. But more than half the staff having dinner together just a couple blocks from the office, and conspicuously without Manager, churned his stomach. *There's going to be hell to pay for this one. And I'll bet I'm the one going to be stuck with the check.*

CHAPTER FIFTEEN

The Long Hour

Eiko arrived fifteen minutes before her lesson was set to start. Martin overheard Mika greet her from his seat in the staff office, and peeked out the door to get a good look at her. She wore long, denim overalls and a tight-fitting white top. Her orange hair was down just past her shoulders, and she ran a slender hand through it while exchanging greetings with Mika. *From here, she almost looks normal.*

He went back to his desk and pulled out one of his lower mid-level texts, then dropped a pair of whiteboard markers into his pocket. Normally, when a particular student desired private lessons it was done in one of two ways. The first was an accelerated version of the current curriculum, designed for extremely aggressive learners. The second, which Yoshiko had desired, was a free-form conversation class. This style was more suited to speakers who had gained at least a modicum of expertise in the language, and were already comfortable expressing themselves on a variety of topics.

After their last meeting, Manager had not told Martin which direction Eiko's lesson should go. In fact, she said nothing about it except for the dates and times. He understood why, of course, but no matter the reason he was still in the dark as to how to prepare for the lesson. His heart sank into his stomach. He looked up at the clock on the wall and watched the second hand sweep across the indices. *This might be the only time in my life I stare at a clock and think that time is passing too fast.* He sighed. The voices of Mika and Eiko subsided after a short while, and Martin took this as his cue to meet his new student.

She sat in the corner of the lobby, her eyes fixed on a book whose title Martin couldn't see. Her eyebrows were furrowed, and she moved her mouth slowly as if trying to sound out each word she was reading. Whatever its contents, Martin could see that she was very serious about it. He held his textbook in both hands against his stomach and approached her with all the caution of a lion tamer.

The closer he came, the more unsure of himself he felt. He walked until he was no more than three feet in front of her, but her eyes kept their focus completely on the book in her hands.

"Uh… um…" he said, clumsily trying to get her attention. Martin's face began burning up. He was standing directly in front of her now, looking down at her as she stared at her text.

"Ah! Ah!" Eiko slammed her book shut and shot up like a rubber band. Martin flinched and instinctively braced himself for an attack.

"Why don't you say something before you come walking up to people!?" She scrunched her face up at him in disapproval. Martin looked down at the book she held in front of her chest. It was bright red, with a water color-style cover showing a portrait of a fat brown bear wearing stars and stripes patterned underwear, with the title *Mr. Bear Goes to America* written in awful pastels above him.

"Is that a picture book?" was the first thing that came out of Martin's mouth.

Eiko looked down at *Mr. Bear* red-faced and quickly shoved it back into her bag. "It's nothing!"

"It looks like an English book. Let me see it." Martin instinctively moved a hand towards her bag that was immediately slapped away.

"Ow!" Martin shook his hand and stepped back.

"Ahem." Mika stood up from behind them. "Why don't you continue this conversation in the classroom?"

"Right..." Martin nodded. "This... this way."

Martin led Eiko down the hall to his room and opened the door with a gulp. *If she's going to kill me, this would be the perfect place.*

He held the door open and gestured at her to step inside. She paused at the entry and looked around at the room. "It's small," was all she could say.

"Well, it's not big." Martin rolled his eyes.

Up until this point, Martin had only been speaking to Eiko in Japanese, but now it was time to test the waters of her English ability. He put his textbooks down on his podium and turned to the whiteboard, writing his name in blue ink. *I'm the teacher. I've got to take the lead now.* He nodded to himself.

"It's going to be English only from here on out, OK?"

Eiko nodded her head and gave Martin a thumbs up. "Okey-dokey!"

Martin sighed. "Good. Now, I know we've already met, but I would like you to introduce yourself in English and tell me about yourself."

"Okey-dokey!" She gave another thumbs up.

Martin stared at her, waiting for her to continue. After a few moments, however, she shuffled around uncomfortably and it became clear she had no idea what he wanted her to do.

"Go ahead." He lifted up a hand towards her.

"*Go... ahead...*" she repeated slowly.

Martin cleared his throat and spoke as slowly as he could. "Why don't I start. My name is Martin Stilwell. I'm a teacher. I live in Takaoka. I'm twenty-four years old. How about you?"

Eiko nodded, her big brown eyes completely glossed over. "Ah!" She snapped up, pounding a fist into an open hand. "Okey-dokey!"

Martin nodded slowly.

"My name Eiko!"

"My name *is* Eiko."

"My names *is* Eiko"

Martin corrected her emphasis. *"My name* is *Eiko."*

"Yes," she said.

Martin buried his head in his hands. *She can't be this bad. She can't be.*

"Okey-dokey!" she shouted. "I from Japan! I am two-ten's old."

"You're what?"

"What?"

"How old are you?"

"How... old... are... you...?" She put a finger on her hand and made like she was spelling something on her palm.

Martin pinched the bridge of his nose between his thumb and finger before turning around to the white board and writing the numbers one through twenty across it. Eiko looked up attentively and took out a notebook and pen from her bag. Martin watched as she wrote the numbers on the first page, and waited for her to look back up.

Martin pointed at the first number.

"One!"

Good enough. He pointed to the next.

"Two! Three! Four!" Eiko went on until Martin pointed at the eleven.

"Ten-one!"

"No." Martin wrote the word eleven under the numbers. "Eleven."

"Oh! Eleven! Okey-dokey!" She jotted down the number. "Yes!" She nodded confidently.

Martin repeated the process for each number up to twenty, giving her a chance to say each number and write it down. At twenty, Eiko realized her previous error and tried again on her own.

"I am twenty years old!"

Martin let out a sigh of relief. "Good. Let's try again."

"My. Name. *Is.* Eiko," she said, making each word deliberate.

"Yes." Martin nodded.

"Yes," Eiko repeated.

Martin motioned for her to continue.

"Oh! I from Japan."

"Are you from Toyama?"

"Toyama." She nodded.

Martin opened his mouth to help her, but decided against it. "How old are you?" he asked instead.

"I am *twenty* years old!" she said proudly.

Martin nodded and clapped his hands together. "All right!"

Eiko smiled. Not her mischievous, scheming smile that Martin had grown accustomed to, but a genuine smile of happiness and accomplishment.

She's cute when she's not scary. Martin snapped the cap of his marker shut, watching her celebrate her small victory.

"Okey-dokey?" she asked.

"Okey-dokey," he repeated. He looked down at his watch that read ten past the hour. *Only ten minutes. That whole ordeal only took ten minutes.* He stared at his now woefully out of place intermediate level textbook and wondered how to fill the time.

"So..." He clapped his hands and rubbed them together.

"So..." she repeated.

Martin let out a small laugh and scratched the shallow stubble that had formed on his chin. Eiko's copy of *Mr. Bear Goes to America* was sticking out of her bag. He thought to ask her about it again, but his hand still throbbed with the quick slap she had given him at his first inquiry. Martin couldn't wrap his head around why she would bring it with her if she didn't want to learn something from it. Out of habit, Martin put his hands together and began to pull on his knuckles.

"Sensei." Eiko broke the silence. Martin looked up at her. Her countenance had changed, revealing a softer, more feminine side that he had not seen in her until now.

"Teach me."

"Right." He resisted the urge to crack his knuckle and instead picked up the textbook he had brought with him. *This is far too advanced. I'll have to improvise.*

He pointed at her bag, motioning to the book inside. "Can I look at that?" he asked.

She looked down and saw the red cover of *Mr. Bear Goes to America* sticking out and quickly shoved it deeper inside.

"Please?"

She rolled her eyes and folded her arms. "You'll just make fun of me," she said in Japanese.

"Do you want to learn English or not?" he asked. The ball was in his court now, and he wasn't stopping until they were knee deep in whatever trouble Mr. Bear had found himself in.

"Hmph." She shook her head, but when it became clear Martin was serious, she acquiesced and took the book out of her bag.

"Very good," Martin said. "Now, let's read it together."

CHAPTER SIXTEEN

The River Matsu

Her intonation was atrocious. Her grammar inconsistent. She mutilated pronunciation at every opportunity, but she never seemed to mind. Even when Martin buried his head in his hands or showed visible frustration, she'd stick up her thumb and just give out her best, "Okey-dokey!"

After a few lessons, Martin's nerves calmed to the point where he no longer dreaded her almost daily appearance. There were times, to his surprise, where it seemed like she would make genuine progress from one class to the next. By the end of the first week she could talk about her likes and dislikes. And by the end of the second week, she was able to form simple questions, which greatly expanded her ability to converse.

He admired her tenacity and growth, but more than that, he admired how Manager would seemingly disappear from sight when she was due to come in for a lesson. Martin watched as Eiko pulled the strings, and the marionette danced beneath her.

"Why don't you ask her out?" Chris said, rolling a tennis ball between his hands.

"No." Martin zipped his backpack shut and set it on his desk.

"Why not?"

"For one, she's crazy. For two, she's a student."

"She doesn't seem that crazy." Chris tossed the tennis ball up in the air. Martin watched as it climbed, hung, then fell back into his waiting hands.

"Oh?" Martin snorted. "Well believe me, she is."

"If you say so." Chris threw the ball up in the air again, but this time it carried too much of a backspin and landed behind him. Martin watched it bounce away under Stacy's desk and shook his head.

"I'm heading out for the night. See you tomorrow, man."

"Oh yeah!" Chris stood up. "Don't forget the dinner on Saturday."

"Uh-huh." Martin picked up his bag and walked out of the staff room.

"And don't forget to make me look good!" Chris called from behind him.

It was a warm, April evening, and the streets were filled with people—young couples, parents with their children at their heels, and elderly men and women bent forward as they hobbled down the sidewalks. They all made their way south, away from the station. Despite the misgivings in his heart about the coming dinner plans, Martin found a spring in his step and, filling his lungs with a deep breath, decided to follow the current of people southward towards the River Matsu.

It was his first time walking south of the office since the snows had melted. The taller buildings of the area gradually shortened as he continued along, and the crude, colorlessness of concrete men in concrete buildings gave way to a more relaxed, residential area filled with apartments, small shops, and restaurants, centered near a bridge that extended over the river itself.

The Matsu was a narrow river. Its current flowed with a patient speed, and crests of rocks dotted the river itself, betraying the shallowness of the water. The street that ran parallel to the river had been blocked off to vehicles, and was instead overrun by a hoard of stalls and stands. The shopkeepers peddled their goods with gusto, and the air smelled of fried chicken and grilled eel.

Martin waded through the masses along the river, stopping to look at each shop. One stall was full of children playing ring toss. Another was surrounded by men holding beers engaged in light conversation and laughter. It was a true festival. Around him, the men's faces were pink with the consumption of sake. Above him, the cherry blossoms bloomed, their petals pink with the tenuity of spring.

After a few minutes of slow progress, Martin found a small path between two stalls that led down to the bank of the Matsu itself. With some effort he squeezed through the flurry of people and started on the path downwards. The steps were steep and narrow, and as he descended, the streetlights above grew dimmer and dimmer, until nothing but a faint orange glow remained to illuminate his steps. When he reached the bottom, he turned around to look back up the way he had come, but could only see the faint silhouette of branches standing above the grassy incline.

Martin continued his journey east unopposed. Rushing water all but obscured even the loudest of voices from above, and even the grassy incline alongside he walked was devoid of drunken businessmen or mischievous teenage couples looking for a moment of privacy. The moon hid behind the foliage above, and for the first time in a while, Martin felt completely alone.

After a quarter of an hour of walking, his legs began chafing against the inside of his suit pants, and his heels became sore. There were no clean benches or seats upon which to sit himself, and after a quick search of the area, fatigue got the better of him and he plopped down in his nice, navy suit atop the grass.

The river was calm. The light of the stars above reflected on its surface and moved with the ripples and waves of the water.

Irregularly, gusts of wind blew the mature cherry blossoms into the current. Martin watched as they were carried helplessly downstream, feeling a sort of kinship with the fallen petals.

He slid his knees up to his chest, a wave of unease washing over him. "I am where I am and there's nowhere else I can be," he repeated to himself. He watched the flowers float out of sight, and his unease was replaced with a profound sadness as the last flower disappeared into the dark.

Martin squeezed his eyes shut and wiped his tears on the shoulder of his jacket. "What am I doing here?" he whispered. But his only answer was the gentle flow of the river Matsu.

"What am I doing here?" he screamed. Martin slammed his hands down on the grass around him and threw himself upward, towards the river. On the ground he faintly made out the shape of a rock, and he bent down to pick it up.

"What the hell am I doing here?" he shouted again, putting all of his might into his arm and launching the rock across the river. It skipped across the surface of the water until Martin heard a loud *crash* on the far bank. He stared into the dark, expecting nothing but silence.

But this time a voice answered him.

"She doesn't belong here."

Martin spun around and peered into the darkness behind him.

"She doesn't belong here," the voice said again.

"She can't leave," Martin replied.

"You have to take it off." This time, the voice had form. It was the little girl from the red truck. She stood next to him and took his hand in hers.

"I don't understand," Martin said again, holding her small hand in his own.

The little girl smiled and moved closer to him, gripping his hand tightly. "It's OK," she said. "But you can't stay here. You shouldn't come here again. Not for a while, anyway."

"Why?" Martin asked in a whisper. The little girl sighed and pointed to the river.

"You see only the sadness of things past, gone beyond your control. This river, it isn't a strong rushing river. It's a calm river. A gentle river. When things are calm and gentle you waste time looking backwards. But when the waves crash upon your body and the earth shakes around you, that's when you look forward. Because if you don't look forward when the world crumbles, you crumble along with it. You need to stay away from calm rivers. Do you understand?"

Martin nodded.

"Come on," she said, urging him to the edge of the water. "Look that way."

Martin turned his head to the west and saw a light hovering over the water in the distance. He focused his eyes on it and soon its shape became clear. It was a small, wooden boat, occupied by a single man. Its oars rose and fell in the water, splashing softly with each motion. Martin turned back around towards the street, but there was nothing left to see. The once orange glow of lights above him had vanished. The sounds of laughter and cheer had disappeared. There was no one left but himself and the little girl whose hand rested peacefully in his.

"I have questions," Martin said, looking back at the girl.

"About the eggs?" She returned his gaze with a smile. "Have you been eating them every day? Aren't the delicious?"

"How did you get them in my apartment?"

The little girl shrugged. "I just opened the door."

"Uh-huh..."

The distant boat floated ever-closer until Martin could almost reach out and touch it. He inched forward, but the little girl squeezed his hand and shook her head.

"Not yet," she cautioned. "Wait for him."

"But it's right here. Even you could jump on it from this distance."

The little girl only shook her head again. Her face was solemn, and had the words "Do as I say" written all over it.

"Well, well!" the man from the boat bellowed. "If it isn't my best customer!"

"I didn't buy anything from you," Martin replied.

The man reached out his hand to the little girl and helped her board the craft. "Come on." He turned to Martin. "Your turn now. Your turn." He stretched his hand out, but Martin backed away.

"Go to hell, you old coot. I remember what you did to me the last time I took your hand."

"What did I do? I didn't do nothin'. Nothin' at all."

"Stop it, the both of you!" The little girl extended her hand to Martin. "You can just take my hand!"

"The boy's too heavy. Just look at him. He'd likely pull you right out with him and take you under."

Martin was incensed. He stuck his hand out at the man and pointed a finger, but before he could unleash his barrage of insults, the man snatched his whole arm and pulled him aboard.

"God damn it!" Martin yelled. "What the hell is wrong with you?" But Yuji turned and went back to his station at the oars.

"Sit down," the little girl said. "We have a way to go yet."

Martin maneuvered to the front of the craft. It was a rickety boat. Every step he took was punctuated by the nervous creaking of wood. Soft yellow light emanated from an old gasoline lantern that hung from the bow. Martin plonked himself down at the front of the craft, opposite the little girl. Behind her, Yuji manned the oars and pressed off the concrete. He seemed different from their last meeting, stronger and more alive. More purposeful. Despite the warmth of the night he wore long, dark jeans with brown boots, and a long brown coat that extended all the way down to the bottom of his calves.

The world was silent, save for the rise and fall of the oars in the water. Martin watched the reflection of the moon on the river's surface, its image distorted by the ripples from the oars' movement. All the while, he felt the constant gaze of the little girl upon him.

"You're watching me," he said, still admiring the silver moon in the river.

"Yes," she responded.

"Are you taking me back to the station? Does this river even turn north?"

"No."

"So where are you taking me?"

"Home."

"You could just let me out and I could go back the way I came. I do know where I am, you know."

"You know some things. Where you are is not one of them."

"I'm on the River Matsu," Martin said confidently. "Just a few blocks south of the station."

"Look around you," the little girl said, motioning her hand to the bank of the river. Martin looked back at the bank from which he had come. It was empty. No stalls, no families, no lights from the windows. But there was movement along the slopes. Sporadic at first, then constant. Wave-like. Martin felt the little girl move past him and dim the lantern hanging from the bow.

As the lantern's glow faded, the light of the moon revealed an audience of hens lining the banks on either side. Some fat, some slim. They paused every few moments and stared at the craft, then moved again, all as one, to follow. There was an army of them, every single patch of earth was covered by fowl.

"I'm not on the Matsu anymore, am I?" Martin asked, half-hoping that no answer would follow the question.

The little girl only stared back at him, her eyes wide.

"But why are they all here? Why are you here? I saw a news report about your farm not too long ago. Why can't you just go back?"

"The lady won't let us, oh no, oh no," Yuji sang, slapping the oars back in the water.

"The lady?"

"The lady with the red umbrella," the little girl responded. She kicked her legs in the air and leaned backwards, staring at the stars.

Martin looked out across the river again. An eerily faint fog had crept up along its concrete banks, and Martin felt at once uneasy.

"Don't worry," Yuji said, sucking on his teeth. "You'll be gone before the fog wraps her cold arms around you. But not us. Oh no, oh no. Someone's gotta stay."

Martin hesitated a moment before mustering up his courage. "Why am I here? What *is* this?" He felt the pain of desperation weighing on his heart. "What am I doing here?" he demanded.

"Only a fool goes to a place and then asks someone else why he has gone there," said Yuji.

"Then I must be quite a fool," Martin whispered under his breath. The small comfort of control he had once felt was slipping away. It was as if his life up until this point had been carried on the backs the actions of others, and that Martin could only watch as they trudged down unclear paths. The little girl stood up and came to his feet. She tilted her head to the side and stared up into Martin's eyes.

"A fool doesn't often think of himself as a fool though," she said.

"Hmph." Yuji grunted. "Well at least he's been eating the eggs. I told you there was nothing wrong with them. Checked them myself. I did, I did."

Martin looked up again. The fog, which been on the riverbanks only moments before, crept slowly towards the side of the boat. Martin's heart grew cold.

"It's time for you to go," Yuji said, bringing the oars up and into the boat. "We continue. But you can go no further."

"Wait," Martin objected. He stood up to face the duo. "You haven't answered my questions yet. And I've barely even had a chance to speak."

"Don't worry," the little girl said. "You won't be gone forever. Before you know it, we'll all be together again!" She turned towards Yuji and went to his side. The fog was bearing over the edge of the boat, its milky tendrils obscuring the pair from Martin's vision. His heart thumped with panic.

"Just close your eyes!" The voice of the little girl was distant.

"And keep eating those eggs!" Yuji shouted in his grizzly voice. "They're good for you!"

Martin's eyelids suddenly felt heavy. The fog was a cocoon around him. He felt the wood of the boat underneath his feet and focused on it. *Just close your eyes. Just close your eyes.*

Slowly, deliberately, the wood beneath him faded. Martin took a deep breath. Something else surrounded him now: the unmistakable coil of human arms wrapped around his chest. He squeezed his eyes shut as tight as he could, and let himself be taken.

CHAPTER SEVENTEEN

Tuba's Room of Shoes

When he opened his eyes again, Martin was back on the riverbank. His whole body shook violently and he gasped for air as if he were taking his first breath. He felt the powerful arms of a man wrapped around him from behind, clutching his chest.

"Let me go!" he shouted. Martin squirmed and kicked, but his feet couldn't find any earth below him. He was at least a foot above solid ground, and powerless to resist.

"Relax, relax!" called a familiar voice from behind him.

"How can I relax!" Martin roared. "You're squeezing the life out of me!"

"Actually, we're trying to squeeze the life back *into* you. If you get my meaning," the familiar voice said. "And it seems we've succeeded. Sami, put him down."

Martin felt the vice-like grip around him ease, and slowly his body fell until his feet landed on solid ground. His legs shook, and before he knew it, he had fallen to his knees. The water of the river flowed peacefully in the dark. There was no fog anymore. He scanned the river but saw no sign of the boat. It was gone.

The familiar man came to his side and put an arm on Martin's shoulder. Martin turned to look at him. It was Tuba. In his hand he held an old gasoline lantern that gave off a soft orange glow.

Martin focused on the light within it and felt his mind ease. Tuba put a hand on Martin's shoulder and sat down on the grass. He was wearing faded blue jeans with a button-down maroon shirt and his black-striped fedora.

"I'm sorry for that." Tuba bowed his head. "We had just the one chance to grab you before you fell in the water, so we did."

Martin nodded. "I guess I should be saying thank you. Although I'm not sure exactly how you found me here. Or what exactly you saved me from."

"Do you know where you were just now?" Tuba asked pointedly.

Martin hesitated, then looked out across the water. "I was there," he said, pointing at the river. "I was, I mean, I wasn't in the river, I was on a boat—"

"There are no boats on the Matsu," Sami interrupted. "It's too shallow. You could walk through the damn river if you wanted to."

"It's true!" Martin objected. "It was a shit boat, but it was a boat." Martin leaned back and relaxed his breathing. The world around him was dark but for the light of the lantern. Its orange hue filled the void around him and warmed him from within.

"How did you get on the boat?" Tuba inquired. "Did you get on willfully or did something take you onboard?"

"Well... a little bit of both I guess. I mean, I meant to get on the boat but the guy on the boat ended up pulling me in." Martin rubbed the goosebumps on his arm where Yuji had grabbed him.

"Is this the first time you've seen this man?"

"No. This would be the second."

"Did he say anything to you?"

"He said a lot of things to me." Martin closed his eyes tightly. "We were talking, but then this fog came over the boat and—"

"Martin," Tuba interrupted. "Sorry, but can we continue this at the bar? I don't want to stay around this river any longer than I have to. The air is too thick tonight. This isn't a good place to talk."

"Do you know something about this guy?" Martin asked.

"Perhaps I do. But there's only one way to find out. Come with us."

Before Martin could respond, Sami's arms wrapped around him and lifted him off the ground again.

"Jesus Christ," Martin protested. "I can walk on my own two feet, damn it."

Sami snorted and let Martin go. "Suit yourself. Come on. Stay close to us, we'll be back at the bar in no time."

The trio began their trek to the bar in the dark. The path from the river took them through the unbroken gloom of the shutter-town. The street was made of stone, and every door was rusted brown. Every sign was missing letters. *This is a dead town.* Martin thought. And he was right. Even the local homeless people made no effort to find shelter here.

"Is it haunted?" Martin finally asked, hoping to break the quiet.

"No," Tuba responded. "Even something as lonely as a ghost wouldn't be caught in a place like this."

"Why not?"

"What purpose would a ghost have here? It's not just dead. It's *empty*. The whole town made an effort to forget this place, and this is the result."

"I guess. But why not just tear it down then? It's just a waste of space. They could build something here that people would come to."

"Like I said." Tuba moved the old gasoline lantern up to his face. "They made an effort to forget this place. If they started talking about it again, then they'd have to acknowledge its existence. And I guess sometimes it's easier to just let some things fade out of mind until there's nothing left at all."

"I don't know about that," Martin said, but Tuba said no more.

After three blocks, the trio turned a corner and headed east. About a hundred feet in front of them, Martin could make out the neon green letters "SORA" at the base of the stairs.

"Mind the bar, will you Sami?" Tuba asked. "And make sure Chris isn't giving away too many drinks for free up there."

"Chris is there?" Martin stopped.

"We had to leave someone at the bar in charge. He's done it for us before... but..." Tuba let out a sigh, and Martin waited for him to continue.

"It would be best if he didn't see us. It would be best if you didn't see him either. Not now."

"Why not?" Martin said anxiously.

"Just trust me this once." Tuba put a hand on Martin's shoulder. "We're here to help."

"And Chris isn't?"

Tuba's eyes lowered. "Come on. We must be discreet." With that, he turned toward the bar, leaving Martin to follow him.

The bar's heavy bass shook the walls of the staircase as they climbed. Sami went in first while Tuba and Martin waited together outside of the door. Martin checked his watch blearily: Five past midnight. *Well so much for making the last train. Maybe one of them can give me a ride home before this gets out of hand.*

After a few minutes the door opened and Tuba hurried Martin inside. It was a busy night, and customers who had probably sought to continue the entertainment from the festival gathered at every table. Martin kept his head down and pushed past them as best he could. Before he realized it, he was standing behind the bar with Sami and Tuba.

"Keep moving," Sami shouted over the music. Martin raised his head and looked forward. The customer-side of the bar ended at a black wall about fifteen feet in front of him, but the wall did not carry over to the service-side of the bar. Instead, there were two black curtains that came down from the ceiling, beyond which he could not see.

Martin kept pace behind Tuba, following him up to the curtained-off area until he held out a hand signaling Martin to wait. Tuba slid his body through the curtain and disappeared for a moment before reemerging with a smile on his face.

"We are ready," he said. "Close your eyes and come through. Open them as soon as you have taken the first step through and you feel the curtain close behind you. Do you understand?"

Martin could only nod. *There's nothing else to do but to cross the precipice now. There's nowhere else I can be.* He took a deep breath, and stepped through the curtains.

*

As he had been told to, Martin opened his eyes at the exact moment he felt the curtains close behind him. Only there was nothing he was opening his eyes to see. The room was pitch black.

"Tuba?" Martin whispered to the darkness. "Where are you?"

Nothing.

Martin reached out with his arms, trying to feel for a wall or something to guide him as he sojourned further on, but there was nothing.

"Stop there." Tuba's voice was stern, and Martin was compelled to obey.

"Good. Now I'm going to ask you some questions. If you answer honestly, you'll get some light."

"What?"

"I just need to make sure."

"Make sure of what? What's going on here?" The hairs on the back of Martin's neck stood on end.

"What is your relationship with the old farmer, Yuji?" Tuba's voice echoed from somewhere in front of Martin.

How does he know? The only person I've told is Shimodoi. And there's no way that kid comes to places like this.

"Answer the question."

"I'm not sure how to answer your question." Martin hesitated. "What exactly is it you want to know?"

"How did you come to know him?" Tuba probed.

Martin tried to recall the exact details of their first meeting the month before. "He came to me at a convenience store late at night. He asked me if I needed eggs."

"Did he give you some eggs?"

"He did."

"Have you eaten them?"

"I have."

"I see." Tuba paused. The room fell quiet again until Martin decided to break the silence with questions of his own.

"Can you tell me who he is? Can you tell me what he wants with me?"

"There are certain things I don't know about Yuji, you must understand." Tuba's voice was solemn. "He's just a man. But like the shanty-town we came through, he's part of this city that everyone has done their best to forget."

"Why? Did he do something wrong?"

"Not exactly. After he disappeared, rumors started circulating. No one could piece together where or why he had gone. A lot of people lost their jobs, and their frustration fueled more speculation. Nowadays, people act like they've never even heard his name."

Martin heard the creaking of footsteps on the wooden floor, followed by the sound of grinding metal, and then a burst of faint orange light. It was the lantern that Tuba had been carrying, standing not ten feet in front of Martin. Martin stared into the light, perplexed.

"Thank you, Martin. Now, close your eyes. This might sting a little."

But before Martin could close his eyes, a massive burst of light from all around him exploded outward. He forced his eyes shut, but was too late to avoid the sting.

"It always happens faster than I think it will!" Tuba let out a hearty laugh and approached Martin, who opened a cautious eye and looked at him. All of his clothes were white, from his fedora to his vest, to the very shoes on his feet.

"You look like a marshmallow," was all that came out of Martin's mouth.

"I'll have you know the ladies dig the white."

"Don't tell me you've brought me to your love lair."

"I have." Tuba spun around and struck a pose.

"Great. I'm honored," Martin said.

After a few moments, his eyes adjusted to the light and he looked around. The room was ringed with sofas and bean-bag chairs, great and small. The walls to either side of Martin were covered top to bottom with books.

On the wall in front of him was a large painting that he recognized: a woman with her back to the viewer, walking in black and white through the rain. The only color, a splash of red that gave life to an umbrella she held in her hands. The detail of it was so incredible that Martin felt like he could reach out and grab the woman by her shoulder. But before Martin could let himself be sucked in by the painting, something else caught his eye from above.

He looked up, and saw shoes.

"Why...?" he stuttered, as he craned his neck around to see all of them. There must have been at least a hundred pairs of shoes stuck to the ceiling above him. *You would think with all these shoes in here the place would stink of feet. But it doesn't. It doesn't smell at all.*

"I'm a collector," Tuba said. He turned and walked to the painting of the woman with the umbrella.

"You bought all these? They're all yours?"

"No. None of them are mine. They all came from people like you."

"What do you mean?"

"I'll tell you a little later. For now, I imagine you have a few other, more important questions."

Martin's eyes narrowed on Tuba and the old metal lantern. There was one part of this situation that stank much worse than the rest.

"Are you in on this with him? Is this some sort of joke?" Martin asked.

"What do you mean?" Tuba stepped back with surprise.

"Come on. How else did you find me tonight? How did you know where I would be? You had to be in contact with him somehow. Is this some sort of game?"

Tuba scratched his chin. "I can assure you, Martin, that is not the case. Oh, how I wish it were, that I could fly so high to meet someone like him. Tried once with Sami. But like Icarus, we just... fell back to earth." Tuba ran a finger over the old lantern, and its light dimmed. "Toyama was never what we would call a famous place, you know. But if we had to name two things that we were known for, well the first of course, would be our beautiful women!"

Martin gave no reply.

"Ba ha ha!" Tuba put a hand on his chest. "No, I jest."

Martin thought about Eiko. *Maybe she's not from Toyama, then.*

"The first thing we are known for is bronze. Statues, figurines, and even lanterns, just like this one."

"I see. And the second?"

"Ah." Tuba paused and reached for something behind the sofa he was sitting on. "Here we are."

It was an umbrella. Ornately crafted in black and gold. The handle was chestnut brown without a curve. Tuba opened it with a flick of his wrist, revealing a pattern of golden stars against a black backdrop. It was gorgeous. Tuba let Martin admire it for a moment before closing it back up and setting it down at his side.

"You see, the craftsman didn't just make these to sell at the market for nickels and dimes. He made them as gifts to the many different Samurai families of the area, in an era when Samurai still existed and a Shogun ruled Japan. They were so prized that many families actually fought over them. His work became legendary, and before long a young nobleman from Kyoto crossed the mountains in search of this craftsman. He carried with him chests upon chests of gold and jewels—a gift for the craftsman in order to secure his services.

"He crossed the River Jinzu on a warm spring day and found the craftsman hard at work on his trade. 'Oh, great craftsman!' he announced as he stepped from his horse. 'I have traveled far in search of you and your masterful works. I have brought you gold and jewels enough for you to live in comfort for the rest of your days, if you would only make for me one umbrella! Just one treasure that I may take home to my sweet Kyoto!'

"But the craftsman did not heed him. He sat with his hammer in hand and continued his work. The townspeople had gathered around the procession to view the exchange between the two men. One man in the crowd shouted, 'You can't buy his work, my lord! He will not hear your words!'

"The young lord grew agitated, and as he did his words became harsher. 'Heed my words, peasant!' he shouted. 'You should be honored that one such as myself has come this far just to see one such as you. I demand that you make me an umbrella immediately!'

"And at those words, the craftsman stopped beating his hammer, and turned to face the young lord. 'I will not make one for you, my lord,' he said.

"The young nobleman's face darkened. 'Do you dare defy me? Do as I say!'

"'I will not make one for you, my lord,' the craftsman said again.

"The young nobleman ground his teeth together. 'I will not be denied by one so low as you. If I wanted to, I could put this disgusting little hamlet to the torch and kill everyone in it. Would you be willing to have their blood on your hands?'

"But the craftsman only shook his head. 'I will not make one for you, my lord,' he said for the third time. The young nobleman screamed with rage, and cut down the craftsman where he stood. With his dying breath, the craftsman looked up at the lord's face and smiled. 'You will never have one, my lord. Not you, nor your children, nor any descendant of yours from this day 'till the sun burns out in the sky.'

"With the murder of the craftsman, the value of any remaining umbrellas skyrocketed. Some grew so attached to them that they requested theirs be buried with them in their graves. Of course, that just made them a prime target for grave robbers. Before anyone knew what was going on, half of Japan was flooded with forgeries and facsimiles, and many of the originals were lost."

Martin looked at the umbrella resting against the sofa. "If it's so valuable, shouldn't you be keeping it locked up tight? Why take it out?"

Tuba grinned. "Where's the fun in that? Besides, it has a purpose."

He reached down into his pocket and produced a remote.

"Watch," he said. He gave the remote a click and the lights shut off all at once, returning the room to complete darkness.

Martin heard a shuffling, then the sound of the umbrella opening again.

"I don't see anything."

"Wait for it."

Martin focused on the spot where Tuba had been sitting and waited.

Gradually, small points of light began to form in front of him. They looked like the most distant stars in the night sky, but slowly they grew closer. One by one, they began to dance together and form a picture in the darkness.

It seemed to be a meadow. The stars swirled together to form the shapes of trees that stood all around him. In front of him stood the image of a small building. Too large to be some kind of shack or shed, but too small to be a home. The biggest concentration of stars stood in front of the structure, taking the form of an umbrella whose handle bent and curved in unnatural ways.

"What am I looking at?" Martin asked.

"It's showing you something that's out of place. Something that is where it isn't supposed to be," Tuba answered.

"But there's nothing here."

"True. I have yet to discern why my umbrella shows me this picture. I can't even determine where it is to try to go and fix it."

"So, you were able to see me on the river this way?"

Martin heard the umbrella close. The golden stars all around him disappeared, and the room was dark once again. He closed his eyes in anticipation of the lights turning back on, but only the flame of Tuba's gas lantern flickered to life between them.

"The umbrellas the artisan crafted weren't all the same. They each had a special purpose. Each had a uniqueness to them. This one shows people that aren't where they are supposed to be. When it glows, I pop it open, take a gander, and then Sami and I get to work on fixing whatever it is that's out of place."

"Why do that at all? What do you get out of it?"

"You've got it all wrong, man!" Tuba stood up. "It's no trouble at all. Besides I find it... morally fulfilling."

"I see." Martin looked up again. "You still haven't told me about the shoe fetish though."

"What can I say?" Tuba licked his lips and walked up to Martin. "It's part of the bargain. Sometimes people ask for something, and this is what I get in return. I'm sure I even have a few from people you know."

"But why do it at all?" Martin looked back up.

"Because," he said, taking off his fedora and looking up with Martin, "I like feet."

CHAPTER EIGHTEEN

Dinner for Four, Table for Two

On Thursday, Eiko called the office and canceled her planned lessons for the rest of the week. When Martin asked Manager why, she only glared back at him and walked away.

It was strange getting through several consecutive days without Eiko's appearance. During the hours that she was scheduled to come, Martin secluded himself in the staff room, picking through different materials for her to study, and tailoring them together to form coherent lessons. On Friday, during his office hour, he borrowed the microphone and CD player in the upstairs office and recorded himself having basic conversations for Eiko to listen to at home for extra practice. It wasn't something Manager would ever approve of, so he found a slender, empty case for the CD and kept it in his bag.

Saturday night came soon enough. Each member of the dinner party left separately and made their own way to the restaurant on the top floor of Mariet. Martin arrived second after Chris, who he found pacing back and forth in front of the elevators.

"Why don't you just go up first and get us a table?" Martin said, undoing the knot in his tie. "Unless you think you can impress her with your pacing skills."

"Shut up, you hobbit." Chris stared into his reflection in the glass of the elevator door. Martin watched as he nodded to himself a few times and brushed his hand through his hair.

"All right then," Martin said, leaning against the glass. He took out his phone and glanced at the time. It was quarter to nine.

"What do you think?" Chris asked after a few moments. "Jacket on or off?" Chris posed for a moment with it on then took it off and flung it over one shoulder.

"Are you posing for a JCPenney advertisement? It looks fine either way." Martin shoved his phone back into his pocket.

"Come on man, help me out."

"Fine. Jacket off then." Martin lifted his phone up to his face again.

8:46.

"Why do you keep looking at your phone." It was a statement more than a question. "You've been acting weird all week."

Martin only grunted in response. For the whole week he had thought of little else but his boat ride on the river, Yuji and the little girl, Sami pulling him from the fog—everything that had happened that night had become hazy, like trying to look back at a harbor after setting sail, he found his memories shrinking and fading in the distance. A chicken farmer and a half-Brazilian with a magic umbrella? A foot fetishist with a room full of shoes hanging from the ceiling? Martin kicked his heels against the glass wall and bit his lower lip.

The more he thought about everything, the more irritated he became. He looked back down at his phone.

8:47.

"I'm going to go up first. I'll get us a table." Martin said with uncharacteristic authority. Chris stammered for a moment, then nodded and called the elevator down.

The restaurant was on the seventh floor on the western side. The window seats looked out above the train station, and there was a small outdoor seating area that couples could relax in to enjoy the scenery. The doors to the balcony were kept open, and a fresh evening breeze flowed in through the eatery. From small speakers above Martin flowed an odd fusion of 80s synth and old-time-y Japanese pop songs that he had no familiarity with. The restaurant itself wasn't crowded, and Martin was seated almost immediately.

He set his phone on the table and texted Chris, "Booth towards the back," to which Chris replied with a simple thumb's up. Martin ordered a beer and began to indulge himself before the others came. By the time they finally did, he was already halfway through.

"Just couldn't wait, huh?" Stacy said, taking the seat in front of Martin. Mika came in next to Stacy. She wore the same tan jacket and long skirt as usual, but she had added a hairpin in the shape of two large peaches being connected by a straw. Chris came in last and took a seat next to Martin. His face was already tinted red, and his jacket was on.

"I didn't know what you guys would want," Martin said, passing the drinks menu over to Stacy and Mika.

As they chatted among themselves about cocktails, Martin leaned over to Chris. "Jacket on?" he whispered.

"I couldn't help it," Chris whispered back. "When I saw her, I started breaking out into a sweat and before I knew it, I looked like I had fallen in the tub."

Martin stifled a laugh. There was already a warmth in his cheeks. The previous irritation that had niggled at him was starting to fade away. Mika called the waitress over to place their order, and as she did Martin reached for his drink and chugged it down as quick as he was able. The other three stared at him.

"Are you all right, Martin?" Mika asked. But before there was any answer the waitress was already there, with her cheap Bic pen and notepad.

"Another!" Martin demanded, raising his empty glass in the air. The waitress, scribbled down their orders and disappeared back towards the kitchen. Before he knew it, Martin was bobbing his head to the 80s synth music and drumming his fingers on the table to the beat.

"Does he always get like this?" Stacy looked at Chris.

"No... no this is a first."

She looked back at Martin, who had become fully enamored in the beat of the music.

"Let's order some food!" Mika interjected. The thought of food snapped Martin back into reality. He stopped drumming, but his head still bobbed to the tune.

"Good idea!" Chris added. "What are you in the mood for?" He lifted a menu up so everyone could see.

"The chicken and veggie dish looks nice." Stacy pointed at a picture on the bottom of the right page.

"OK sounds good," Chris agreed. "What else? Mika do you like spicy food? They have some spicy won tons over here."

Mika gave an emphatic nod.

"The portions are pretty big here, so we can grab a few small plates and share everything. Let's get some fried rice too." Chris turned to Martin, who was still bobbing his head back and forth. "You uh, you good on food there, buddy?"

"I want the shriiiiimp." Martin elongated the "i" long enough to annoy Stacy, who summarily kicked him in his shin underneath the table. "Ow!"

"Would you get a hold of yourself? We haven't even gotten our drinks yet and you're over there having a one-man riot."

Before Martin could say anything in his defense, Mika burst into laughter. "I didn't know you three had so much fun together." Her laugh was staggered and ugly. To Martin, it matched the rest of her, but as he looked over at Chris, he saw only the eyes of someone completely head over heels.

The drinks they had ordered came quickly and the mood at the table relaxed. Chris eventually took his jacket off, and his voice and tone turned back to his usual self. Stacy facilitated conversation as she often did whenever there was a moment of quiet, and Martin continued to drown himself in a new glass every few minutes until his body felt limp as a noodle, and he leaned back in his seat with a big sigh.

The food came out as Martin was starting on his fourth drink. Mika talked about how she had moved into a new apartment since she had started her job. A company owned complex, much the same as the ones the three teachers lived in.

"Wow. They don't even spring for something a bit nicer for Assistant Managers!" Chris remarked.

"I know." Mika gave a deep nod. Martin listened as their conversation hopped from topic to topic, completely indifferent to what was being said.

Halfway through the meal, Martin felt his shins being kicked again.

"Ow! What now?" He gave Stacy the best angry look he could muster.

"Over there." Stacy raised her chin, her eyes pointed to the patio area. "Isn't that your student? What's her name?"

Martin turned around and tried to focus his eyes on the patio tables. Sure enough, Eiko was seated at the furthest table, facing their direction. Martin snapped back around.

"What's she doing here?" he said.

Chris and Mika raised their heads up and looked over.

"What else do you think she's doing here? She's obviously eating dinner." Stacy took a sip of her cocktail.

Martin snuck a peek back at Eiko. Her orange hair was in a ponytail to the side, and she was wearing a long black and gold dress. Martin stared for a moment.

"Didn't you say she was crazy?" Chris asked.

"What?" Martin turned back around. "Oh yeah. One-hundred percent. Certifiable." He fidgeted uncomfortably in his seat.

"Really?" Mika leaned in. "But you know, she's always very polite when she comes in. And she always comes in early and studies in the lobby."

"Now that you mention it," Stacy added. "I saw her at the café right below the station on my way home on Wednesday with an English book. I was impressed. Most of the girls in my classes that are her age don't study half as hard."

"Study…" Martin muttered to himself, straining to remember something. He looked back at Eiko and her orange hair. Her eyes were cast down and she had on half a smile.

"Oh," Mika said. "She's with a guy. They must be—"

"That's right!" Martin interrupted. He picked up his bag from the floor beneath his legs and set it in his lap, elbowing Chris in the process.

"What are you doing?" he asked, slapping Martin's arm out of his face.

"I forgot I had her CD. I should go give it to her."

"Martin, I don't think that's a good idea. She's obviously having dinner with someone."

"It's fine." Martin fished the CD out of his bag and took a long gulp of water.

"Can't it wait until Monday?" Chris asked, but it was already too late. Martin had stumbled up, CD in hand, and started to walk over.

If someone had asked him what he was doing in that moment, Martin could not have given an answer. Something compelled him, and before any sort of logical thought could take the reins in his mind, he had already marched halfway over to Eiko's seat. He puffed his chest out and focused his eyes on her.

"Eiko!" he called out her name. She glanced over, then back at her dinner companion, then back at Martin. Her eyes grew like saucers. She held out a hand and shook it under the table, but Martin was so singularly focused on keeping one foot in front of the other that he failed to notice.

As soon as he approached the table, the half-drunken courage that had inspired him to get up in the first place deflated and puttered out. There he was. Holding up a CD in both hands to Eiko, who had turned white as a ghost. Martin felt drops of sweat forming and running down his sides.

Oh God. What have I done?

"Who in the hell are you?"

"Huh?" Martin turned and looked down at the man who sat across from Eiko. He had a rugged, ragged face. Not quite the level of Yuji, but close. Martin guessed that he was at least forty. His jaw seemed misaligned and his nose was a stubby glob of grease. He looked out of two beady eyes at Martin.

"Sorry, uh..." Martin stammered, but Eiko quickly snapped out of her shock and broke in.

"Ah, ah! Thank you!" She stood up from her seat and took the CD out of Martin's hands. "Thank you so much for returning this to me. I didn't realize I had left it downstairs! Ah ha ha ha!" Her smile begged Martin to understand, and her eyes threatened death if he didn't.

"Ha ha... ha ha." Martin played along. "Well I'm glad I was able to find you and return this to you!"

"Yep! Yep! Great, well it was good to see you, thank you, have a good night!" She turned Martin away back towards his table and pinched his arm.

"Ow, ow, oh! Yes! Good to see you too! I'll see you on Monday then!"

Eiko froze. Martin froze.

"See you on Monday?" The greasy-nosed man stood up. "Now what in the name of—"

He spoke with an Osaka accent that was as thick as sludge, and Martin lost his understanding of what he was trying to say after the first sentence. He had never heard such a long string of foreign profanity, and all he could do was stand there in inebriated awe of the speed and quality of which he was being yelled at.

At this point, the entire restaurant had turned their attention towards the two men, but Martin could do nothing to pacify the situation. The man stood a full head taller than he, and was so close that Martin choked on the alcohol on his breath.

"Stop!" Eiko tried to intervene. Martin looked at her, then back at the man.

"I'm sorry," he said, taking a step back. But the man grabbed him by the collar and shoved him backwards into an empty table. Martin heard the gasps of the other customers, the crashing of silverware, and the breaking of glass. The back of his head slammed into something hard, and he felt the hot sting of blood running down his neck.

"Martin!" he heard Chris shout from somewhere. He felt Chris's hands on his arm, but he could only look forward. His blood, which was already hot with embarrassment, boiled with anger at what he saw before him. Eiko ran towards Martin, but the brusque man grabbed her by the arm.

"Get off of me!" she yelled. She tried to tear herself from his grip, but as she did the man spun her around and slapped her down to the floor.

"You no good cunt!" he spat.

That was enough. Martin couldn't hear the crowd around them. He couldn't see the face of Chris as he pulled him up off the floor.

"Let's go, Martin," Chris said, but Martin tucked his right arm in and rocketed forward.

"What. You got something else to say to me you little shi—"

Martin had never been in a real fight before. In high school, his mother had worried about him being bullied at school because of his size, but somehow Martin never really found himself as the object of another boy's ire. In fact, he never found himself on either side of any fence. But now, here he was. He felt a sharp shooting pain as his knuckles connected upwards with the other man's chin, and heard the cracking of bone as he launched him off his feet then back down onto the table behind him.

His breathing was heavy, his face hot. He looked down at the man at his feet in disbelief. *I did it.* He looked at his fist, then over at Eiko on the floor next to him. *I got him.* He couldn't help but smile.

"I got him!" He turned around and met the eyes of a horrified crowd. His smile faded instantly.

"Someone, call the police!" A voice shouted. "This foreigner started a fight!"

Martin froze again. *What did I do? What have I done?* His mind spun, and the room began to spin with it.

"Sensei," Eiko said, grabbing the leg of his pants. He reached down and helped her up. She was as light as he had imagined, and in one swift motion she was up and holding onto his arm. Her hand was all bone, but her skin was soft and cool. She put a hand on her face where the man had slapped her and wiped away a tear.

She looked up at him, still holding onto his arm, and did her best to give him a smile. "Your suit's all messed up," she said.

"I'm sorry," Martin said, but Eiko just shook her head.

"Take me out of here, will you? Take me home."

He took her arm in his, and walked towards the crowd that had gathered by the entrance, giving a brief look to Chris and the others, letting them know not to interfere.

"Please let us through," Martin said to the crowd as they approached.

"Now hang on here." One of the men in the crowd stepped forward. "You can't be breaking people's faces in and just leaving that simply—"

"Huh?" Eiko responded. Her eyes flared the way they did when she had chased Martin down after they had first met. "If you want to stop someone and arrest them, arrest that shit-head lying on his ass over there!" She pointed at the man still on the floor.

"Now little miss, just because you say so," the man responded, but Eiko was now back to being Eiko. "Get out of the way!" She slammed her heel down on the foot of the man who had blocked their path and pulled Martin along.

"You bitch!" the man yelled, but Martin and Eiko had already started running—down the escalators, through the front of the mall, and out into the warm April night.

CHAPTER NINETEEN

David Duchovny's UFO Catcher

Eiko's apartment was a twenty-minute walk from Mariet. The pair spent most of the journey without saying much of anything beyond simple directions and affirmations. Martin was grateful for the quiet. The back of his head throbbed and he occasionally felt the tingle of warm blood running down his neck. After a few blocks he tried to press his hand against the wound on his head, only to have Eiko slap it away.

"Don't touch it. You'll get blood all over your hand and then you'll look like you just committed murder."

"But it hurts," Martin moaned. They came to a red light, and Eiko folded her arms across her chest. No cars were coming, but she kept her eyes fixated on the walk sign ahead of them. They had passed over the Matsu River, leaving the hustle and bustle of downtown behind them. Martin heard the sound of laughter far away, and in the distance, he watched the flashing lights of a plane on its descent towards Toyama Airport.

Is it really all right for me to do this? The walk light ahead of them turned green, but Eiko made no effort to move forward.

"It's green," Martin said.

"I know."

Martin looked at her. Neon reflections danced across her eyes, and the gold in her dress shimmered under a lusterless streetlamp. He watched her chest rise and fall with each breath, not quite knowing the right thing to say. The light in front of them eventually turned red again, and Martin sighed.

"Why did you help me back there?" she finally said.

"I don't think I really helped. None of that would have happened if I had just let you be." He stuffed his hands in his pockets and looked the other way.

"So, do you regret that it happened?" Eiko turned and looked up at him.

Martin thought for a moment. "If I caused you trouble, then I suppose the answer is yes." He rubbed his hands on his flushed cheeks.

Eiko smiled. Not the forced smile she had at the dinner table with the greasy-nosed man. Not the fake smile she had on when greeting Manager before their lessons. She smiled a genuine smile. A smile not for anyone else, just for herself. She took Martin by the arm again and led him forward.

"Come on. We're almost there."

Eiko's flat was on the tenth floor of a building with the name "Asai" written on the front. The first floor was connected to a FamilyMart that the pair slipped into before heading upstairs. Eiko picked up a few bandages and a bottle of disinfectant, and Martin bought a can of café au lait for himself.

The lobby of the Asai building was luxurious by Toyama's standards, with marble flooring and a great mahogany desk at the front, where a security guard sat reading through a sports publication. Behind him was an elevator that they rode up to the tenth floor. The entire complex had the smell of fresh furniture, and Martin wondered if Eiko had actually not been lying about her father who worked for a large newspaper.

The door opened to the tenth floor and they made an immediate left. Eiko's room was number 1001. "It's just me on this floor," she said, taking out a silver key and sliding it into the doorknob.

"The whole floor?" Martin asked. He followed her into the entry way. There was a small alcove that lead straight to another door. They took their shoes off and moved forward into the living room.

It was incredibly spacious, and was on its own about four times larger than Martin's whole apartment. The back wall was entirely made of windows that looked out north towards downtown Toyama and the train station. On one side of the room was a three-seat couch that faced a flat-screen television on the opposite wall. Taped to the wall above the TV was an enormous poster of a UFO flying over some trees with the words *I WANT TO BELIEVE* written across the bottom.

Martin stared at it without speaking until Eiko came up behind him.

"I like 'The X-Files,'" she said matter-of-factly.

"Oh," Martin said. "I never really got into it. I always thought it was creepy."

Eiko frowned. "Do you know Gillian Anderson? The woman who plays Agent Scully? She's the reason I dyed my hair. She's so cool!"

Martin hesitated. "I guess," he said, but no sooner had the words left his mouth did he feel a finger digging into the back of his head.

"Ow!" he shouted, jumping up into the air. "What the hell is wrong with you?"

"What's wrong with *me?* What's wrong with *you?* Why don't you try showing some interest when a girl is telling you about what she likes?" Eiko folded her arms across her chest again and pouted.

Martin lightly rubbed the back of his head and looked back towards Eiko. He opened his mouth to speak, but she turned around and walked off down the hall. *So much for that.*

After a few minutes, he heard the sound of the bath being drawn. Suddenly thirsty, he made his way into the kitchen for a glass of water. The kitchen itself wasn't especially clean. Dirty dishes were piled up in the sink and the trash was filled to the top with food wrappers and other items of miscellany. Martin went down the line of cupboards, opening each one until he found one with a clean, yellow mug inside. He retrieved it and shuffled over to the fridge, finding a bottle of mineral water in the inside door compartment.

As he began to pour, a sudden fright overtook him. He remembered the Eiko who had chased him down outside the convenience store. The Eiko that had stalked him and found where he worked, and who had smashed his kidney in before forcing herself upon his daily schedule. *Why the hell did I come up here?* His eyes focused on an array of cutlery stored neatly by the stovetop. *She's crazy. She's crazy? She's crazy, right?*

From down the hall he heard the bath being turned off, followed by water splashing.

Relax. He looked down at the bottle of mineral water in his hand. *If she was going to kill you, she would have done it before taking a bath, right?* Martin nodded to himself.

"Right," he said out loud. He nodded, and slowly started to pour himself a drink, then closed the bottle of mineral water and held it against the back of his head. The sensation against the swollen warmth of his wound sent shivers of relief down his spine. He rested his lower back against the counter and held the bottle up as long as he was able before switching hands and rotating the bottle to the cooler side. Outside, he watched as a train approached Toyama station from the west. He could make out the lights of the car windows as they passed over the Jinzu River Bridge and disappeared inside the station. It was past eleven o'clock now, and Martin imagined that no other trains would be rolling in tonight.

He put the bottle down, then walked up to the window till his nose touched it and looked down at the street. It was a magnificent view. He could make out Mariet in the distance, and though he couldn't see it directly, he traced his finger down the street where Sora was. He pictured Tuba in his secret back room, and Sami in the front lifting kegs of beer around while customers laughed and danced together.

He took a sip of his drink and turned back towards the couch. *What are the others doing now?* He instinctively reached for his phone, but soon realized he had left it on the table at the restaurant. There was no way he could contact them and tell them what had happened.

He looked up at the poster on the wall. It wasn't the only piece of "X-Files" fandom in the apartment. DVD cases lined the cabinet beneath the TV, and next to them was an autographed picture of Gillian Anderson and David Duchovny that looked like it was taken when the show had just kicked off. Martin unfastened the top few buttons of his shirt and fell backwards onto the couch. On the table was the English textbook that Eiko had been working on. With nothing else to do, Martin reached for it and began flipping through the first few chapters.

Mika had said during dinner that she'd seen Eiko studying hard, and looking through the textbook, Martin could see the truth of it. Each page was brimming with notes written in the margins. There were red circles around things that she had trouble with, and silly-looking happy faces next to questions she had answered correctly. He couldn't help but smile as he turned each page at the satisfaction of knowing that his lessons were bearing fruit.

Before long he heard the sound of footsteps coming from down the hall and quickly put the book down back where it had sat.

"Sensei," Eiko called as she opened the door. She had put on long sweatpants and a black tank top, and her hair was up in a towel. In her hands were the bandages that she had bought in the store, along with a wet cloth and some disinfectant.

"Take off your shirt," she ordered.

"Now hang on here..." Martin objected.

She sat down next to him and put the items on the table, then stared him down until he started unbuttoning.

"Good, now face that way and be quiet," she said.

Martin obeyed.

Eiko shuffled around for a moment behind him, and then pressed the warm cloth against the back of his head.

"Ow." Martin winced. "Can't you be gentler?"

"Shush." Eiko began humming a tune he didn't recognize. There was nothing to do but sit still and wait for her to finish.

"What song is that?" he asked as she began to rub the disinfectant into his cut.

"It's called 'Summer.'"

"'Summer?'"

"Yeah. It's by Joe Hisaishi. Do you know him?"

"No. I've never heard of him." Eiko continued humming along while applying the bandage to Martin's head. "It sounds nice."

"All done!" She slapped the top of his head as if to give him her personal seal of approval. Martin buttoned his shirt halfway and turned back around.

"Thanks." He touched the back of his head where the bandage now was.

Eiko smiled and reached for her phone. "I think I have that song on here somewhere," she said, flipping through a long list of music. "Here!" She pressed a button on her phone, and an array of speakers around the room crackled to life. "It's from a movie, I think."

Eiko tucked her knees in to her chest and rocked back and forth with the beat. Martin sat still, listening to the lighthearted piano rhythm rise and fall. It lasted four or five minutes, after which she turned down the volume and let her playlist continue on its preselected course.

Eiko reached across the table and picked up the can of café au lait that Martin had bought for himself. She played with it in her hands for a bit before popping it open and taking a sip.

"It's good."

"Uh, yeah. That's why I bought it. For me."

Eiko ignored the comment and took another sip.

He sighed. "I hope the others didn't have any trouble getting out of there. I wish I had a way to contact them."

"Where's your phone?"

"On the table at the restaurant." He reached over and plucked the can out of her hands and took a sip himself. "It's too late now to go and get it but if I'm lucky Chris picked it up and took it home with him."

"I see." Eiko took the towel off her head and threw it on the other chair in the room. Martin shuffled around uncomfortably. His drunken adrenaline had long since worn off, and sitting in Eiko's apartment, he found himself without a clue as to what to talk about. Martin looked back up at "The X-Files" poster on the wall.

"'I want to believe,'" he read aloud. Eiko looked up at it with him. "Where did you get that poster anyway? It must be hard to find things like that for a show that ended back in the 90s."

"Oh, I won it at a UFO-catcher game." Eiko giggled.

Martin stared blankly at her. "Did you just make a joke?"

"What? Don't you know? It's that game they have at arcades. You know, where you use a joystick-thing to control a claw, and then the claw drops down and you try to pick up a prize from the bin?"

"Oh yeah." Martin nodded.

"What do you call it in English?"

"I think it's just called a Claw Game." Martin tilted his head to one side, unsure of his answer.

"Well that's boring. I must've spent three thousand yen trying to win that thing. But I was catching a UFO with a UFO catcher! And David Duchovny's UFO to boot!" Eiko was clearly pleased with herself.

She circled around the table and took a seat next to Martin, taking the can of café au lait out of his hands and back into hers. Martin chuckled.

"Have you ever seen a UFO?" she asked.

"No. I've seen some weird stuff, but never a UFO."

"America seems like the kind of place where you could see one if you tried," she said, taking another sip of his drink.

"I guess so. But 'The X-Files' isn't just about UFOs, right? There's a lot of things about cults and science-gone-wrong. People with weird abilities and monsters and the like, right?"

"That's true." Eiko stared blankly across the room for a few moments, lost in thought. Martin watched her and waited for her to continue, but her gaze seemed fixed at the poster on the wall.

"But you know." Martin scratched an itch on his knee. "Even if you saw one, what would you do then?"

Eiko turned back around and locked eyes with Martin. "What do you mean?"

"I mean, who would you tell? Where would you go? What would you do? The people who you wanted to believe, wouldn't. And the people who would believe would be the ones you didn't care about. In the end, you'd just be alone with your own knowledge. And nothing would change."

"It sounds like you've already given up," Eiko said. "You don't know who might believe you if you don't try."

Martin laid his head back against the couch. In his heart, there was nothing more he wanted than to reach out and talk to someone about his recent experiences. Against his better judgment, he had entered into a world that didn't obey the normal, logical order of life. A pair of uncle-and-niece egg farmers on the run, a boat ride lost in the mist, visions of giant roosters and a bartender with some sort of cosmic feng shui umbrella. With every passing day it seemed like reality had slipped an inch further away from his grasp.

"Sensei," Eiko called. "Are you listening?"

Martin turned his head and looked at Eiko, who had come so close their noses were practically touching.

"Woah!" Martin recoiled, but there was nowhere behind him to move.

"What's wrong?" Eiko whispered. "Am I not your type?"

Martin's heart thumped in his chest. *What is this, all of a sudden?*

"I, uh." He fumbled. Her eyes were like daggers that pierced into his mind. "I mean, I don't not like you?"

"I didn't ask if you liked me."

"Oh! Right."

"Hmph!" Eiko scowled. In one motion she turned to grab the pillow behind her, then spun around with all of her might and slapped it against Martin's unsuspecting cheek.

Before he could respond, she was already up and halfway to the door. "You can sleep there. The bathroom is down this hall on the right. Peek into my room and I'll eat your eyes out of your thick head."

"I—" Martin started, but was interrupted by the door slamming behind her.

CHAPTER TWENTY

The Morning After

He woke up as the first light of the sun began to shine through the windows. His body was still sore from the previous night's altercation, and despite the fact that his small stature allowed him to fit neatly on Eiko's couch, his back cracked and ached as he rose to meet the morning.

He looked around for a bit and let his eyes focus before standing up and pouring himself a glass of water from the kitchen sink. His mouth still had the taste of beer in it, and swallowing felt like he was forcing cotton down his throat. He wanted nothing more at this point than to take a shower, brush his teeth, and crawl into his own bed.

There was no noise coming from down the hall, and he surmised Eiko was probably still fast asleep. *It's better this way. There's no reason to wait and to tell her I'm heading out. Better just to get a head start now.* Martin instinctively checked each of his pockets, making sure he had collected all of his belongings before unlocking the front door and sneaking out into the hall. Only his phone was missing, and for that he could only hope that Chris had picked it up and taken it home with him the night before.

The way back to the station was easy enough. He had seen it from Eiko's room, and remembered most of the trip they had taken the night before to get there without issue. He boarded the 6:00 A.M. train for Takaoka, and by 6:30 he was halfway home and coming up to Shimodoi's store.

Against his desire to return home, he decided to pop in first. As far as he knew, Shimodoi didn't work the morning shift, but Martin wanted to pick up a fresh toothbrush and some toothpaste before getting back. He pushed open the door with a heave of his shoulder. As before, there was no one in the shop except for himself. *Maybe he is here after all?*

"Shimodoi!" Martin's voice was hoarse. "Stop napping in the back room and come serve your customer!"

Martin turned around and leaned against the register. At the end of the aisle stood a wall of refrigerators, each brimming with enough beer and schnapps to wash his memory clean of what had happened the night before. Tempted as he was, something was nagging him from the inside. A certain pride that he had never experienced before. He dragged himself past the row of liquor and over to the sandwich section. After a few ponderous seconds, he picked up a turkey and Swiss and unwrapped it on the spot.

"Shimodoi!" he called. "I'm eating your merchandise without paying first!" He grabbed a can of coffee from the cabinet next to the register and opened it.

No sooner did the words "without paying" escape his lips than Shimodoi shot up like a rocket from behind the counter.

"Thief!" he shouted. "Thief and foreigner!"

"Calm down," Martin urged. "Someone might hear you and actually take you seriously."

"I should call the police on you, you know. Ten Yen gets shipped out of the country with a snap of my finger. Who got the power now, huh? Not you, honkey!"

"Honkey? Where the hell did you learn the word honkey?" Martin asked.

"You didn't see the James Bond movie?" Shimodoi asked back.

"Which one?"

"That new one. *Live and Let Die.* With Roger Moore. He's a honkey!"

"New one?" Martin asked, puzzled. "Didn't that come out in the 70s? Roger Moore is just some old geezer now. He wasn't even a good Bond. And I doubt someone calls a British spy a 'honkey.'"

"It was on at the theater last night, so it must be new!" Shimodoi balled up his fists defensively. "And Roger Moore was great! You don't know anything, Ten Yen."

Martin slid the open can of coffee over to Shimodoi. "You know, now that I think about it, I don't think I've ever even seen that one," he said. "What's it about?"

"It's a spy movie."

"Yes, I know that. It's a James Bond flick."

"Well if you know that why are you asking me about it?"

"You're a little shit, Shimodoi. You know what I'm talking about. Tell me what happens in the movie."

"Oh, it's good movie for you. All about Yankee-Doodle Americans and their drugs. Do you do drugs, Ten Yen?"

"No. Do you?"

"Oh! Oh! You dare question the morality of a Japanese!" he said, slamming Martin's open can of coffee onto the counter. "I'll have you know that I'm not a degenerate!"

"I don't know what you are." Martin shook his head. "So how about the girl? She cute in this one?"

"Oh yeah, she's cute! Jane Seymour is the best Bond girl, you know. Better than any of these Japanese girls. A Japanese girl could never be a Bond girl, you know?"

"There was a Japanese Bond girl, you idiot. She was hot, too."

"What!?" Shimodoi slammed Martin's coffee into the counter again, sending the contents up onto Martin's face. "That can't be! I know all the Bond girls!"

"Well, then you should know there was a Japanese Bond girl."

"Oh? If you so smart, what's her name then?"

"I don't remember. Akiko or something like that."

"Akiko!" Shimodoi shouted. "Half of all the girls in Japan are named Akiko! It's not even a cute name. No cute girls named 'Akiko.'"

Martin had little knowledge of names in Japan—which ones were "cute" or which ones were "cool." Which ones were old-fashioned or which ones sounded pleasant to the ear. He loathed to say that they all sounded similar, but when it came to women in Japan, Martin was nearly hopeless in the field of remembering names. The ones he knew nearly all had the same variation of "ko." Akiko. Eiko. Yoshiko. It had been one of the saving graces upon meeting the Assistant Manager. The girl whose name ended in something other than "ko," even if it was just one letter off.

"So, what's special about Jane Seymour's character?" Martin asked.

"Her name's Solitaire. She's got a superpower. She can see the future!"

"How?"

"She uses these cards. Um, what do you call them? Rot cards? Root cards?"

"Tarot cards?"

"Yeah, that's the one." Shimodoi nodded. "But there's a catch. She can only use her powers if she stays a virgin."

"What kind of condition is that?"

"It's a Bond film, right? So, you know none of the girls can stay virgins!" Shimodoi laughed with a perverted snort.

"I guess so. I wish she was here to see my future. I could use someone with that kind of ability."

"Oh yeah? You know, my Gram-Gram can read the future."

Martin retrieved his coffee and began rapping his fingers on the lid. "Your Gram-Gram, huh. Is she a virgin too?"

"Ha! No. She not like you. Have you even taken that thing of yours out of its original packaging? It doesn't increase in value, you know," Shimodoi said, imitating the way Martin rapped on his can.

"What would you know about anything?"

"I've been with lots of girls. *Lots*," he said emphatically.

"Yeah, OK." Martin leaned back against the counter and said nothing further. He thought about Eiko, her orange hair, still wet underneath her towel. The soft lines of her face. He took another sip of his coffee and began to wonder if he had made the right decision to leave without telling her.

"What are you doing here, Ten Yen?"

"What do you mean?"

Shimodoi sighed uncharacteristically. "Have you ever seen the movie, 'Ikiru?'"

"No. What's it about?"

"It's about a guy like you. Except he finds out he has cancer and will only live another six months. He realizes that he has wasted his life, and with the short time he has left, he tries to do something meaningful. In the end, he succumbs to his illness on a swing in a park he helped build. But before he dies, he sings this song—'Gondola no Uta' is the name. You ever hear it?"

Martin shook his head.

Shimodoi cleared his throat. "*Inochi mijikashi...*" his adolescent voice cracked as he sang.

"Life is short?" Martin asked.

Shimodoi didn't answer, but kept humming the tune.

Outside, a large van stopped at a red light, reflecting the morning sun from its passenger side window. Martin watched the driver as he tapped his fingers against the wheel. As if sensing his gaze, he looked back at Martin, who immediately turned away.

"I used to believe something—" Martin put his coffee down on the counter and ran his fingers over the back of his head on the bandage that Eiko had carefully placed "—that I couldn't help but be where I am, and that it was pointless to try and change anything. But now, I'm not so sure."

"Oh." Shimodoi continued humming. He pressed no further. And they stood together in silence for quite some time.

"Next weekend, I'm going to be staying in Tateyama with an acquaintance of mine," Martin said. "I'm hoping it will give me a chance to think about some things."

"Ten Yen always thinking. Ten Yen never doing. That's why Ten Yen's penis is still in shrink-wrap."

Martin elbowed him hard enough to get a good yelp of pain as a reward.

From outside came the noise of a slamming car door. Shimodoi jumped.

"Oh no!" He said, moving his can of coffee under the counter. "You should get out of here, Ten Yen. If an actual customer sees us like this it might cause trouble."

"Yeah," Martin agreed. "I guess I'll see you later then. Good luck."

"Ten Yen!" Shimodoi called as Martin walked away. "You going to Tateyama for vacation, right?"

"Yeah. What about it?"

"You met the egg farmer, Yuji, right?"

"Yeah. And the little girl that is always trailing behind him. His niece I think it was. Why? What about him?"

"To be honest, he hasn't come in the past couple weeks for his normal morning deliveries. You remember, you met him here?" The way he spoke had somehow become more rigid.

"Where is he?" Martin asked.

"No one knows. Not that anyone really knew where he stays in the first place."

Martin frowned. He hadn't seen the duo since their cryptic boat ride earlier in the month. "I'll keep that in mind. And I'll let you know if I find out anything."

Shimodoi nodded, and then clapped his hands together as if suddenly remembering something important.

"That's right! You'll need an umbrella if you're going to stay in Tateyama. It rains a lot."

Martin looked at the rack of cheap plastic umbrellas hanging from the rack on the door and moved to pick one of them up.

"Not one of those. Those cheap umbrellas are so bad you'll get wet on a sunny day."

"So, what should I do?"

"I'll give you mine. Just check outside your door the morning you're supposed to leave," Shimodoi said. "It will be there."

"All right then. Thanks. I leave next Sunday morning."

Martin pushed the door open with his shoulder and waved goodbye as he left.

"See you, honkey!" Shimodoi shouted. "And remember to look for the umbrella!"

CHAPTER TWENTY-ONE

The Running Rooster

Martin's phone was waiting for him on his desk when he got in on Tuesday, along with the two of the three coworkers who had been with him just a couple of nights prior. Martin hadn't shaved, and the anxiety of what might happen as he stepped into his office this morning had robbed him of a good night's sleep.

Chris looked up at him as soon as the door opened. "Oh, thank God!" He shot out of his chair and embraced Martin. "Are you OK? Jesus, man, why didn't you come over? None of us knew what happened to you after you broke the shit out of that guy's jaw!"

"I'm OK, I'm OK." Martin tried to push Chris away. "Get off of me."

"Right." Chris took a few steps back. "Well, Mika and I are very glad you're safe and well. Tell him, Mika."

"Y—yes." She hesitated. "But you caused quite a bit of trouble for us after you left."

"What do you mean?" Martin asked.

Mika opened her mouth to answer, but before she could the door opened from behind Martin.

"She means this." Martin turned around only to be met with a slap across the face from Stacy. She glowered at him, her fists clenched as she spoke.

"What does she mean? What do you think happened after you just strolled out of there? Do you think they just let us walk out? Do you think the police weren't called after you bashed that man's face in? They had to carry him out of there in a stretcher, you know. And instead of sticking around and accepting the consequences of what you did, you left us with the check. You're lucky. So lucky that other witnesses there were able to corroborate that he hit you first. But plenty of them were saying that you walked up to him piss drunk and started it."

"But Stacy, you know that's not true," Chris interjected. "You know what he did was right. That rat bastard slapped one of our students square in the face, so hard that she fell to the ground and Martin stood up for her!"

"Right? Do you think this is about right or wrong? Do you think that anyone will care about the right or wrong of it if this story gets out? You live out here in the sticks, Martin. The damn sticks. You live between a rice field and an old folks' home. You think any of them will take anything from this other than the fact that an angry foreigner fought it out with a Japanese guy and broke his jaw? You should know better. You shouldn't put yourself or us in that kind of position."

"Since when did you become such a slave to the mentality out here?" Chris pushed Martin out of the way and walked up to Stacy. "Or has it finally gotten to you? The nail that sticks out gets hammered down, so just keep your head low and be the polite, obedient gaijin? You know Martin didn't go over there looking for a fight. It's not his fault. And you're starting to sound just like Colby."

"Both of you, stop!" Mika's usually timid voice roared. The three looked back at her diminutive figure. She put a hand over her mouth, as if surprised but her own sudden authority. "I mean,

I think we should just forget about this whole thing. We can't change what happened, so let's just move on, OK?"

Stacy rolled her eyes in frustration and stormed out.

"Don't worry about that clod." Chris turned around and went back to his desk.

"What happened after we left?" Martin rubbed his cheek and sat down.

"Nothing, really. Just like Stacy said, the cops came and asked us a ton of questions. That guy whose foot Eiko smashed was throwing out accusations left and right, but fortunately a number of people who saw the whole thing were able to corroborate our version of events and the police left with just that guy you messed up."

"It was scary," Mika chirped.

"It was kind of awesome," Chris whispered. "I never would've thought you had that in you, Martin. You really put that guy in his place!"

"Martin." Mika sat down in Stacy's chair. "What happened after you left? You were hurt too, right? Did Eiko take you to the hospital?"

"No, not exactly. She asked me to take her home, so I did," he hesitated, not sure how much information he was willing to provide.

"And?" Chris asked with a perverted grin.

"And nothing. She patched up the cut I had on the back of my head and then I went home. Nothing happened." It wasn't a total lie, but a nuanced truth Martin could live with.

"Be careful," Mika warned. "The way the two of you walked out of there looked like... well, let's just say the way it looked could lead to misunderstandings. Above anything else, you're her teacher and she's your student."

"I know." Martin leaned back in his chair. "I'm sorry for leaving you guys like that. I don't know what happened or what got into me. Before I knew it, I was already outside with Eiko. I didn't even realize that I had left my phone there until later."

"It's all right," Chris said. "Besides we've got some vacation time coming up. It'll give Stacy time to clear her head about all this."

The three carried on for a few minutes until it was time to start prepping their morning classes. In a stroke of luck, Manager had gotten a call to cover for another Manager who was out sick, leaving Mika in charge. At five o'clock, Martin got a call from one of his private lessons asking to cancel, leaving him with an empty hour between six and seven. With some free time, he went up to the front desk to help Mika out in the lobby.

His seven o'clock lesson was with Eiko. "Shouldn't you prepare for it?" Mika asked as they sat together.

"I've got a few weeks of lessons pre-planned. I'm just following a script at this point with her until she has a better grasp on the basics."

"Hm. Well your lessons seem to be working well, don't you think?"

"I hope so." Martin spun his chair around to face the back wall.

Martin looked up. "Hey, was that painting always there?" It was the woman with the red umbrella, walking away from the perspective of the artist. She seemed different this time. Taller, more powerful. The focus of the painting was clearly meant to draw the eyes to the umbrella. It was the only source of color in the photo, after all. But as he looked now his eyes were drawn more to the dark lines, the details in the rain. the curvature of her legs as she walked.

"Oh, that?" Mika turned around. "I just brought that out from Manager's office today, actually. It's such a pretty painting. I thought it would bring some flair to the lobby. What do you think?"

"It certainly does draw attention to itself. Was Manager OK with you taking it?"

"Oh, I didn't think she would care. That thing has probably been sitting in her cramped little office for years. It deserves some light."

"I guess." Martin spun his chair back around. The two made light conversation while working for the rest of the hour. Most of the evening classes were heavily populated by high school and college-aged students, and at 6:30 P.M. they started trickling in by ones and twos. Despite them not being his direct pupils, Martin enjoyed engaging and talking with them about their school lives and hobbies.

Eiko came promptly at 6:45, but Martin immediately noticed something different about her. Her hair was done up in a ponytail, and she wore a short skirt and a loose collared shirt not unlike the school girls she stood near. Her lipstick was as orange as her hair, and as soon as she walked into the building conversation stopped and all eyes were on her. She gave a brief bow and approached Mika, who ushered her into the interview room, no doubt to apologize for the trouble that Martin had caused at the restaurant. His instinct was to walk into the room after them, but he soon realized that he was the only staff member among the crowd, and decided to remain and entertain the group until the other teachers came out.

After a few minutes, the two emerged with smiles on their faces, and Martin breathed a sigh of relief. Eiko took a seat across the room and fixed her eyes on him. At this point, however, he had become completely encumbered by high-school girls asking him all sorts of questions and chitter-chattering about nothing in particular. Martin tried to call out to Eiko, but couldn't fit a word in edgewise. She only sat, her hands in her lap, and watched.

"Sensei!" one of the girls called out over the others. "Are you married?" The girls all laughed.

"Idiot, you can't ask a teacher that question!" another girl interjected.

"Oh!" The first girl pouted. "But I want to know!" Several other girls nodded in agreement.

Martin sighed. "No. No, I'm not married." It wasn't the first time he had been asked this question. At times he felt more like a spectacle than an actual teacher. Something more commonly seen at a museum with a plaque that read, *Martin Stilwell, American, Single, Early 21st Century.*

"How old are you?" asked another girl.

"I'm twenty-four."

"How tall are you?" asked another.

"That's none of your business." Martin pointed a finger at her nose, and everyone laughed.

Despite the feeling of being a specimen, he loved these small moments with the kids. Although he was only six or seven years apart from the majority of them, he exuded an air of playful adulthood that most of them gravitated to. Martin thought of his own self at their age, looking up to those who were graduating college and moving into real society. To them, it might have been just another step on the road, but to him, they looked like giants.

"Do you have a girlfriend?" the first girl asked. The crowd hushed instantly. Martin looked over to where Eiko was sitting, locking eyes with her from across the room.

"I, uh..." Martin stammered and stood up, looking around.

"That's not the kind of question you ask a teacher." Stacy came forward to collect her group.

The girls moaned collectively. "Come on, now. Let's get started." Stacy gave Martin a cold glance before ushering her students out. One-by-one they went down the hall until the lobby had emptied. He looked over to where Eiko was sitting—only now, she was gone.

"Mika?" he asked, still searching. "Did you see where Eiko went?"

"Eiko? Why, she was just sitting there, wasn't she?"

"Yeah. She was." Martin walked down the hall to his own classroom to see if she had gone ahead of him, but found her desk empty. At a loss, he walked down the hall and checked the bathroom, but it too was empty. He walked back up to the front desk. "I can't find her anywhere."

A thought occurred to him to check outside, but before he took even the first step towards the door, he saw something familiar form behind the glass. A thick, white fog had crept in, swallowing the outside world. The same fog that had enveloped him as he rode the raft with Yuji and the girl along the Matsu River.

His heartbeat quickened. He stepped forward, not following his own will, but moving as if being pulled in by some force he couldn't yet comprehend. Everything around him became still. Quiet. He pushed the door open slowly, and reached out his hand into the night fog. It was cold, damp. As fog tends to be. He swallowed the lump in his throat and pushed his arm further in, until finally he felt something. It was smooth, organic. At first, he thought it the hand of some other person, but it quickly slithered up the rest of his arm and yanked him forward.

"What's this, then?" a woman's voice asked. "Another fly?"

"Eiko?" Martin called out. He couldn't see more than a few feet in front of him, and what he could see was all the same: white fog in every direction. It surrounded him, touched him. He breathed it with every inhale, and it chilled his lungs.

"Eiko?" the woman's voice repeated. "Hmm... hmm."

"Who are you?" Martin tried to get a read on where her voice was coming from, but when she spoke her voice seemed to come from everywhere.

"Me?" Her voice was thick and seductive. Every word she spoke poured into his body, like waves of the ocean washing over his mind. "I'm no one, really. Just a visitor, you could say. But you, little fly, I know you. You're Yuji's little pet."

Martin's body seized up. He wanted to back away, but there was no direction to run in. The sound of her voice seeped through his courage, a creeping terror that stole away any reasonable thought from his mind.

"What have you done to him?" His voice was nothing more than a pathetic squeak.

"Do you want to see him? I can show you." She laughed. Martin did not have the stomach to respond. In front of him, the white fog began to turn a shade of crimson, and behind that he heard clicking of heels against the concrete.

"It won't hurt a bit," she whispered. The clicking of her heels came to an abrupt stop. She was there. He couldn't see her, but she was there—just beyond the crimson veil. He closed his eyes and waited. It was all he could do now. He waited, and waited, and waited.

But nothing came. The voice from the fog was quiet. He kept his eyes shut and listened. Slowly, faintly, the sound of footsteps appeared from behind. Martin turned his head around and squinted through the fog.

"Don't believe those lies, now," a voice rang out. "It'll hurt plenty."

"You're supposed to stay in your forest," another voice said. "I suppose you need us to show you the way back?"

"Hmph." The lady's voice was more distant than before. "And who do you think *you* are?"

From behind the fog, the slim figure of Tuba emerged, complete with his striped fedora and holding the black and gold umbrella that Martin had seen at the bar.

"We're just a couple of bartenders out for a stroll." Tuba pulled a lighter from his pocket and flicked it open, lighting the cigarette in his mouth. "Isn't that right, bro?"

Sami appeared from the fog holding something against his chest that Martin could not make out. He was huge, seemingly bigger than before. A spectacle of human muscle contained in a tight collared shirt and a pair of cargo pants. Martin stared at the pair, and as he did his heartbeat began to relax.

"How did you guys get here?" he finally managed to ask.

Tuba flashed a smile and tapped his umbrella against the asphalt. "She never leads me astray. And this is the second time she's had me find you. You're just as a moth to the flame with this one." He raised his head towards the red fog beyond them.

"That umbrella," the voice from the fog asked. "Where did you get it?" Her tone shifted from anger to seduction.

"Sami," Tuba whispered. "Send Martin on his way."

Sami nodded and opened his arms, revealing a tuft of black feathers.

"A gift from our mutual friend," Sami said.

It was the rooster from the vents at Shimodoi's shop. The rooster Martin had dreamed about in front of the cave, black within black pinions that were lit by the crimson light of the lady behind the fog. Sami eased the rooster to the ground and let it go. Martin looked at it, then traced the lines of Sami's boar tattoo back up his arm till their eyes met.

"Follow it," he said. "Don't let it out of your sight. Don't look at anything else. No matter what you hear, don't look back. When you're out, you'll know," he said, stepping around Martin.

His first instinct was to look back at Sami—something Sami himself must have sensed, because the next thing Martin felt were Sami's hands holding the back of his neck. "Don't. Look. Back." He gave Martin a push forward.

"Sacrilege!" The woman in the fog's voice was almost a whisper, sending shivers right down to Martin's knees. There was nothing else he could do.

The fog thickened around him, and he would have given up right there and then if the rooster had not darted forward.

"Wait!" Martin yelled after it.

His legs carried him forward. He ran and ran, barely able to keep pace. Never looking back. Not when he heard the screams. Not when he heard the silence. He ran until he could run no further, until he collapsed on the ground right back where he started. In the street in front of the office, with Eiko nowhere to be found.

CHAPTER TWENTY-TWO

This One

She didn't come to class the next evening. Or the evening after that. Mika called her multiple times each day to check on her, but never got further than her voicemail. For his part, Martin did not know where to start. He didn't know what had happened, and the two people he had thought to ask—Tuba and Sami—were nowhere to be found. He visited the bar every night after work, but was met by a locked door.

The rooster that he had followed out of the fog had also evaporated into thin air. He thought about stopping by Shimodoi's shop to see if it had run back over to his air ducts, but decided that chasing roosters was the least of his concerns.

Yoshiko came for her weekly lesson on Thursday morning with the usual ginger in her step. They spent most of their lesson going over the plan for visiting that weekend. She had arranged for her driver to pick Martin up at his apartment on Sunday morning. From there he would be escorted straight to her home in the woods.

"The estate is quite large. You'll have plenty of time to wander around and take it all in." She smiled as she spoke. "It's been so long since we've had a guest. And our nearest neighbor lives ten kilometers down the road!"

Martin listened and nodded. He was still excited about the trip, but his heart dwelt on Eiko and the happenings two nights before.

"You seem distracted, Sensei," Yoshiko said after a moment of silence.

She sees right through me.

"I'm sorry, Yoshiko. I am very excited to come and visit." He scratched his arm and leaned back a little in his chair. "Actually, I have something on my mind. But it's nothing too big. I'm sorry for being distracted."

"Hmm..." Yoshiko tilted her head. "Why don't you say what's on your mind? You'll feel better if you do."

Martin folded his arms. He didn't want to blurt out everything that had happened. Yoshiko would just think he had lost his mind. "I—I—I have another student, and she's been missing her classes. It's a private lesson, like yours, and I'm concerned about her."

"Have you called her?"

"Well yes, I mean, not me personally but the Assistant Manager has. She never seems to pick up the phone. She's usually very enthusiastic. In fact, she's never even been late to a lesson the whole time I've been teaching her."

"Did you get into an argument?"

"What?" Martin shook his head. "No, no. I mean, she's a student and I'm her teacher. There's nothing to argue about. She comes to class and I teach her. That's it."

"Maybe that's the problem?" Yoshiko put her hands on her cheeks.

"Oh. Do you think my way of teaching isn't suited for her? Or maybe my lessons got dull? She always seemed to like them, though." Martin rubbed his chin, perplexed.

"Oh, Sensei, you're an idiot." Yoshiko covered her mouth as she laughed. "Why don't you just go find out yourself?"

"But I can't. She never picks up her phone."

"Why don't you write her a letter?"

This time, it was Martin's turn to laugh. He couldn't imagine penning a letter in this day and age. "I don't even know where the post office is in Toyama. And what would I even put in a letter to a student?"

They both smiled. The laughter had lifted his spirits somewhat, and the rest of the day passed smoothly.

Despite his initial resistance to the idea, he found himself with pen in hand alone in his classroom the hour that Eiko was supposed to come. *This should be easy, right? Just write something simple.* He tapped his pen against the desk. *Something simple.* He thought.

Eiko. He wrote the letters of her name on the top of the page.

"Eiko," he whispered. "Eiko."

Before long, he found himself doodling a picture of a UFO on the page. Martin's doodles had always been solid, seventh-grade-level masterpieces. There were many types of spaceships and UFOs from different movies and TV shows, but he decided to go with the one he had seen on the poster in Eiko's apartment. The classic flying saucer.

He carefully outlined the shape, starting with the half-dome on top for the cockpit, then working down to the edge of the saucer, and back in before squaring off the bottom. After this, he started adding the little details. Ridges on the saucer section. A reflection of light on the cockpit, and finally speed lines underneath the craft.

When he was satisfied, he held up his artistic tour de force in front of the clock that already read 6:45. "Shit." He dropped the page on his desk. Forty-five minutes of work for four letters and a wicked-sick UFO sketch. The appeal of writing a letter quickly faded.

Saturday was the last day before vacation started. He kept the UFO doodle in his bag in case the urge to write something struck him, but it never did. After the last lesson, he waved goodbye to the other teachers and proceeded out the front door. It was the beginning of May.

With few options left to him, Martin began the long walk to the Asai building and Eiko's tenth floor apartment. He didn't have any plan in particular. In fact, he had no idea whether she would even be home or not. But after today there was going to be a full week of vacation, and something told him that if he couldn't try to resolve what had happened, there wouldn't be another chance.

In the back of his mind, he thought about the lady in the fog. Had Eiko gotten lost the same way he had? And if she had, the only people he could think to turn to for help—Tuba and Sami—had been all swallowed up with her by the lady in the fog that night.

He did his best to cast off his doubts and, after a few missteps and wrong turns, he found himself in the lobby of her apartment building. The same security guard sat at his mahogany desk, reading a newspaper and drinking coffee. Martin did his best to act natural and slid into the waiting elevator behind the guard, pressing the button for the tenth floor as he did.

As expected, there was no one there when the door opened. He stepped into the hall and over to Room 1001. It was quiet. No sounds of any occupation on the whole floor. He pressed his ear against her door for a few seconds, then began tapping his fingers against the frame.

Without much thought, he set down his backpack and opened the zipper, pulling out the doodle of the UFO he had done with her name on it. Even now, as he stood in front of her door, he had no idea what he would say.

"This is stupid," he said as he tapped his knuckles against the wood. There was no answer.

Martin sighed heavily and took out his pen. *Maybe I'll just leave her a note. But what do I write?* He looked down at the UFO, and imagined the poster hanging on her wall above the TV. That blurry image of an alien craft flying low over some trees, *I WANT TO BELIEVE* printed in huge text at the bottom. It radiated 90s nostalgia, and even though Martin had barely seen more than a few episodes, it reminded him of an innocence long past.

The mundaneness of his early adult life had come to this. Was there really a chicken farmer and his niece making midnight deliveries from the back of an old red truck? Was there really a monster behind a veil of fog that he had evaded twice? Was there really a girl named Eiko behind this door, who had only months before assailed him over not taking his receipt? Was there a girl who had completely pulled the wool over Manager's eyes just to get free English lessons? A girl who he had gotten into a fight for, and who had taken him into the very room in front of him now?

He took out a pen and sat down in front of the door, and wrote the only thing he thought he could write.

Eiko, I want to believe.

*

He saved his preparations for the trip till the next morning. Just as Shimodoi had promised, there was an umbrella leaning against his front door when he woke up. It was an odd thing, a mixture of yellow and orange hues that looked like a sunset. It had an old-timey feel, and was more akin to a parasol than a proper umbrella that one might find at a department store. He packed a single bag with a couple of days' worth of underwear, shirts, and socks. There was not much else Martin could think to bring with him. He shoved his toothbrush into a plastic bag, and threw it with a stick of deodorant in the front pouch.

At precisely nine o'clock, his phone buzzed with a number Martin did not recognize.

"Mr. Stilwell." A dry voice cracked on the other end. "The lady requests that Mr. Stilwell be standing outside of his apartment in a quarter of an hour."

"Are you the driver?"

"This one fulfills that duty, among many others."

His Japanese was formal to the point of being honorific, and Martin was unsure of how to address him properly. "All right," he said. "I'll meet you downstairs in fifteen minutes."

"Very well. This one eagerly looks forward to our meeting. Goodbye."

The phone call ended with a mechanical beep in his ear. Martin scratched his head with the edge of his phone before shoving it into his pocket along with his wallet and keys. With everything prepared, he closed the apartment window and grabbed his travel bag. He looked over the room once more until he was satisfied that nothing had been forgotten, then slung his bag over his shoulder and exited.

It was an exceptionally warm May morning. A few spring clouds patched the sky, but there was no hint of bad weather. He made his way downstairs and out to the parking lot where he leaned against the bicycle rack and waited.

At 9:15 on the dot, a black 1960s Rolls Royce pulled into the lot and stopped in front of him. He didn't know much about cars, but he knew enough to be impressed by the vehicle. It was sleek and spotless—like it had just been bought brand-new and driven from the lot straight to his apartment. The driver kept the engine running and emerged from the car.

The driver, much like the car, was immaculately groomed. White gloves covered his hands, and a long, tailed suit fitted his slender form.

"I've seen you before," Martin said, recalling the day he had escorted Yoshiko out to this very car.

"Indeed. This one owes the gentleman a debt of gratitude. The lady often speaks fondly of her English lessons."

"What's your name?"

"This one was not meant to be named."

"What does that mean?" Martin asked, puzzled.

"Forgiveness. This one has offended the gentleman's balance of humors with babbling. Let this one take your bag."

Martin unslung the bag from his shoulder and held it in front of him.

"Forgiveness," he said, grasping the bag in both hands and bowing his head. Martin kicked a nervous foot against the concrete as he watched the man's slow, deliberate stride towards the back of the car. There was an off-putting way he carried himself, like a machine that was running a preset program. Deep wrinkles in his skin, coupled with a ring of liver spots on his forehead, led Martin to guess he was nearly as old as Yoshiko. Maybe even older.

He opened the rear door and ushered Martin in with a gloved hand.

"No seatbelts?" He looked up at the driver.

"Forgiveness." The driver bowed his head.

"Yeah, well I don't think forgiveness is going to save my life if you crash into an eighteen-wheeler."

"This one will drive with the utmost caution."

"Uh-huh."

He closed the door behind Martin and circled around to the driver's side, seating himself gently. The interior of the car was just as pristine as the outside. So much so that he felt like he cheapened its value just by being in it. The driver shifted gears and tapped on the gas, and before long they were well beyond the Toyama that Martin knew.

"How long will it take to get to Yoshiko's house?" Martin asked as they passed by a run-down supermarket.

"This one cannot say for sure," his driving companion replied.

"You mean because of the traffic?"

He gave a brief nod. "There are many that drive to the mountains. But the roads are few."

Martin craned his head around and looked out of the rear mirror. "Hmm."

"Does something trouble the gentleman?"

Martin watched the scenery disappear behind them for a moment before turning back around to answer.

"Nothing troubles me. But I have a question."

"This one has little knowledge. But if it will satisfy the gentleman's curiosity, this one will try to answer."

Martin leaned against the door. "What can you tell me about Yoshiko?"

"The lady of the house is kind."

"Yes... yes, I know that, but I mean, what do you know about her? How long have you worked for her?"

"I have been in the service of the lady since she came to us."

"How long is that?"

"This one cannot say. It is rude to speak on matters that might betray the gentle lady's age."

Martin opened his mouth to object, but common sense got the better of him and he retreated back into his own thoughts instead.

"This one notices your inquisitiveness. The lady would be flattered."

"What? I don't mean to flatter. She's told me many stories, and sometimes I wonder just how much more there is to her that I still don't know."

"There is always more to know about the lady."

"She told me about the bombings. About the war."

"The manner in which the lady came to our house is as the gentleman says."

Martin scratched at something behind his ear and looked back out the window. Urban residences had given way to sprawling rice fields and the occasional farmstead. He tried to imagine the sound of the planes above. The sound of bombs exploding in the distance. The night sky reddened by the glow of fire and destruction. But for all the good it did him, he couldn't picture the scenery before him in any other state. There was a timeless quality to it that warmed Martin's heart and made him forget about the troubles of the world.

"Is it true about the rain up there?" Martin asked on a whim.

"The gentleman is well informed. Tateyama's rainfall is not to be underestimated. I see that the gentleman packed appropriately."

"Oh, this?" Martin lifted up the handle of the umbrella at his side.

"Indeed. The craftsmanship is exquisite."

Martin held on to the wooden handle of the umbrella and turned it in his hand. "It's not mine. I just borrowed it."

"A high-quality umbrella the gentleman possesses," the driver glanced at him through the rearview mirror.

"How can you tell?" Martin asked. "I just got it this morning from some punk kid who works at a convenience store. Not the kind of guy who would possess anything high quality. Or stylish for that matter."

"Forgiveness," the driver said with a shrug of his shoulders.

"Why are you apologizing?" Martin asked.

But the driver kept his silence.

It was another half an hour before they entered the mountain pass. For a while the street ran parallel to a river whose name Martin did not know, but after a short time the driver turned onto a narrow road amongst the trees.

"It's beautiful," Martin commented as he admired his ever-changing surroundings.

"The gentleman's words are kind. The lady's residence is a beautiful place as well," the driver said with several nods.

"Have you lived here all your life?" Martin asked.

"This one has lived long under the roof of the lady and longer under her husband."

"You live with them too? Wow." Martin leaned back. "Must be hard."

"The road becomes steep ahead," the driver said. "The gentleman may feel uncomfortable."

"Don't worry about me," Martin said. "Are we almost there?"

"The house will be visible from the peak of this incline," the driver said.

Martin watched as the road ahead became steeper and steeper. He felt the car sputter and struggle every inch until it felt as if the road bent ninety degrees upward into the sky. Martin's stomach began to churn. But when he finally felt that his body was ready to retch up all of its contents, the road began to straighten, and within moments they had cleared the incline and came to a halt at the edge of what felt like a large crater hidden within the foothills.

The driver silently exited the car and came around to Martin's door, opening it gently.

"Come." He smiled. "The gentleman can see clearly now."

Martin emerged from the car and followed the driver forward until they reached a small vantage point on the side of the road. He let out a gasp. His eyes followed the road down until it twisted and turned between the trees. Enormous, old pine trees that swallowed the road whole, and a great swathe of land in the middle of the crater that had cradled an old wooden temple.

"Is the house behind the temple there?" Martin asked.

"The temple is the house the gentleman sees," the driver responded. "But before we descend into the woods and the land beyond, there are certain rules that the gentleman must know."

CHAPTER TWENTY-THREE

A Man is Only as Good as the World Around Him

The path to Yoshiko's house was much longer than it looked from the top of the crater. The road itself was hardly ever straight. It curved and coiled like a snake during the descent, then opened up to a long stretch of road leading through the forest.

"The gentleman must observe some rules before he enters," the driver said. "This one will explain to the best of his abilities."

"All right. Shoot," Martin responded.

"The gentleman must keep himself to the grounds of the lady's home and the temple. He must not venture into the woods at any point or for any reason."

"That's easy enough. Wouldn't want to get eaten by a bear or something." Martin feigned a laugh but got no reaction from the driver.

"When the gentleman is outdoors, he must carry his umbrella with him at all times."

Martin scrunched his face up, perplexed. "Why?" he asked. "I didn't see any rain on the forecast. Hell, the sky was blue the whole ride here, wasn't it?"

"Forgiveness," he said. "The gentleman is confused, but this one can explain no further on the issue. Please, for the lady's benefit."

The lady's benefit? What does that mean? Martin clutched the umbrella between his hands and nodded.

"Fine," he said. "I'll try not to forget it."

"This one appreciates the gentleman's understanding."

I don't understand shit.

"OK, so avoid wandering out in the woods and always bring an umbrella around on a clear day. Any other house rules for me?" Martin asked, spinning the umbrella in place on the floor.

"The gentleman is not to leave the main house after dark."

"Not even to tinkle?"

"The gentleman will be provided with facilities for tinkling."

Did he just say tinkling? Martin's confused expression turned into wide, toothy smile. "Okey-dokey then, my good man. As long as my tinkling facilities are provided for, I solemnly swear that I will not leave the house after hours."

"This one is pleased." The driver nodded, turning his eyes back to the road ahead.

They spent the rest of the ride in silence, short as it was. After a few minutes they passed through a large, wooden, Japanese gate which seemed to cut the world in two. No sooner had the car crossed that threshold did Martin see the vast property that stood before him. The trees lining the road were replaced with statues of all sorts and sizes. A large horse. A small, wily fox. A masked warrior with a sword in his hand. A bare-breasted woman with her hands outstretched to the world. Martin tried to see more, but they came and went too fast for him to fully appreciate any of them meaningfully.

The driver had mentioned that the house and temple were separate, but as it came into view, it was clear that this building was all temple and no house at all. He opened his mouth to ask the driver, but thought better of the answer he was likely to get and stopped himself. Regardless of what name they attached to the building that stood before him, there was no questioning its age or its beauty. Patterned green shingles adorned the roof, and the outer walls were covered in murals that Martin guessed must have been at least a hundred years older than he was.

In front of the main doors stood Yoshiko. She wore a smile atop a yellow and green kimono, and carried an umbrella of the same hue in her hands.

"Sensei!" she called as Martin emerged from the car. His knees cracked loudly as he stood, but he gave her a smile and a wave.

"The gentleman must not forget his umbrella," the driver said, appearing behind Martin.

"What, now? But it's not—" Martin cut himself off and looked down at his feet. "All right, all right. But hey, why don't you have one?"

"This one has no need," the driver responded. He reached deftly into the trunk and pulled Martin's belongings out.

"Thanks," Martin said. He unfurled his umbrella, thrust it open towards the sky and began walking towards Yoshiko and the front door.

"Your umbrella is beautiful!" Yoshiko exclaimed as Martin drew closer. She covered her mouth with one hand and gave him a slight bow.

"It's not mine," Martin confessed for the second time. "I just borrowed it from a friend."

"Why... what a courteous friend you must have made here. To have something such as this that he would just lend to someone!" She giggled.

Martin looked up at the inside of his borrowed umbrella. "Why wouldn't he lend this to me? I mean it's a nice umbrella, but it's just an umbrella, right?"

"Oh, Sensei, you jest!" She returned a hand over her mouth to cover her own bemusement. But when Martin didn't make any hint of a joke, she straightened up and looked into his eyes. "You mean you don't know?"

"Know what?"

"Oh!" Yoshiko's voice wavered. "Didn't you tell him?" she asked, looking at the driver.

"Forgiveness, my lady. This one did not inform him of the rarity of his possession."

"Rarity?" Martin's eyes widened.

"Yes. The gentleman holds a Soken-brand umbrella. A masterpiece of Japanese craftsmanship and design. Elegant, beautiful, and made for royalty. The lady has the pleasure of owning more of them than the Emperor himself," the driver said with pride.

"Oh, that old buzzard wouldn't know good design if it hit him in that big forehead of his!" Yoshiko stomped a foot down.

"Are Japanese people allowed to refer to the Emperor as an old buzzard?" Martin asked.

Yoshiko's back straightened and she looked around in a panic as if someone might have been listening to her comment. "Oh!" She looked at Martin. "Sensei is correct. We should be polite. Even when talking about old buzzards!" Her laughter was infectious, and before he knew it, Martin was howling right along with her.

After the amusement had settled, Yoshiko took Martin on a grand tour of the grounds. Just as he had suspected, nothing in the house looked at all house-like. The floors were all hardwood and polished to perfection. The sliding doors that lead into each room had murals of all different sizes and styles depicted on them, similar to the ones that adorned the outer walls. There was nothing modern in the house to speak of. No phone. No computer. Not even a microwave stood in the kitchen.

A MAN IS ONLY AS GOOD AS THE WORLD AROUND HIM

But Martin noticed one thing above all else—the emptiness. Aside from the driver who dutifully followed them to each and every room they toured, there were no other servants, maids, family members, or anyone at all to speak of. Even the sounds of nature were hushed by the thick walls of the house, leaving behind nothing but their footsteps and the echo of Yoshiko's voice.

After moving in and out of several rooms, they at last came to the back door of the house. Yoshiko motioned the driver over to the door and, after taking a seat on his knees, he dutifully opened it, revealing a lushly expansive stone garden.

"I've never seen anything like this," Martin commented as he took the first steps out on the patio.

"I imagine you haven't, Sensei," Yoshiko remarked with pride in her voice. "It is the only one like it in all of Japan."

The garden's rock formations had long been overrun with brilliant green moss. Stone paths disappeared behind thick, giant trees and, just as they had in front of the house, statues lined each path. Some of them looked as smooth and fresh as if they had been built yesterday, others stood with broken limbs and cracked eyes, half overrun by the encroachment of nature and time.

"How far does it go?" Martin asked, peering beyond the barrier of foliage.

"Farther than I've gone in my lifetime," Yoshiko said quietly. "The garden extends onto old lands. Properties that were not originally ours, but were subsumed by the tides of forgetfulness."

"You mean other people live here?"

"Other people once lived here," Yoshiko said, taking a cautious step down the stairs to join Martin. "But it is only us now. This land may be forgotten by most of our people. But we remember it. We keep it alive."

Martin turned around to help Yoshiko down the stairs. Behind her was the driver, still sitting on his knees at the door of the house. Martin smiled at him, but his gaze was elsewhere. *What is he looking at?* Martin wondered as he turned back to the garden. But nothing caught his attention.

"Sensei," Yoshiko began. "This garden is my special place. Do you like it?"

"It's incredible. I feel like I could get lost in here if I wandered too far out," he answered.

"Come," she said, taking his arm in her own. "Let us walk down this path here. There's a nice little tea house down the way where we can relax."

"What about him?" Martin said, turning a finger towards the driver.

"Oh? Nonsense, the butler's duty is to the household, and there he will remain. Besides. My husband is waiting for us in the tea house, and he is eager to meet you."

Martin acquiesced and they began to move down the center path, away from Yoshiko's house and into the woods. Martin kept Yoshiko's arm locked inside his own, and though their pace was slow, there was no shortage of things for Martin to see along the way.

As they progressed, the statues that lined the path changed. At first, Martin half expected each one to be slightly more degraded than the one before, but slowly he realized that the opposite was true. The statues themselves seemed to come alive the further they went, until finally they came across the visage of a large wild boar that Martin couldn't help but stop and admire.

"Now here is a fierce creature," Yoshiko said, unlocking her arm from Martin's and gliding towards the statue. "I've always admired this one."

"It feels so alive," Martin said coming to her side. "Like someone took a snapshot of a charging boar and captured it in stone."

"I thought of it in much the same way, Sensei," she said, resting her hand on its outstretched snout."

"Your husband's waiting for us at the tea house, right?" Martin looked away from the boar and back down the path.

"Of course. Can't you hear him?"

Martin narrowed his eyes and listened carefully.

"Dum dum dum." Yoshiko hummed behind him. "No? Nothing?"

Martin pointed his ear towards the silence and listened as hard as he could.

"*Somewhere, over the rainbow...*" Yoshiko began to sing, "*way up high...*"

A trio of notes responded from the distance.

"A trombone?"

Yoshiko clapped her hands together with excitement. "I'm glad you remembered, Sensei!" she said cheerfully. "Come on! We should hurry along to see him before our tea gets cold!"

They rushed along the path as quickly as a seventy-something-year-old woman could rush. They followed the path left and right and left and right until finally they came before a building almost as large as the mansion they had come from.

"It's huge," Martin exclaimed. "Is this a tea house or just a normal house?"

Yoshiko climbed the steps and opened the door for him. "Come in and find out." She smiled.

He took off his shoes in the entryway and stepped up into the hall. The room in front of him was perfectly square, with a rectangular table in the center that was covered in all manner of snacks and edible delights. Musical instruments of all kinds adorned the walls. Guitars, violins, even woodwinds and horns. Many of them he didn't recognize. In each corner, larger instruments stood proudly. A grand piano, a concert harp, and a long, flat wooden instrument with strings that Martin had never seen before. Three small chairs were prepared at the table, and Yoshiko ushered Martin to the one seated opposite the other two.

"I took the liberty of preparing meat," a voice said from the doorway. Martin turned his head back to the entrance and saw the figure of Yoshiko's husband. "We don't usually eat meat."

Martin stood to greet him. "I appreciate that," he said, bowing his head. "Everything here looks delicious."

The man took a few steps forward into the room, keeping one hand behind his back and the other rigidly to his side. He had every bit of the dignified stateliness that Yoshiko had. Perhaps even more. His face was weathered and worn, but his eyes were wide open and he moved with the speed of a much younger man.

"I told you that he could eat fish," Yoshiko started, "you didn't have to go through all the trouble."

Yoshiko's husband waved a dismissive hand in her direction and walked towards Martin. "Nonsense," he said. "We don't often get to cook for guests anymore. It's a pleasure to cook for someone else's palate than our own."

"You cook everything yourself?" Martin asked.

"Are you surprised?"

"Well, you have the driver who brought me here. I guess I just assumed that you would have others living and working here to help take care of you."

"There were others," he said. "But I always preferred to do the cooking myself."

"And he cooks very well," Yoshiko added.

Her husband stepped forward until he was just inches from Martin and outstretched a leathery old hand. Martin gave it a good shake and smiled.

"It's nice to meet you, sir," he said.

"Indeed. Yoshiko talks frequently about you. Sometimes I think she aims to make me jealous. But looking at you I can see I have nothing to worry about."

Half of Martin's smile faded. *Did he just call me ugly?* Tension filled the air, and it seemed like both of his hosts were waiting for a good response.

"Thank you?" Martin stammered and looked around nervously.

Her husband's face turned red. "It's not every day a foreigner comes into my house and then thanks me for calling him ugly either!" He roared with laughter so hard that even Yoshiko began to snicker and snort. Martin was at a loss for words.

"Sensei!" Yoshiko called in between bouts of laughter. "Sensei, you must not take this old fool so seriously! Oh, Masa, stop laughing so hard!"

All pretense of the old aristocratic couple living in a mansion high in the mountains vanished, and before Martin knew it, he was dining and making conversation with such ease that he felt as if he was in his own home.

They spent a leisurely afternoon in the tea house. Martin ate until he could stomach no more and talked until his voice was hoarse. Yoshiko's husband spoke about how he had been born and raised on the grounds—the only son of the previous head groundskeeper who had inherited the lands quite by accident after the local monks decided to abandon the property during the war.

"It became a terribly lonely place," he explained after taking a sip of tea. "At that time the war was in full swing. Of course, you would never know it in a place like this. But news would come from visitors, and we would hear about how well the Empire was doing. You would have thought that Japan was going to rule the whole world in those days."

Martin said nothing, listening intently.

"But then after a while the refugees began to appear. Although maybe 'refugee' isn't the right word for them. Families whose homes had been destroyed in the bombings. Orphans, cripples, deserters. At first, we didn't pay much attention to it. But then..." He ran a finger around the rim of his cup.

Martin's eyes were completely focused on Masa. His ears hanging on every word. He urged Masa to continue with a nod.

"My father and I went into town one day on an errand. It was a hot, midsummer day in 1945. And that's when we saw them. Hundreds of Japanese lining the streets. Homeless, wounded. Some of them were crying for food. Some of them were crying for their mothers. Some of them were just crying because there was nothing else they could do but cry."

Yoshiko placed a hand on her husband's shoulder and nodded. "I remember," she said.

"You were there too?" Martin asked.

"Oh, yes. Yes. It was the first time I saw the man who would become my husband."

"Didn't you tell me you were from another prefecture?"

"I was. We all were," she said with a frown.

Yoshiko's husband raised his head and spoke. "We were isolated. Far from the troubles of the war. But on the other side of Hokuriku, machines of industry churned day and night supplying the war effort, in a city called Fukui. Fukui was no prize of a place. But its contributions to Japan's war machine did not go unnoticed by the Americans."

Martin looked at Yoshiko. "But didn't you tell me you were on a farm, far from the city during the attack?"

"I was. The city was destroyed, but not even a stray piece of shrapnel came within a kilometer of our house. No, Sensei. It wasn't the Americans that destroyed my home. It was the Japanese."

Martin tilted his head in surprise. "How?" he asked.

Yoshiko's husband was the one to respond. "War can make men desperate. The survivors of Fukui had lost everything. Their homes. Their families. Their jobs. But they also lost their food. Their money. And when they couldn't turn to their government for support—"

"They came to our farm one night," Yoshiko interrupted. "A group of men. Demanding food and shelter. They accused us of hoarding for ourselves. They said they knew that we had piles and piles of rice just hidden away somewhere. They told us that if we didn't give it to them, they would burn the farm down with us inside."

"What did you do?"

"What could we do? Fukui had no more police. No more army. No more order. My father was gone, fighting in China. We surrendered the house. My mother showed them to our last reserves of rice and told them to take everything. But it was a paltry amount. The leader of their group started shouting at us. Demanding that we show him where our real reserves were. And when we could not, they burned the farm to the ground with my mother still inside."

Martin had no response to give. No words of comfort. Her words fell upon him like rain in an open field.

"I was just a child. Barely seven years old at the time. I remember one of the men in the group had been another farmer on the other side of town, who we often met in the market. He took me by the hand when no one else was looking and we ran away from that place as fast as a seven-year-old and a seventy-year-old could run."

"What happened to him? Why did he decide to help you?" Martin asked.

"I don't think I'll ever know. He was a good man. But I think all of the men who burned down our farm had been good men once. A man can only be as good as the world around him allows him to be. And in those days Japan was no country for good men. He died at the border of Toyama, too old and weak to carry on. That was the same day that my would-be husband came into town."

Bittersweet smiles came over Yoshiko and Masa's faces.

"It's amazing how one person can change everything," Yoshiko said, giving Masa a nudge.

He nodded. "Like I said, that day my father and I had come into town on some errands. My father was a kind man. He knew nothing of where they had come from or what had happened. But that same day he took as many people as were willing back with him to this place."

"Here?" Martin looked around.

"Of course. After all, by then it was just the two of us living with all this to our name. We had no shortage of rooms or beds. The farm at the other end of the valley kept us supplied with more than enough provisions to feed a hundred men. Although we ended up taking about only half that amount back with us that day."

"There weren't any problems? Having all those strangers around living under the same roof?"

"Oh, of course there was the occasional disagreement or clash of personalities. But it was surprisingly peaceful. As long as they were willing to help us tend the grounds and keep the house up and running, then they were welcome to stay. We had everything we needed. Even after the war ended and Japan was occupied by the Americans, their army never came here. Fifty people came with us that day to live. And fifty people stayed here to die many years later."

"No one left? Not even a single person?"

"Not of the original fifty, no. They had seen enough of the horrors of the outside world and were content to stay. My father adopted Yoshiko, as she had arrived without a single person, and she stayed with us in our room."

Martin leaned back in his chair, rubbing a thoughtful hand across his chin as he did. The conflicts of his lifetime felt insignificant and petty.

Yoshiko's husband took another sip of tea before slapping his hands on his knees. "Well!" he said. "Why don't I lighten the mood with some music. Stay here, you two, I'll be right back."

He disappeared through the back door, leaving Martin alone with Yoshiko. Martin searched for something to say, but before he could grasp at anything, she spoke.

"You're wondering about all the people. What happened to them. Aren't you?" she asked.

"Well... I just figured they had passed away. If most of the people who had come here were already grown men and women then it just figures that... well, you know."

"Hmm." Yoshiko frowned. "Many of the women and men ended up getting married and having children of their own. Before we knew it, we had a bustling miniature society."

"What happened to the kids, then?"

"Children that grow up in peace are restless. They seek adventure and yearn for more than the world they are born into. We were isolated, but not completely cut off from the rest of the world. When they saw what the bigger cities had to offer, what reason did they have to stay?"

"I see."

"And so, they all left. And one by one the original fifty began to pass away until just my husband and I remained. We never had children of our own. If we had, they would have only gone away like the rest, I imagine." Yoshiko looked at Martin. "Just like writing letters on the sand of some beautiful beach. No matter how deeply you inscribe the letters, the waves will come and wash them all away."

"What do you mean?" Martin asked.

"It's just the same here, Sensei. We brought up a society of people together. A group of survivors who knew well enough to stay here with other like-minded men and women. But all of them are gone now. I, too, am getting old. Soon the waves will come to wash my mark from the sands of this world. We fifty will be forgotten. The lessons we learned. The wisdom we had. All faded away into nothingness. That is the way of things now."

"I don't think so." Martin came to his feet and walked to Yoshiko's side. "I won't forget the things you have told me. I won't let your good lessons fade into nothing. I promise."

Yoshiko smiled and lifted herself up. "Thank you, Sensei," she said with a deep bow. "Please keep us alive in your heart."

Outside, rain had begun to fall. Her husband returned with his trombone, and soon all the words that had been spoken were transformed into the long, deep notes of a lone trombonist, playing melodies against the downpour.

CHAPTER TWENTY-FOUR

Partners

They returned to the estate as night fell. Yoshiko instructed her butler to show Martin the room where he would be spending the weekend. She and her husband stayed on the first floor. Their years had made it too taxing for them to climb the stairs more than once or twice a week. As such, the upkeep of the upper floors had fallen to her butler, who had more than dutifully kept each room immaculate.

"The gentleman will follow," he instructed. The stairwell itself was narrow and steep, and the floorboards creaked with every step. They climbed two separate flights until reaching a long, well-lit corridor on the third floor.

"It feels like a hotel," Martin commented. The hall stretched at least fifty yards in each direction. Art lined the walls, just as statues had lined the paths in the garden. They made a right turn and after a few doors they came to an open room with a large futon prepared in the center.

"The gentleman's belongings are in the closet." The butler motioned toward the far wall. "The lavatory is behind the door opposite the gentleman's room. If the gentleman requires aid, there is a hand chime on the desk by the window. Ring it three times. That will suffice. If the gentleman wishes, he may visit the other rooms on this floor, but take care not to wander outside the estate."

"Right." Martin nodded. "No going out after dark. Got it."

"Very well. This one will return to the lady. Good night."

"Good night." Martin watched the butler shut the door behind him, then let out a sigh of exhaustion.

The bedroom was sparsely furnished, but provided a spectacular view of the garden below. Martin set his borrowed umbrella down carefully against the desk and walked across the room to the balcony door. There was just enough light left to make out the tea house in the distance, though it was mostly obscured by pine trees much taller than the house itself. Martin stepped outside and looked down at the path he had walked with Yoshiko. Even from above, the statues dotting the path seemed to spring to life. He couldn't quite see the boar statue from his room, but he imagined it breaking out of its stone prison at night to wander the forest before returning every morning when the sun rose.

After a few minutes, a cold breeze forced him back inside, where he took a seat at the desk and removed his phone from his pocket. He didn't expect to get any signal up here, but still felt a slight pang of disappointment when his expectations were confirmed. No signal. No internet. For all intents and purposes, he was cut off from the outside world. Alone in the woods.

In his newfound silence, his mind began to wander. Though he couldn't see it from here, Martin knew that Yuji's farmlands lay in the same general area as Yoshiko's home. Somehow during their hours of conversation, he had failed to broach the subject. It had now been a month since he had seen the duo—since that boat ride along the Matsu River. He thought back to Shimodoi's remark that Yuji hadn't made a delivery in more than a couple weeks. Had he simply given up? Or had he moved on? Martin searched his thoughts but found no answer.

Then there was the woman in the fog. Tuba had said something about sending her back to where she belonged. But he and Sami too had gone missing. They stayed to fight whatever that thing was, while Martin had run. *And that rooster. Where did you go? Where did you come from?*

He crossed his right leg over his left and leaned back against his chair, where he stayed swimming in his own mind until the soft pitter-patter of rain caught his attention. The clock on his phone read a quarter past eight. Too late to go downstairs and find something to do, too early to call it a night and go to bed. With nothing else to do he stared out the glass door to the balcony and listened to the rain. For a while, it was all he could hear. But slowly, almost unnoticeably, he began to hear a thumping noise coming from outside. Martin perked his ears up and listened. *Thump. Thump thump.* There was a pause, followed by the loud creaking of wood, then silence.

Martin stood up and walked to the light switch and quickly shut it off, leaving him in the dark with his eyes unadjusted. At first, the silence continued, but there it was again—*thump thump. Thump thump thump.* Then another long creaking noise. Martin cautiously approached the door, never for a moment taking his eyes off the balcony. His eyes, now gradually becoming accustomed to the low light, could see just out to the handrail outside but no further.

The irregular thumping continued. Closer, closer, and closer until Martin felt like something was about to burst up from below. But after the last set of thumps and creaks, he heard something else.

"Ah."

"Ah?" Martin whispered. He focused his eyes harder on the balcony.

"Ah." He heard again.

There was a short burst of thumps, then suddenly the image of a hand shot up in front of him, grabbing the wooden railing from the other side.

"*Ah*!" he shouted.

"*Ah*!" the voice replied. Martin watched, horrified at the single hand grasping the rail outside. He thought to run, but as he did so the voice called out again. "Ah! Help!"

He turned back around towards the door and saw the hand still grasping at the rails, while another one appeared and then disappeared several times.

"Help!" the voice cried again. "Help me, you idiot!"

Martin slid the door open and tip-toed out until he could peek over the railing. Ever so faintly, he made out a tuft of orange hair about a foot or two below him.

"Eiko?" Martin stood astonished.

"Sensei!" She looked up. Her whole body was rocking back and forth in the air with nothing below but leaves and earth.

"How did you get there?"

"Are you seriously asking me questions while I'm hanging here?" she shouted. "Help me up!" She waved her free arm frantically.

"Oh, yeah." Martin nodded. He grabbed her wrist and began to pull.

"Pull harder!" Eiko shouted from below.

"I'm pulling as hard as I can!" He took a step back. "You're so heavy!"

"I'll kill you, Martin!"

"I'll let you go, Eiko."

"Ah!" she screamed again. Martin took another step back and heaved until the top of her head was level with his. Her free arm finally grasped at the rail, and Martin rushed in and put his arms around her. He put all his strength into one last pull backward and before he knew it, she had flown over onto the balcony and crash landed on top of him.

"Are you OK?" Martin asked, his arms still wrapped around her. The heat of her labored breaths brushed his face. She was too exhausted to speak, but gave a couple of quick nods in response.

"Can you stand up?" he asked.

"Not yet." She rested her head against his chest. "Not yet."

Her hair was done in a ponytail, and she was wearing a black blazer over a white collared shirt. Naturally, almost instinctually, Martin ran his hand through her hair while she calmed her breathing. Her small chest rose and fell against him, and all the apprehension and fear he had felt just moments before were swept away.

"Sensei?" she asked, lifting her head up and looking him in the eyes. "I should punch you for calling me heavy. But I'll forgive you this time." She pushed herself off of him and stood up.

"Thanks?" He stood up after her and brushed himself off. "Wait here. I'll turn on the light."

Martin made his way through the room and flipped on the switch. He looked back at Eiko and watched as she slid off her shoes and stepped inside. She wore long, tight pants that matched her blazer, and other than looking like she had just fallen in a pool, she seemed unharmed by the ordeal.

He opened his mouth to ask her a question, but she stopped him with a wave of her hand.

"Sensei," she said. "Could you show me where the bathroom is first?"

"Yeah, it's right here." Martin opened the door behind him and pointed across the hall. Eiko nodded, but didn't move.

"What is it?" he asked.

"Can I...?" She motioned to Martin's bag in the corner. "Can I borrow some clothes for a while?"

Martin looked over at his bag, then back at Eiko. "I don't think they'll fit very well. But I guess you can't sit around here sopping wet either." He unzipped his bag and took out a clean pair of jeans and a brown T-shirt.

"Here," he said. "You'll need a belt or those will fall straight off, though."

"I've got that covered." She tapped on her waistband. "I'll be right back."

Eiko crossed the hall and opened the door to the bathroom, then looked back at Martin. "No peeking." She smiled, and shut the door behind her.

Martin sat back down at the desk and waited, though it was only a few brief moments before she emerged again clad in his long blue jeans and baggy T-shirt. Their heights were not so different, but his waist size had more than a few more inches. He tried not to laugh as she walked in and collapsed on the futon in the middle of the room.

"Ah!" She let out a long sigh of relief. "What a day!"

"Eiko," Martin said sternly. She sat up on her knees and looked at him. "Where the hell have you been?"

"Hmph! *That's* the first thing you ask me? What do you care?" She put her hands on her hips and puffed out her cheeks defiantly.

"What do you mean? You disappeared just before your lesson on Monday, and didn't show up to any classes after that. You didn't pick up your phone either."

"Oh yeah? Well maybe I don't want to be your student anymore."

Martin scratched his head, then folded his arms around his chest. "Did I do something?"

"I bet you haven't even thought about our class. I bet it's been a relief for you that I haven't been showing up. 'Finally! Crazy Eiko is out of the picture. Now I can go back to being surrounded by cute high school girls every night!' That's what you've been thinking, haven't you?"

Martin's face began to betray his annoyance. "What's your problem? And what the hell are you talking about, 'surrounded by high school girls?' Do you mean the ones from Monday? They aren't even my students."

"But you wish they were your students. I saw how you were with them."

Martin buried his face in his palm and shook his head. "Think whatever you want. I don't care."

"See!" She stood up and shoved a finger in his cheek. "You don't care. I knew you didn't care. You're such a jerk!"

"Ugh." Martin slapped her finger out of his face. "How did you even get here, anyway? Were you stalking me here just like you stalked me to my work?"

"Stalking? Ha! Don't make me laugh. I didn't stalk you here. I followed you here!"

"That's what stalking is!" Martin was almost yelling.

"Hmph!" Eiko shoved her hand in her pocket and took out a folded piece of paper. "It's not stalking someone if you're invited!" She pushed it into his hands and turned around.

Martin unfolded it and stared. It was the letter he had written her with the sketch of a UFO. "Eiko, I want to believe." The only words scrawled upon it.

"This isn't an invitation anywhere," Martin said.

"Then what is it?"

He was stumped. He looked down at it, not quite understanding what he had wanted to accomplish with those five words. "It's..." he hesitated, not knowing what to say next. He knew what it had started out as. An idea. A last-ditch effort at communication with someone who he thought might not be there anymore. "I was worried," Martin started.

"Liar. You never even tried to call me."

"That's not true. We called you every day. Twice a day. You're the one who never picked up."

"*We?* What 'we' is there? You never called me. The Assistant Manager did. But you didn't. Not even once."

"What difference does it make? You still ignored it."

"It makes all the difference!" Eiko turned back around and pointed a finger at his nose. "Is that all this is, then? A business relationship? You're my teacher and I'm your student, right?"

"I mean, I am your teacher. And you are my student." Martin scratched the back of his head again, more violently than before. "And none of this addresses how you stalked me from my apartment in Takaoka all the way to the middle of the damn woods."

"How could I not follow you? I saw you being taken into a big black car by a man in a suit and figured that you needed help! That's what this is, right? Some kind of compound!"

"This isn't 'The X-Files,' you know! There's no FBI here, no mysteries to solve in this country-bumpkin-ass-shantytown of a prefecture."

That was it for Eiko. She shot a hand straight across his cheek and pushed him back down into the chair behind him. "You take that back," she commanded.

Martin rubbed his hand against his cheek, astonished by the force of the blow. Tears were welling up in her eyes, and he immediately felt regret for the words he had spoken.

"I'm sorry," he said. "I don't know why we're fighting." He got back up from the chair and walked over to where she stood. "And it's not that I'm not happy to see you. In fact, I'm relieved."

"You don't seem very relieved." Eiko looked away from him again, her arms still folded around her chest.

"It's true. I know we haven't had a chance to talk since that night. And I'm sorry I left in the morning without telling you. There's been so much I've wanted to say, I've just not known how to say it."

She wiped her tears on the shirt he had lent her and sat back down on the futon. "Are you really sorry?"

"Is there some way I can prove it to you?" he asked.

She looked back up at him, the light on the ceiling reflected in her eyes. "I'm hungry," she said.

Martin half smiled and looked at the chime on his desk. "I think I can fix that. But you might have to hide in the closet for a minute."

Convincing the butler to bring up a small meal was a simple enough request, and after a short wait he reappeared with a tray of leftovers from their lunch as well as a glass of water. Martin thanked him and waited until he heard his footsteps in the stairwell before opening up the closet and letting Eiko back out.

Her stomach growled, even as she ate. Martin watched as she shoved spoonful after spoonful in her mouth, with barely enough time to breath in-between bites.

"Is it good?" he asked.

She looked up at him, seemingly suddenly aware of her appearance, and pushed him away. "Don't watch me eat." She said through a mouth full of food. Martin laughed and sat back down on the futon.

When she finished eating, she swallowed the entire glass of water down in one big gulp and leaned back against the chair, satisfied.

"Hey, Eiko," he said after a few minutes of silence.

"Yeah?"

"How did you find me?"

"I told you, I saw you getting into that car with the guy in the suit and followed you here." She got up from the chair and sat down on the floor in front of him.

"I mean before that. How did you even know where I lived?"

"Oh, that?" She hesitated. "Well. I could tell you, but you promise not to laugh?"

"You haven't been following me home at night?"

Eiko was not amused. "Promise you won't laugh. And promise you'll believe me?"

"OK." Martin nodded. "I promise."

"Well, I wasn't going to come. I was going to just tear up that stupid letter right there I was so mad. But then Rodney appeared and told me that I needed to follow him.

"Who?" Martin turned his head. "Who is Rodney?"

"Rodney isn't really a who." She shuffled around uncomfortably. "You promised you'd believe me. right? You won't laugh?"

Martin nodded, and waited for her to continue.

"His name isn't really Rodney. I just called him Rodney because he didn't have a name and I didn't know what else to call him."

"I thought you said he wasn't a person?"

"He's not." She looked from side to side, then leaned in close. "He's a chicken."

CHAPTER TWENTY-FIVE

The Room at the End of the Hall

"A chicken?" Martin leaned forward. "What kind of chicken?"

"A big old black one." Eiko stretched her arms out, demonstrating its size. There was no doubt about it. This "chicken" Eiko had seen was no chicken at all, but the rooster Martin had encountered twice before.

"A rooster, then," Martin said.

"A what?"

"A rooster. You know, a male chicken. And you named him Rodney?"

"Yep. He looks like a Rodney." Eiko nodded. "At first it was kind of creepy. Just having a big old black chicken-rooster-thing show up out of nowhere. But it told me how to find you, and here I am!"

Martin rubbed his hand against his chin. "Where is he now?"

"I don't know. He was with me in my car up until I got to your apartment and saw you getting into that Rolls-Royce, then he was gone. Pretty cool, huh?" She scooched in closer. "But how do *you* know Rodney?"

Aside from Shimodoi, no one else really knew about the rooster. He had brought it up in passing conversation with Chris once, but never again after that. It had all started with that rooster in the air ducts of Shimodoi's shop, but the more he strained to reason out what had happened since then, the more muddled everything became.

"Do you believe in the supernatural?" Martin asked. "I don't just mean the idea of the supernatural. Do you believe that there are some things that exist in this world that are beyond explaining?"

"Like ghosts?" Eiko asked.

"No." Martin shook his head. "I'm not sure how to describe it."

"It's kind of hard to say yes or no if I don't know what I'm saying yes or no to. Why don't you try saying everything that's happened out loud? Sometimes it's better to hear things come out of your own mouth than just look at images in your mind."

"I guess I can try," he said. "But a lot has happened and it might take some time to tell you about all of it."

"I'm not going anywhere." Eiko smiled.

Martin took a deep breath, then took his time recalling each event as it came to him. The rooster in the air ducts; Yuji and his chickens; the boat ride and the bartenders who had saved him; the lady in the fog; everything. He took care to tell her every detail, from the umbrella that Tuba had to the news report he had heard of Yuji's farm being shut down and all the chickens disappearing overnight. Eiko listened intently, and though Martin was sure that at some point she would find his claims laughable, she never interrupted. When there was a pause, she would nod and urge him to continue, but she said nothing.

"It's ridiculous, I know. Saying it out loud makes me feel like it's more of a series of coincidences, rather than something supernatural. And now the people I would talk to about this are all gone. Yuji and his niece. Tuba and Sami. They're the ones who know things."

Eiko put her hands behind her and leaned back. "You know, when Mulder is investigating a case, he usually calls Scully and she does some research or runs some tests for him. Then she calls him back and tells him what he needs to know before he can finally solve the mystery."

"Yeah but we're not—"

"In 'The X-Files,' I know, I know," she finished. "But what I'm saying is, you have a mystery, and in order to solve the mystery, you need knowledge."

"So where would I find more knowledge?" Martin asked.

"Are you dense?" Eiko stood up and motioned towards the walls. "Just look at this place. You're staying in a mansion owned by an old rich couple, right?"

"Yeah? So what?"

"So, they probably have a study or some such room where they keep a lot of books and the like. Think about it. This Yuji person you're telling me about had a farm right here in the mountains, right? Practically next door. The owners of this place would know about their neighbors and about what happened. Maybe even have newspapers or something about the farm!" Her excitement was palpable.

Martin stood up. "Even if that's the case, we can't just go snooping around their house." But his voice fell on deaf ears. She was already in the doorway, ready to hunt down whatever she thought they could find hidden inside the mansion's walls.

"Come on, partner!" she called to him as she rushed out. "Let's go!"

Searching the mansion room by room was no easy task. They split up and each went separate ways down the hall. For his part, Martin found only a long series of bedrooms and what seemed to be a recreational room near the end of the hall, with a second bathroom on the left-hand side. Eiko's findings were much the same, the only difference being a small second kitchen and dining area.

"This really is more of a hotel than a home," Martin said as they met back up at his room.

"Yeah." Eiko nodded. "I don't think it was ever meant for just two people and a man-servant. Where should we go next? There's one floor above us, right?"

"Yeah. Let's look upstairs first," he said. They crept up the stairs, but no matter how lightly they stepped, the floor creaked under them.

"We wouldn't make very good spies," Eiko whispered as they cleared the last step.

Martin shrugged. This story was entirely different from the last, with an entirely open floor plan. Boxes piled upon boxes lined the walls. Antique clocks and wooden sculptures stood here, there and everywhere. The air was thick and heavy with dust, and it was clear that no one had been up here for some time.

"I don't think we'll find anything up here," Martin said. Eiko slid past him, intent on taking a look around.

"Let's check it out anyway. I'll take the left side again and you take the right."

They split up again, but in the maze of boxes and old art, Martin quickly lost sight of her. Everything on the fourth floor felt like it had come from an entirely different era. Boxes were labeled in words that he couldn't read, and most of the art pieces looked like they'd crumble apart at the faintest touch from his hand.

It wasn't long before he heard Eiko calling his name from across the room. He squeezed and pushed his way through the dust-filled attic until he caught sight of her leaning over something long and wooden.

"Check this out!" she said.

"What is it?" Martin peeked over her shoulder. It was a wooden plank, about five feet long and one foot wide, with ten or so strings that stretched across the whole thing. Martin had seen something just like it in the tea house earlier in the day.

"It's a koto. An instrument like a harp but you play it sitting on your knees. I used to take lessons when I was a little girl."

"It looks difficult to play." Martin ran his hand along the side if the instrument. It had deep, faded engravings and several cuts in the wood that showed its years of use. "It's cool."

"I hated it." Eiko laughed quietly. But my step-dad always made me play it when we had company over. He was always like that. Making me do stuff to put on a show."

"He sounds like a real pain in the ass." Martin sat on his knees next to her.

"Oh?" She looked over at him. "You should know more than anyone. I'm pretty sure you broke his jaw, after all."

Martin turned back to her, his eyes wide. "Eiko, I'm so sorry," he said. "I didn't know."

"Ha!" She laughed louder this time. "That old shit got what was coming to him. I was never able to stand up to him like you did. It was really cool."

Martin's face turned red. "Thanks," was all he could say, which made her laugh even more. Eiko spent a few minutes lightly plucking at the koto strings, dwelling on memories that Martin didn't quite yet know.

"Eiko," he said, breaking the silence. "I think we're looking in the wrong direction."

"What do you mean?" she asked.

"Well, Yoshiko and her husband don't have much in the way of entertainment up here, and what they do have would probably have to be somewhere easily accessible, right? They can't travel up and down flights of stairs like they used to, after all." Martin stood up and brushed off his knees. "They gave me a tour of most of the home when I got here, but there were a few rooms I didn't see. If there is a study, I bet it's downstairs."

Eiko stood up and put her hands on her hips. "But they sleep down there, right? What if we open the wrong door and walk in on them... you know." Eiko nudged him with her elbow.

"Stop." Martin laughed. "We're supposed to be on a mission here."

"Right, right." Eiko put her hands together. "What should we do, then?"

"Let's do this," he said. "I'll go down first and check things out. If the they or the butler catch me, I'll just say I was looking to get a glass of water or something. I'll take a quick look around, then come back for you."

"Okey-dokey!" She nodded enthusiastically. "I'll wait for you at the top of the stairs, then."

They left the old koto where it was and proceeded back down the stairs, parting ways on the second floor. He moved as quietly as he could down the stairs into the main hall, stopping every so often to listen for any sounds of activity. When he got to the bottom, he looked around. Four of the rooms he had already been through during his brief tour with Yoshiko, and he counted those out immediately. That left the room directly in front of him and the room at the end of the hall, across from the kitchen. Both doors were shut, leaving him with a fifty-fifty chance to guess which one it could be.

There must be some way to narrow this down. He thought as he looked back and forth at each set of doors. There was no distinct difference between the two. No markings nor paintings nor convenient sign that said *Study* above either of them. After a minute of deliberating, he approached the door across from the stairwell and put his ear against it.

Nothing, but as he slid his feet closer, he felt something move against them.

Slippers? He kneeled down and picked one of them up. It was soft and light, with fur lining the inside. *This has to be the bedroom.* He stood back up and walked to the other set of doors at the end of the hall. Sure enough, there was no footwear, and no sound of occupation coming from behind them. He rested his hand on the door and slid it open just barely enough to peek inside. The lights were off, but moonlight illuminated outlines of desks and bookcases that stretched as high as the ceiling.

"Jackpot," he whispered.

Martin left the door slightly ajar and returned to the stairwell, where he found Eiko waiting patiently at the top. He signaled her to come down, and pointed to the doors at the end of the hall with a nod.

The pair entered the study, sliding the doors shut behind them as they did. Eiko moved her hand against the wall until she found the light switch. She flicked it on, activating the overhead lamp. It was dim, but lit the room well enough that they could easily see how extensive the study was. Rows and rows of bookshelves stretched from the front of the room all the way to the back. In the center was an enormous desk with its own lamp and a leather chair.

"Where should we start?" Martin whispered.

Eiko scratched at her chin and walked towards one of the shelves. "We're looking for newspapers, remember? Magazines, publications, things like that. Those kinds of things probably wouldn't be mixed in with normal books."

"Hmm." Martin plucked the book closest to him from the shelf and brushed off the cover with his hand. He studied the characters on it for a moment before looking up at Eiko. "What does it say?"

"I thought you could read Japanese?" She took the book from his hands.

"I thought I could too, but I've never seen these characters before." He looked around at the other titles in the shelf. "I can hardly make out any of these."

"Whole lot of good you are," she teased. "This one's about old European symphonies. In fact, all of these seem to have to do with music and music history. Mostly western, from the looks of it. A couple Japanese ones too." She placed the book back in the shelf.

They spent some time walking up and down the rows, looking for anything that would stand out. Each row had a common theme to it: art, history, science and much more. Yoshiko and Masa were clearly a well-read couple, though none of this helped Martin and Eiko's quest. After they had circled the study for a second time, he took a seat at the desk and let out a frustrated sigh.

"There's nothing here," he grumbled.

"Maybe we're just looking in the wrong place?" Eiko rested her elbows on the desk and closed her eyes in thought.

"Where else could we look? We've looked everywhere." He put his hand on one of the drawers and slid it open and closed.

"Don't whine. We haven't looked *everywhere*."

"Even if we did." He slid the drawer open and closed again. "This whole thing is probably just a wild goose chase."

"Would you stop playing with the drawers? You're making too much noise."

"It's not that loud." He slid the drawer open again, but this time Eiko caught it with one hand and slapped Martin in the forehead with the other.

"Ow," he whispered. "What was that for."

"Shush." She reached into the open drawer and pulled out a thick, green text with another title that Martin couldn't read.

"What does that one say?" he asked.

"This?" She pointed at the characters. "It means collection. And the one next to it means... hmm." She scratched the back of her neck. "Ghost? Spirit? Creatures? I'm not sure how to best say it. Look here. There's a bookmark in it." She set the book on the table and opened it to the marked page about a third of the way in.

"Now that's familiar," Martin said, rubbing his hand on the left page. It was a picture, faded, but easily recognizable. A woman in the rain, holding an umbrella and walking away from the viewer. The color had long disappeared, but he knew it was the same picture he had seen many times before.

"What is it?" he asked.

"It says, 'kasa-obake,'" she said.

"Umbrella-monster?" Martin looked back at the portrait. "She looks like a normal person to me."

"Let me see." Eiko picked it up and started reading.

"'The kasa-obake, history and recorded encounters. She initially appeared in the house of a powerful noble after he had returned home from a long journey to the northern-central prefectures. Upon the noble's return, he gifted his young and beautiful wife with a stunning red umbrella made by a famous northern craftsman. His wife was instantly enthralled by its deep crimson hues, and was never seen without it. Rumors in the upper court said she was so compelled by its beauty that she even slept with it in her bed for fear that someone might come and steal it.

"'A month after the noble's return, several murders were reported, and the victims were the nobleman's housemaids and servants. The murders occurred over the course of several weeks, until finally the noble ordered a permanent guard stationed at every door of the manor. But this too, proved ineffective, as soon even the guards were found one after another, massacred by an unknown assailant.

"'Eventually it was thought that the house was cursed. The nobleman, now fearing for his life, ordered the mansion to be burned to the ground and that a new one should be built in a separate location. Before this could be carried out, however, he too was found massacred in his own bedchambers. The remaining members of the household now strongly suspected the young wife of being responsible, and sought to set a trap for her. A fortnight after the nobleman's murder, they sprung their trap and attacked the young wife in the middle of the night. Fifteen men were sent to kill her, and the doors were barred behind them. A sixteenth man, the youngest son of one of the murdered lord's samurai, was ordered to set the manor ablaze should they not succeed.

"'After several minutes of listening to his comrades being slaughtered from behind the door, he put everything he could to the torch, and fled into the night. The survivors of the fire were able to recover the charred and mangled bodies of the fifteen men who were sent to kill her, but found nothing of the young wife herself.

"'It became known that the umbrella was made by the crafter Masahiro Soken, famously murdered by the selfsame nobleman who had gifted the umbrella to his wife. People believed that the murder had cursed the nobleman's house, and led to his death and the downfall of his entire family.'" Eiko flipped the page. "Look. There are notes in the margin."

"'Each night, I play my trombone for an hour in the tea house to calm her. She seems to have a vague memory of song. Something from her distant past that pacifies what little soul she has left within her. I have continued this practice for decades—since my father before me, and the masters of our home before him—but I am old now. And there is no one left here to play her song.

"'Last night, she appeared in front of the tea house. The first time I've seen her in over fifty years. Still beautiful. Untouched. It is as if her entire being defies time and nature itself. She looked at me for a time with some intent before disappearing back into the fog from whence she came. Why did she look at me so? Has she known this whole time that it was I who played those notes that calmed her? I cannot say.

"'I sought to ask the neighbors for help on this issue. The poultry farmer Yuji, and his cute little niece. But I arrived too late. She was there. Her eyes were different now. What little semblance of humanity I had seen in her before was gone, replaced by madness and bloodlust. I can only hope that Yuji made it out of there before she arrived.

"'I bear the guilt of it, now. I feel myself wearing thin. I play her song now only once or twice a week, and even then, only for ten minutes or so before my strength leaves me. Is she still listening? Do my melodies reach her? I do not know. There is nothing left for me to do but carry on as long as I can. For Yoshiko's sake. For all of our sakes.'"

Eiko turned to the next page, but found it blank. That was the end. She and Martin sat together in utter silence, both knowing full well what the other was thinking. It was real. She was real. And she was here.

CHAPTER TWENTY-SIX

The Kasa-Obake

They took care to leave everything exactly as they had found it, before turning the lights off and sneaking their way back up to Martin's room on the third floor.

"What do we do?" Eiko asked after they had both taken a seat on the futon.

Martin put his hands together and cracked his knuckles one by one. "What can we do?" he asked. "Think about it. Yoshiko and her husband have known about this thing and tried to keep it subdued for more than half a century now. You would think that they would have found something out in all that time."

"What are you saying?" Eiko asked.

"I'm saying that there's nothing to find out. This isn't just some crazy person in the woods that we can call the police about. It's a monster. Something that shouldn't even exist. We have no way to do anything about it."

She sighed dejectedly. "Something just doesn't add up."

"What else could there be?" he asked, but Eiko could offer no answer. They sat together quietly again for some time before Martin broke the silence. "Why don't we get some sleep for tonight. Tomorrow I'll explain to Yoshiko and her husband about how you ended up here and apologize for the whole thing. Then we can ask them about all of this together."

"Yeah." Eiko nodded. "That's probably best."

Martin looked at her, then down at the futon. "There's only one," he said. "I'll go check the other rooms and see if I can find another blanket or something—"

Eiko grabbed his hand before he could finish. "It's OK," she said. "I don't mind."

"Right." He blushed. "I'm going to go brush my teeth. I'll be right back."

He crossed the hall to the restroom and closed the door. Eiko's clothes were still hanging from a rack meant for towels. Her black blazer and pants still seemed a bit damp, but no worse for what they had gone through. He turned the sink on and splashed hot water on his face, then stared at his reflection in the mirror. In a way, he felt some measure of relief. Reading the book and Yoshiko's husband's notes had helped him affirm that everything he had experienced was real. And yet now he had nothing to do with that knowledge.

She doesn't belong here. Martin thought back on the words Yuji's niece had shared. *She can't leave.* He now knew of whom she spoke, and how she came to be. The murder her husband committed had tainted his prize, and that taint had cursed her to become the being she was now.

He finished brushing his teeth and crossed the hall back to his room. To his surprise, Eiko was fast asleep, sprawled out in the center of his futon leaving him with barely a foot of space. Not wanting to disturb her, he took a seat at his desk and took out his phone. No messages. No voicemail. And still no signal. He flipped back and forth between his old messages and his contacts a few times before tossing the phone down on the desk with a thud. The rain had come to a stop outside, leaving only the sound of Eiko's deep inhales and exhales behind him.

He turned his chair around to look at her. She was still wearing his clothes, and the curves of her body were completely obscured. But the lines of her face. The shape of her chin. The slight twitches of her lips and nose as she breathed. These things he could see, and as he watched her, he felt the exhaustion of the day slowly overtake him until his eyes closed shut and he faded into a deep slumber.

It was still dark outside when he heard a voice call out to him.

"Martin," she said. He felt the warmth of her hand on his arm. "Martin," she called again. He stirred slowly. "Martin, wake up." He heard Eiko's voice more distinctly now.

"What is it?" he asked. His eyelids were heavy and his vision out of focus, but he felt her next to him.

"Listen," she said.

Martin leaned forward. His neck and back were sore from sleeping against the hardwood chair, but he did his best to silence his inner aches and listen.

"I don't hear anything," he whispered.

"Shh." She squeezed his arm. "There. Do you hear it?"

Martin turned his head. It was faint. So faint that if no one had pointed it out, he never would have noticed. But the sound was unmistakable. Musical notes. Small, weak notes coming from a horn. A song he had heard once before.

"*Nen, nen korori yo. Okorori yo,*" he sang.

"*Boya wa yoi ko da, nen nen shina,*" the horn replied.

A surge of emotion overwhelmed him in the span of a quarter-second, then disappeared out the window, gone.

"How do you know that lullaby?" Eiko asked. "It's so old."

He forced himself up and opened the door to the balcony. The notes were instantly clearer, only now another instrument joined. A string, picking up where the horn left off. Through the trees, he spotted a glimmer of light coming from the tea house. Unmistakably where the music was originating.

"They're playing her song," Eiko said.

Martin looked back at her. She was wearing her clothes now—the ones she had been wearing when he found her hanging from the balcony. Her orange hair was messy and untamed, and her eyes were totally focused on the small light coming from the window of the tea house.

The song went on, yet Martin couldn't help but notice something wrong. Each note sounded distressed, like it was coming from an instrument that didn't want to be played. A far cry from the gentle tunes that Yoshiko's husband had played for him during their lunch hour. Each passing minute, the notes seemed to become more disjointed until they suddenly stopped altogether.

"We should go check it out," Martin said, rubbing his eyes.

"Wait, really?" Eiko stood up straight.

"What is it?" he asked.

"No, nothing." She pulled him towards the door. "Let's go investigate!"

"Wait." Martin grabbed the umbrella from the corner and gave it a shake. "We'll take this."

Eiko started to ask, but shut her mouth just as quickly and nodded in agreement.

There was no need for subtlety this time. They raced down each flight of stairs without regard for being discovered, pausing only once at the back door to slip on their shoes. From the ground, it was no longer possible to see the tea house through the trees. Eiko took out her phone and turned on its flashlight.

They followed the path as Martin remembered it, past all the animal statues until they arrived at the giant boar, whose dulled stone tusks pointed the way towards the tea house. From here, they could see the faint hints of light from distant windows.

"Martin." Eiko stopped suddenly. "What do we do when we get there?"

He turned around and looked at her, then his eyes fell downward at the ground. "I hadn't really thought that far ahead," he admitted. "But the music they were playing stopped suddenly, right? They might need our help."

She took a step towards him. "I know, but what if we have to defend ourselves? All I have is a cell phone and all you have is that umbrella." She pointed a finger at it. "Unless you've got something hidden in there that I don't know about."

Martin lifted the umbrella up in his hand. "The butler told me I was to have it on me at all times. This monster—the kasa-obake—she became obsessed with hers, right? Maybe she won't go after the person holding it for fear of damaging it?"

Eiko scrunched her nose. "That's pretty flimsy. Didn't you tell me that your bartender friend had one of these? That if you looked at it in the dark you could see images of things where they didn't belong?"

"Something like that." He nodded.

"What does that one do, then?"

Martin rubbed his hand over the orange canopy, hoping for some kind of reaction. "I don't know." He shrugged. "It's orange."

"Orange is a feature, not a capability." She pinched his arm.

"I don't know. I don't know, OK?" He recoiled. "Look—" he started, but Eiko rushed past him.

"What is it?" he asked.

"Something just ran across the path." She pointed her flashlight of her phone ahead. "I think it was an animal."

Martin stepped ahead of her and peered into the brush. He heard the rustling of leaves. Small, quick movements in the dark, but impossible to tell from where. "Shine your light over here," he said as he came to a larger hedge along the path.

She came up behind him and did as he asked. The rustling stopped, and through the foliage, something round and black reflected the light from Eiko's phone. "There's definitely something there," he said. "It's small."

"Be careful." She came closer.

Martin turned around. "Don't worry. It's probably just a cat or someth—"

Caw! A voice from the bushes interrupted. He turned back around and was immediately assaulted by a familiar set of talons on the feet of black feathers. In a panic, he fell backwards and scurried as fast as he could back towards Eiko.

"Get off! Get off me!" he shouted. But the creature only answered in a loud throng of "coos" and "caws".

"Rodney!" Eiko rushed forward. As soon as she said the name, the avian attack ceased. Martin looked up to see the rooster run up to her and rub itself against her ankles. "It's so good to see you!" She picked him up and gave him a hug.

"Eiko, what the hell." Martin got up to his feet. There she was, smiling in absolute bliss as she rubbed the tuft of the rooster's little head. Martin brushed the dirt and leaves off his clothes and stared. "I ought to pluck out those feathers one by one and boil that runt for dinner."

"No!" She cradled Rodney tighter and backed away. "You can't eat Rodney!"

"Caw!" Rodney agreed.

Martin shook his head in utter disgust. "What are we going to do with him?" he asked. "What am I going to say to Yoshiko when I show up with a girl who shouldn't be here holding on to that overstuffed monstrosity."

"Don't insult him! You'll hurt his feelings."

"Caw, caw!" Rodney responded. He jumped down from Eiko's arms and pecked at the ground a few times before moving forward.

"Where are you going?" Eiko walked after him. In the dark, his black feathers were nearly impossible to see, and it was all she could do to keep the flashlight of her phone on him as he began to pick up pace. Walking after him turned to jogging, jogging to running, and running to outright sprinting, as he wove his way through the path ahead.

Martin did his best to keep up with them, and after just a few minutes they found themselves at the entrance of the teahouse. Rodney darted up the stairs until he got to the doorway, where he stopped suddenly and scratched his talons against the wooden porch in hesitation.

"He stopped," Martin said, gasping for air.

Eiko ran up the short staircase and joined Rodney at the door. Several times, the rooster approached the threshold, but was rebuffed just as he would try to set foot inside. It was as if some invisible wall had been erected in front of him, and he didn't know how to surmount it.

"Something's wrong." Eiko bent down and tried to calm him, but he hopped away in distress. "Ah, Rodney! Don't leave now!"

But it was too late. He vanished into the night. Martin walked up next to Eiko and listened for voices coming from within.

"I don't hear anything," he said. He took a step through the door and tiptoed into the hall.

"There's another door leading inside," he whispered. "It's ajar."

Eiko stood up and followed him in. A light from inside the house illuminated the small open space where the door had been left open, giving them just enough light to see without the use of her flashlight. Martin slid forward until he could rest his hand against the door, then held his breath and peeked through the crack.

"It's useless," a voice from beyond said. Another voice answered, but it was too muffled to hear clearly. Through the opening, he spotted the table where they had eaten lunch earlier that day. Beyond that, he could see the edge of the back door, and between the two he spied some clutter on the floor. Instruments that had before adorned the walls were strewn about: a violin broken in two, a fractured clarinet, and a guitar whose strings had been plucked.

"What do you see?" Eiko asked.

"I don't see Yoshiko or her husband," Martin replied. "But I can't see much of anything in there from here. If I can just slide it open a bit further..." He stuck his fingers in the gap and pushed as lightly as he could. But before even half an inch budged, another hand shot through the gap and flung the door open.

It was the woman from the painting. She grabbed Martin by the collar and tossed him across the room like a ragdoll. He crashed onto the table and slid off the end, still clutching his umbrella as his body recoiled from the force of the throw.

"Sensei!" He heard Yoshiko's voice, and spotted her by the door, hunched over a koto even larger than the one they had found in the attic. Lying on the floor on the other side of the room was Masa. He clenched his trombone in his hands, and was being embraced by the butler, who was speaking words Martin could not hear.

In front of Martin was the woman from the painting. The kasa-obake. He did not know her real name, but he knew her form. She was tall, much taller than he. Her hair was black and flowed down past the small of her back. Her skin was as white as snow, and she wore a kimono of autumn reds. She was beautiful, terribly so, and in her hand was the crimson umbrella of which he had read. Intermittent lines formed and faded across its canopy, seemingly in random careless motions. Like the veins of a beast, they pulsated and stretched, forming outlines of human faces. The more he watched, the more he was drawn to it, more so than he had been drawn to anything in his life. Its visage was as seductive and sinister as the woman holding it.

He traced its lines up to the handle—or what should have been the handle. It wrapped and coiled around her hand, coming in and out of her skin in places. Grotesque as he could have found it, it seemed to be almost naturally a part of her now—as if this was the form it had been meant to take since its creation those hundreds of years prior.

"Ah ha." She slithered past the table and stood over him, folding the umbrella back in as she did. "I know you. You're the one who was looking for that girl. Aiko? Eiko? Oh, I hope you found her." She put a hand over her mouth and giggled.

Martin came to one knee and tried to stand.

"Stop," she said, putting the tip of her umbrella to his chin. "There's no need to stand. In fact, I like it better to see a man bend his knee."

"Where are Tuba and Sami?" he asked.

"Hmph." Her smile faded. "Lost some more friends, have you? Well don't worry. I know where those two are." She pointed down at the canopy of her umbrella. "Just here. Adding their color to my beauty."

Martin said nothing as she unfurled the canopy.

"Watch," she said.

Once again, black lines danced and quivered, until they finally settled into the horrid façade of the brothers Tuba and Sami. Martin averted his eyes and tried not to heave.

"Oh my..." She turned her attention to the umbrella in his hand. "Now, where did you get this?" She bent down and tried to lift it with her hand—her human hand—but Martin held on to it, refusing to let go.

"It's mine," he said. It hurt to breathe. Each inhale he felt like his lungs were being stabbed, but he held on.

"Oh, dear fly. Dear little insect. Must you struggle so?" She took a step back and raised her umbrella up, resting her free hand at the base of the shaft, just above the point where wood melded with flesh.

"It's beautiful, isn't it? Such craftsmanship. Such *color*. It's as vivid and alive as the day it came to me. I see the way you are looking at it. You *want* it, don't you? Don't be shy. Everyone else did too."

"Is that why you killed them?" Martin asked.

"Oh, no!" She laughed, closing the canopy once again. "Does a carpenter bemoan the loss of the trees felled in order to fuel his craft? Does the chef stay awake at night haunted by the animals that were slaughtered so that he could design his dishes?" She slowly stroked the umbrella's red flesh.

"It's been so long, cooped up in this forest. We yearn for more now. Don't we?" She turned around and walked towards Yoshiko and Masa. "How many years have I waited for your *incessant* songs to stop?" She lifted up her leg and crushed a violin under foot. "This entire room is an insult to my very being."

She turned back towards Martin and, with a flick of her wrist, popped the canopy open and raised the umbrella over her head. One by one, the metal ribs that held it aloft twisted and extended, contorting and stretching out across the room like a pit of cobras, each searching for a target. They coiled around the instruments still left decorating the walls then, without warning, flung them to the floor with such force that wooden chips and other debris shot up in every direction.

She worked her way around the room, destroying each instrument until the floor was covered in their shattered remnants. She laughed. Between the crashing and breaking that filled Martin's ears, he could hear her. A giggle at first, then outright hysteria. He used the table for cover as best he could, peering over it only briefly to try to spot Eiko in the hall, but he could not make out her figure in the chaos.

After every string, horn, and drum had been sufficiently smashed to bits, the kasa-obake turned her attention back to Martin.

"Don't worry," she said. "You will add to the color of my masterpiece too. You will be part of something truly beautiful."

She pointed the umbrella forward, and sent each metal rib towards him until he was completely surrounded. Yoshiko was still slumped over her koto. Her butler had collapsed alongside her husband, covered by a mountain of musical debris. Eiko was nowhere to be found. *Thank God. At least she got out.* With no defense left, he turned his gaze back towards the kasa-obake, who smiled back at him.

He closed his eyes, but instead of hearing the sound of metal and laughter, he heard a loud *crack*, not unlike the sound of breaking a piggy bank with a hammer.

"A bad egg, this one. But not one of mine. Oh no, oh no," a man said.

"Uncle, this one seems pretty rotten. Can I throw it too?" a girl said.

Martin opened one eye. The kasa-obake was still there, only now she wasn't smiling. Thick yellow egg yolk dripped down the side of her head, tiny pieces of broken shell mixed in. Before he could blink, another one hit her smack in the temple, exploding its gooey contents all over the side of her face.

"Ha!" The little girl cheered. "Got her!"

Martin looked towards the back door. On the right was the little girl. She held a basket full of brown eggs in one hand and tossed a fresh projectile up and down like a baseball pitcher in the other. Next to her was Yuji. His cheeks still fat and his eyes barely half open, but on his shoulder perched Rodney, who cawed his loudest caw, and jumped in for the attack.

"Ugh!" the kasa-obake screamed. A third egg missed its mark, but splattered against the canopy of her umbrella. "No!" she shouted, redirecting the metal ribs towards the girl, but before they could find their mark Rodney had already reached her, tearing and scratching at her face with his talons.

In the chaos, Martin ran over to Yoshiko and pulled her up.

"Sensei," she said weakly. "I'll be all right."

Her hands were shaking, and there were several cuts along her arms. He pulled her back until she could lean comfortably against the wall.

"I'm sorry," he said. "I wish there was something more I could do."

"No. I should be the one to apologize." She looked over at her husband, who lay unmoving on the floor. "It just became too much for us."

"Martin." He heard Eiko's voice from the hall, and turned around to see her head poking through the doorway. "What should we do?"

"Eiko! Come help me!" he said.

Yoshiko craned her neck towards Eiko and narrowed her eyes.

"I know you," she said. "You're the girl from Sensei's class."

"Nice to meet you." Eiko bowed. "I'm Eiko. Eiko Nigawa"

Yoshiko looked back and forth between the two of them and managed to crack a smile. "Sensei. I didn't know you were that type of man."

Eiko blushed. "It's not like that." She waved her hand in front of her face like she was swatting away a mosquito.

"Can we talk about this some other time, please?" Martin interjected. The sound of battle continued on behind them, with neither side seeming to take the upper hand.

"Go on and help the others," Eiko said. "I think I know what I can do." She took Yoshiko by the hands and slid the koto picks off her fingers. "Can I borrow these?"

Yoshiko nodded. "Hurry."

There was a loud yelp from behind them. The kasa-obake had managed to ensnare Rodney, who let out a cry before being smashed against the floor.

"I'll kill you all!" she shouted after tossing his lifeless body to the side. Yuji and the little girl were next. The kasa-obake coiled the ribs of her umbrella around each of them and pulled them into the air above her. Without any thought or hesitation, Martin picked up the nearest thing he could find—the top half of a saxophone—and threw it at the back of her head. This time, one of the canopy ribs was ready and deflected the attack. With nothing left, Martin rushed at her as fast as he could and jumped, grabbing her by the arm that was attached to the umbrella.

"You have to take it off!" The little girl yelled from above. Martin looked up, then back down at the arm of the kasa-obake. He finally understood. It was the umbrella. It had to come off somehow. *But how? It's part of her arm. It's part of who she is now.*

"Enough of this," the kasa-obake yelled, dropping both her victims to the floor and wrapping every metal limb of her umbrella around Martin instead. She wasted no time squeezing the life from him, until he felt himself beginning to lose consciousness from the pressure.

He didn't hear the first notes play, but at the moment the world began to turn black, he saw Eiko. Sitting there with her knees on a pillow behind the koto, plucking at its strings to form the beautiful lullaby they had heard from the mansion. She kept her eyes focused on the instrument, never once looking away from it. She played and played until the vicelike grip of the kasa-obake deadened and Martin struggled free.

"Stop," the kasa-obake protested, but the strength in her voice had begun to vanish.

Yuji wrapped his arms around her from behind and held her tight. His eyes were open now. Fiercely so, and he looked squarely at Martin.

"Pull!" he shouted.

The ribs of the umbrella had retracted into their proper place. Martin folded it shut and grabbed a hold of it as tight as he could, then pulled.

"It's no good!" he shouted. "I'll tear her whole arm off doing this!"

"Tear it off, then!" Eiko yelled. She looked up, and as she did a string of the koto popped, sending out a wry *pang* across the room. The kasa-obake came to life immediately, pulling her arm back in.

"Get off!" she screeched. Her face, which had once been beautiful and white, was now a mess of blood and scratches. Her kimono was stained and sticky, and the stench of rotten eggs made Martin's stomach churn. With the last of his strength, he gripped the umbrella with both hands and planted a foot in her stomach, then threw every ounce of himself behind one last pull.

As he did, the fabric of the canopy began to tear, and the umbrella itself seemed to cry out in pain.

There was a loud snap. Yuji and Martin fell backwards, the kasa-obake still trapped in his powerful arms. She screamed.

"My beauty! My beauty!" Martin flung the umbrella as far away as he could, and when it landed it began to bend and writhe against the floor, sending its ribs shooting out in every direction. One of them flew towards him, striking him in the head before he had a second to react.

His vision blurred and, with his heart pounding out of his chest, he looked back over at Yuji, whose eyes had begun to roll back in his head. The lights around them began to flicker, then in an instant, there was darkness.

Amidst the umbra, he heard voices. Thousands and thousands of voices, like a chorus whose verse had risen to its crescendo. He didn't know if it was the blow he had taken to the head, or if it was just a hallucination, but as the lights sparked back to life, he saw the flock—just as it had appeared to him along the banks of the River Matsu those long weeks ago. Only now, the ravenous brood flooded into the room by the hundreds. Their black eyes focused on only one thing: the kasa-obake, both the woman and the monster from who she had been forcibly separated. They pecked and tore and rent until there was nothing left, not even a splinter.

When the chaos settled, he looked back at Eiko, who had turned the koto on its side and taken cover behind it. She raised her head slightly, checking to see if the danger had passed, before rushing to Martin's side.

"Are you all right?" she asked, lifting him onto his feet.

Martin nodded as he surveyed the damage. The little girl stood over Yuji, who moaned in exhaustion but seemed mostly unhurt. The butler, who had used his own body to protect Yoshiko's husband from the indiscriminate destruction, rose up to one knee and stayed there. A still sadness in his eyes told Martin all he needed to know. Masa was gone.

"Sensei." He heard Yoshiko call from the corner. He ran over to her and fell to his knees at her side. Her breathing was labored, and her voice was nothing more than a whisper. She looked over at the butler and the unmoving body of her husband, but instead of crying out in agony, she looked back at Martin and forced a smile.

"Thank you," she whispered, taking his hand in hers. She mustered the last of her strength and spoke slowly. "But I have to go now, too. Masa is calling me. I can hear his song."

Martin shook his head, not knowing what to say. He opened his mouth, but as he did, she squeezed his hand, begging him to let her finish. With her last breath, she leaned in close to him.

"Remember us," she whispered. "Remember… that we once lived."

CHAPTER TWENTY-SEVEN

The Pyre

Martin placed Yoshiko's body next to her husband's. Her hands were still warm to the touch, and she still smiled as if she could spring back to life at any moment. Martin knew that she was gone, though. The light in her eyes had dulled, and despite the last smile on her lips, her chest no longer rose and fell with the beat of her heart. He did his best to clean the dust and debris from her face and hair before finally taking a step back to say goodbye.

The butler was doing much the same with Masa's body. When he was satisfied, he took his place next to the survivors, who watched over the departed couple in silence. There was a lump in Martin's throat where his voice had been, stifling all words. He wanted to apologize, but Yoshiko and Masa were not there to hear him anymore. In place of words, tears welled in his eyes. He looked at them until he could look no more, then turned away, his body trembling.

Eiko took his arm in her hands and buried her face in his shirt, but she too had no words of comfort to steal away his grief. Amidst quiet tears, the butler stepped forward, placing his hand on his chest and began to sing. His baritone voice trilled a Japanese song that Martin had heard only once before, and wouldn't have understood if the little girl had not come to his side to translate.

As the sound of his voice grew, she managed to say in English the words that he was singing:

> *"Life is brief.*
> *Fall in love, maidens*
> *before the crimson bloom*
> *fades from your lips*
> *before the tides of passion*
> *cool within you,*
> *for those of you*
> *who know no tomorrow.*
>
> *"Life is brief.*
> *Fall in love, maidens*
> *before his hands*
> *take up his boat*
> *before the flush of his cheeks fades*
> *for those of you*
> *who will never return here.*
>
> *"Life is brief.*
> *Fall in love, maidens*
> *before the boat drifts away*
> *on the waves*
> *before the hand resting on your shoulder*
> *becomes frail*
> *for those who will never*
> *be seen here again.*
>
> *"Life is brief.*
> *Fall in love, maidens*

before the raven tresses
begin to fade
before the flame in your hearts
flicker and die
for today, once passed
is never to come again."

At the song's peak, something happened. Through tears streaming unbroken from his eyes, he spied the umbrella that Shimodoi had given him. An invisible hand began to draw upon it, changing every detail as it did. Its orange hues turned to indigo, and small, distant stars began to form across its upper hemisphere. Martin quietly picked it up and unfurled it, and its expanded interior turned into a sunrise sky. Under the canopy, the stars gathered to form the image of a landscape: a line of trees, and below them, a rooster standing in front of a cave.

Martin ran his hand over the image of the rooster, as the sky of the umbrella turned a pre-dawn blue. Where in his dreams he had once seen the flock of hens, there now stood a line of people, hundreds and hundreds of them, stretching around the circumference of the canopy. At the very front, just where the mouth of the cave opened, were the two bartenders that had saved him.

When the song ended, the butler gave a solemn bow along with Yuji and the little girl. Wiping the tears from his eyes, Martin closed the umbrella and bowed as deeply as he could. One by one, they exited the tea house and gathered together at the base of the stairs that lead back towards the mansion.

"This one will stay behind. There is one final duty that he must perform," the butler said. He turned to Martin and bowed his head. "Forgiveness. this one would ask the good man Yuji to escort you back to Toyama City."

Yuji stepped forward and put his giant hand on Martin's shoulder. "It's for the best. It is, it is," he said.

"It doesn't feel right to leave." Martin looked at the butler. "Please, let me stay. Let me help out. It's the least I can do." He began to choke on his own words. "If I had gotten here sooner. If I had just moved quicker, then maybe…"

The butler put up his hand and shook his head. "The gentleman must not blame himself. It is this one who should be ashamed, for he could not protect them."

"You killed the monster!" the little girl piped up. "And Lady Yoshiko smiled at the end. I'm sure she was grateful!" Her face was puffy and red with insistence. The rest of the group agreed. Martin tried to protest, but Yuji squeezed his shoulder and began to pull him away.

"We'll be seein' ya. We will, we will." Yuji gave the butler a wave.

"One moment," the butler called out. He put his hand in his coat pocket and produced a thin, folded envelope. "A gift." He pressed the envelope into Martin's hand.

"A letter?" Martin asked.

"A message, one might say." The butler gave the slightest hint of a smile. "To be opened when the gentleman feels ready to do so. No sooner. No later." There was something small and round inside the envelope, but Martin had no idea what. He looked at it for a time then folded it back in half and slid it into his pocket.

They each said their goodbyes, then parted ways. Martin and Eiko followed Yuji on the path back through the woods, but when they came to the boar statue, they kept going straight instead of turning towards the mansion. They walked in silence for nearly a half an hour. The trees slowly became less sparse, until they came to a dirt road at the top of a steep hill. Yuji's rusted red truck sat parked overlooking the land below.

"The chickens are back in their coops. They are, they are," he said, pointing a finger out towards the valley below. Martin came up beside him and looked down in surprise. Even in the moonlight, he could clearly make out the rooftops of what seemed like a hundred large-scale chicken coops. Beyond them stood a giant barn, and beyond that, barely visible in the distant dark, was a house.

"Is this your farm?" Martin asked.

"It is, it is," Yuji answered. "Come and visit us, when you've the chance. We could use another farmhand since all of ours are gone."

"Uncle," the little girl chided. "He's not a farmer."

"Oh ho! That's right, that's right. But come anyway. I'm sure the hens would enjoy the company."

Yuji turned around and opened the rear door to the truck, ushering Martin and Eiko inside. The old leather seats were torn and their color was faded, but no less comfortable despite the cramped cabin. Eiko followed him in, taking the seat behind the little girl.

"How are you feeling?" she asked after buckling her seatbelt.

"Like I'm in a dream," he said. "Like I'm in a nightmare."

Yuji turned the key and the truck sputtered to life. Then, they were off. Eiko took Martin's hand in hers and put it over her heart.

"Does this feel real?" she asked. Martin cleared his throat, suddenly aware of his own embarrassment. She brought his hand up to her cheek and rested her face against it.

"How about this?" she asked again. Her brown eyes were bright and alive. Her skin was soft and smooth. Her nose was small, and her lips were thin, but he found himself captivated by just how full of life she was. An irresistible vigor that stood in such stark contrast to the way Martin had lived until now. With her head still nestled in his hand, he leaned over and pressed his lips against hers. It was a brief but passionate kiss that was interrupted when the truck began to lurch up a severe and uneven incline.

When they reached the top, the bright light of a distant light caught their attention. It was the tea house, set ablaze as a funeral pyre against the night sky. Without stopping, Yuji whispered a quiet prayer under his breath. Martin watched the flames, entranced by the way they stretched up and licked the sky. He took a deep breath, and waved goodbye to the home he would never see again.

As they moved on and the fire faded behind them, he began to say the words of the last verse that the butler had sung in eulogy. His voice cracked and broke, but after the first line, the others in the car picked up the verse and sang with him.

> *"Life is brief.*
> *Fall in love, maidens*
> *before the raven tresses*
> *begin to fade*
> *before the flame in your hearts*
> *flicker and die*
> *for today, once passed*
> *is never to come again."*

*

At some point as they began their descent from the hills towards Toyama City, Martin and Eiko were overtaken by exhaustion, and fell asleep in the old leather seats of Yuji's truck. He dreamed of nothing and nowhere, and when he awoke, he and Eiko were lying in the grass along the banks of the River Matsu.

Martin looked at Eiko, still sleeping, and nudged her softly until she began to stir. The early rays of dawn illuminated the world around them, and the sound of moving cars and people's voices were distinctly clear from above where they lay.

"Eiko." He nudged her again. "We're back."

She slowly opened her eyes and stretched her body out in the grass like a cat. "Back where?"

"Back in Toyama. Where else?"

"Oh!" She shot up and almost slipped in the grass. "Why are we in the grass by a river?"

"I don't know," Martin answered. He stood up and looked around. It was a familiar scene, almost exactly where Yuji and the little girl had picked him up on their rickety riverboat almost a full month before.

"I think I know about where we are though. If we go up these stairs and down that road we should end up at the station," he said, brushing grass off of his pants.

"Which means my apartment should be over there." She pointed across the bridge, then looked back at him. "Shall we?"

They ascended the staircase up to the road above and began their trek.

"Sheesh," Eiko said as they crossed the bridge. "It would've been nice if they had at least asked us where we wanted to be dropped off. How did they even get us down there, anyway? Did they roll us down?"

Martin looked over to where they had come from and paused. "I think there was something they wanted me to see," he said. He looked down into the river below, his own reflection staring back up at him. The man in the reflection was someone he had never seen before. He studied the contours of his face in the water. There was someone there that hadn't been there before:

A Martin he had never known, or had long forgotten. Before he could get too attached, a rock splashed against the surface of the water, distorting his image.

"Gotcha!" Eiko laughed. She leaned against him and stared into the water below.

"You're dumb," he said, flicking a pebble from the arm rails.

"Oh, yeah? Is that what you think?" she said, pulling a piece of paper from her pocket and unfolding it.

"What is that?" he asked before immediately realizing what it was. "Oh, no."

"Hee hee." She giggled as she traced her fingers over the UFO sketch.

"What's so funny?" Martin asked. "I thought it was a pretty good little drawing."

"It's not that." She looked up. "It's my first love letter."

"I don't know if you can call that a love letter. It's five words and a doodle of a spaceship."

"Are you saying it's not?"

"I..." Martin shrugged. "I guess it is. But it seems pretty pathetic for a love letter. Don't you think?"

"It's perfect." She folded it back carefully and put it in her pocket.

They left the bridge and continued down the street towards Eiko's apartment. The sun was barely visible as it rose above the distant mountains, and more and more people and vehicles crowded the streets with each passing minute. They found her car in the parking garage across the street, but neither of them questioned how it had gotten there.

"Sensei," she said as they came to the front door of the lobby. She bit her lower lip, and looked away. "Do you think it's all right if I keep taking your class?"

"Why wouldn't it be?"

"I don't know. I thought it might be awkward." She folded her arms across her chest.

"Were you worried about it being awkward while you were lying to my boss about me getting you pregnant and punching me in the gut?"

"No. Not one bit," she said.

Martin sighed. "Then why would you be worried about it now? Although in class you're not my girlfriend. You're my student. So, you have to do as I say."

"Hmph," she protested. "Who said I was your girlfriend, hmm?"

"Are you saying you're not?" He laughed.

"No…" She smiled. "Well, if that's the case, why don't we have a lesson right now? I have missed some classes, after all." He put his arm around her waist and called the elevator down. There was no more need for words. The elevator door opened, and they stepped through, together.

CHAPTER TWENTY-EIGHT

The Rooster Crows

He spent the majority of his vacation with Eiko in her apartment. It was only natural. Riding the train back and forth to his apartment in Takaoka every day was a burden, and his own apartment paled in comparison to hers. They spent their mornings at various cafés and eateries throughout the city. In the afternoons they would go to the mall or catch a movie. With the warmer weather they occasionally ventured out of the city to other towns. The town of Himi along the coast was his favorite. They spent the day at a botanical garden there and then took a small boat tour afterward.

During the evenings, they went grocery shopping for different ingredients, then mixed and mashed them into various delicacies. Neither of them was particularly talented in the kitchen, but they did their best and had fun while they were at it. At night, they watched old reruns of "The X-Files" until Martin could no longer take it.

The week passed quickly, and before he knew it, it was Monday night. He kissed Eiko goodbye and took the last train back to Takaoka. It was just before midnight when the train pulled into the station. Martin took the south exit as he always did and walked the two blocks until he reached the store where Shimodoi worked. He hadn't an opportunity to meet him since his trip to Yoshiko's mansion, so he crossed the street and pushed the front door open.

"Shimodoi!" he called out as he walked to the liquor cabinet in the back. The shop was empty.

"Shimodoi!" he called again. He grabbed the first six-pack he could get his hands on and walked back towards the front of the store. There was no one at the register, but the door to the back room was open. Cans of soda and boxes of food lined the walls. He waited for a moment before taking a look around to make sure no one else was coming in, then slid across the counter and passed through the open door.

A ladder was set out in the middle of the room, leading up to the air duct that Martin had climbed up into several months prior. He peeked back out, making sure that there was still no one else in the store, then silently grabbed on to the rails and tip-toed up the steps. When he reached the top, he stuck his head into the open vent and poked around. He didn't know what to expect, but when his eyes met with nothing but an empty duct, his heart sank.

"Excuse me?" A voice from below startled him.

"Oh!" Martin rushed back down the steps of the ladder. "I'm sorry, I just, I—" He faltered. In front of him was a short, middle-aged man wearing the same blue and white shop uniform that Shimodoi wore. The name on his tag said, "Tanaka", and he looked at Martin with eyes that were half reprehensive and half frightened.

"No one was here," he lied, "and I thought I heard something, so I came back here and—"

"Can you leave?" the little man said.

"Right. Right, sorry." Martin bowed and quickly exited out to the store. The little man followed, closing the door behind them as he did.

Martin pointed at the six-pack on the counter and took out his wallet. "I don't need a bag," he said. The little man still looked skeptical, but took his money and rang up the till.

"No Shimodoi tonight?" Martin asked.

"Shimo-who?" the little man said.

"Shimodoi. The teenage brat who's usually working nights here?"

The little man shook his head and handed Martin his change. "Thank you for shopping with us. Have a good night," he said, ending the conversation.

"Uh, thanks," he replied. *Maybe it's a new guy?* He picked up his beer and walked out the front.

When he got home, he flicked on his bedroom lights and dropped the six-pack in his fridge. He hadn't spent too much time in his own room over the past week, and the air had a musky stench to it from being closed off for too long. After taking off his clothes and changing into his pajamas, Martin opened up the one large window his room had and looked out into the May night. It was cool, but not cold enough to keep him from staring at the night stars. The same stars that dotted the umbrella which he now kept hung inside his closet.

He took care to set his alarm, and laid out everything he needed for work the next morning. On his desk was the letter that the old butler had given him, still unopened. Martin had thought to open it several times before. He picked it up for a moment and ran his hands along the edges. Whenever he thought it was about time to open it, a sharp sting of regret would overtake him and he would set it back down.

"To be opened whenever the gentleman feels ready to do so. No sooner. No later," the butler had said. It had been a full week since the events in the mountains, but for Martin, the grief was still too near. For now, the letter wasn't going anywhere, so he placed it back on his desk and climbed into bed.

The ringing of his phone woke him before his alarm the next morning. It was a group text from Manager, requesting all staff be present for a mandatory meeting thirty minutes early. Martin sighed. Trains from Takaoka only left once an hour, and the 8:47 A.M. train had already come and gone. There was nothing to do but take his normal train there and arrive at his usual time. Nor was there a point in responding. He would get an earful either way, so he buried his phone back underneath his pillow and stared at the ceiling for a few minutes before rolling out of bed and starting his day.

As expected, texts started coming in from Chris just after he boarded his train at Takaoka Station.

>Manager threat level: Chernobyl. Where the hell are you?

On the train<

>WHAT!? ETA?

30 mins<

>Your funeral

If she wanted me there so badly, she should've come and picked me up herself<

She knows when my train leaves<

>OK Martin, you go ahead and tell that to her when you get here

Martin didn't respond, and instead dropped his phone back into his jacket pocket. A deep-seated resentment stirred within him, which he hadn't realized was there until that very moment. His phone buzzed again a few more times during the ride, but he ignored it. Instead, he ground his teeth together and watched the scenery pass until he arrived at Toyama Station.

He made no effort to hurry. Instead, he meandered his way down the road, stopping properly at intersections and waiting until the walk sign flashed each time. By the time he strolled in, it was 10:25. Chaos had already engulfed the office—and not just yelling, but outright screaming could be heard from the main lobby. He shrugged his bag off his shoulder and stopped in the staff room first, setting it on his desk before straightening his jacket and joining his fellow instructors.

They stood all with their heads bowed down, staring at the floor like whipped dogs who had just been caught tearing up the upholstery. On the floor were shards of glass, and behind the main desk, the painting of the woman in the rain—the kasa-obake as he now knew it to be—had fallen from the spot Mika had placed it and shattered into a thousand pieces.

"Martin!" Manager yawped as she saw him come down the hall. "Where the hell have you been?" Her face was beet red and puffy, and by the looks of things she had been yelling at them for the better part of half an hour. Mika stood behind her, pale as a ghost. She raised her head ever so slightly to acknowledge him, then shot it back down.

"On the train," he answered flatly. There was no point in making up stories or apologizing now. "I do live in Takaoka, you know. It's not close."

Chris looked up, only to shake his head at Martin. "Don't do it." His eyes said everything that his mouth couldn't.

"Excuse me?" she said. "Did I hear you right? Was that an... an *excuse*?"

"Did I stutter?"

Her expression soured. "Just when I thought you were starting to get it. You're a sorry excuse for an employee and an even sorrier excuse for a teacher. You're trash. Garbage. A stain on the pride of this company!" She seethed.

"I'm sorry you feel that way." Martin leaned against the counter. "But I'm here now, so why don't you tell me what I've missed?"

She slammed her hand down on the counter so hard that her own purse fell to the floor. Her eyes were bloodshot, and her breathing was so heavy that Martin thought she might have a stroke right then and there.

"Manager!" Mika called from behind her. "P-please, calm down!" Absolute terror was written on her face. As Manager turned to look at her, she began to visibly tremble.

"Calm down? Calm down, is that what you said?" Martin stepped forward to interrupt, but as he did, his stepped on something hard that had fallen out of Manager's purse. He looked down to see a short, green lanyard. When he moved his foot, he saw a key at its end.

"What is this?" He said, bending down to pick it up. But the Manager did not hear him. She tore into Mika with such vulgarity that Mika began to break down and cry. Tears mixed with mascara, sending black lines down her face. Martin turned to Chris, but Chris's eyes had emptied. He stared on like a gargoyle at the scene that unfolded before him, unable to act.

"What is this?" Martin asked again, louder this time. Colby and Stacy looked up at the key in his hands.

"Martin..." Colby started, but Stacy grabbed his arm and shook her head.

He walked up behind Manager and grabbed her by the shoulder, spinning her around and shoving the key in her face.

"What the hell is this?" he asked for the third time.

For a moment, she looked as if she was about to strike Martin with the back of her hand, but then her face paled as the key took shape in front of her. There was a chink in her armor now, and he pressed at it.

"You lied to me," he said. "You said *I* lost this. You held this over my head for months. Then, you tried to use me to get Mika fired. I knew I hadn't lost it. I knew it, but you made me believe that I had. You lied to me."

"Hmph." She snorted. "What makes you think that's your key?"

"You're lying to me right now. This is my key. This is the lanyard it was on."

"You don't know what you're talking about. And even if it were true, what are you going to do about it, huh? You're my employee. My property. You speak when spoken to. I say jump, you say how high. You teach because I will it so. What would you ever do without this job?"

"I'll start my own cram school," he shot back. "I don't need you or this job. I can make my own way."

"Ha!" She chortled. "*You* start a school? *You*? You can barely keep your own students at this one!"

"We'll see about that," he said. Martin looked over at Colby and Stacy. "You knew about this didn't you? You knew about this, and you let me believe her lies."

The two teachers were silent, which was all the answer he needed.

"I thought so," he said, throwing the key on the floor in front of the Manager. He took one last look at everyone around him, then turned and walked away.

"Get back here!" Manager shouted. "You'll never work in this industry again! I'll send your name out to every other company in the country. I'll blacklist you! You'll be through!" Her voice cracked, but Martin kept walking.

"Martin!" she shouted as he picked up his bag from the staff room. "Martin, get back here!" She shouted and shouted and shouted until the door closed behind him and he could hear her shout no more.

*

It was eleven o'clock when Eiko opened the door for him, wearing nothing but underwear and a tank top.

"What are you doing here?" she asked.

His face was still red hot with anger, and his fists had been clenched so tightly that his fingernails had dug into the skin of his palms.

"What's wrong?" She took him in her arms and led him inside.

"I quit my job," he said. "I quit and I'm never going back."

She sat him on the couch and fetched him a glass of water, listening as he described the events that had just happened. As the words poured out, he began to understand the gravity of what he had done, and suddenly became fearful that he had made the wrong decision. When he was finished, he buried his head in his hands.

"So, when are we going to start?" she asked.

"Start what?"

"Your school. You told her you're going to start one, right? Or was that just the empty posturing of an angry man?"

"You aren't mad?" he asked

"Mad at what?" She put her hands on her hips and leaned over him.

THE ROOSTER CROWS

Martin looked up at her. Her orange hair was a tangled and messy, her lips were thin and serious. On the outside, he saw a small woman in pink boy-shorts and a white tank top, but in her heart, he saw a colossus that put his own misplaced doubts at ease.

"Well?" She poked a finger in his cheek. "What are we waiting for? We need to come up with a plan. A name. A way to get students. Study materials and lesson plans. Do you remember that CD you made for me? We'll have to have you do more of those. They were helpful. Oh, and we'll need a place. Can't very well do it in your apartment. Wait, doesn't your company own your apartment?"

"Oh, crap." Martin had forgotten that small detail. He let out a loud moan and threw his hands up in the air.

"It's OK, it's OK!" She reassured him. "We can do it here, but we should probably move your stuff over as soon as possible. I don't think your former boss will waste much time getting you off the company payroll."

"Right," he agreed.

"Let me take a shower and get dressed," she said, taking off her shirt and walking down the hall. "We'll get your stuff all packed up and over here today. Then we can go to work!"

They took Eiko's car back to Takaoka after sharing a brief lunch together. It was an exceptionally warm May afternoon, and they drove with the windows down and the radio blaring. It was a slightly longer drive than it was a train ride to get to his apartment, but fortunately for him, everything was as he had left it.

Martin had always kept the minimum number of things in his apartment to sustain his day-to-day life, but despite this, the process of packing and cleaning took several hours. When the room was finally empty and his bags were packed, he laid down with Eiko on the carpet and stared up at the ceiling he had looked at every morning for the past half-year.

"When I woke up this morning," he said. "I didn't think that any of this would happen."

He looked over at the table. The only items remaining unpacked were his umbrella, which sat unfurled in the corner, and the envelope that the butler had given him. He lifted the letter up and ran his hands over it, as he had done many times before. Eiko stood up and came beside him.

"Why don't you open it?" she said. "Now's as good a time as any."

Martin nodded. He ran his finger slowly beneath the seal until it tore open. There was no paper inside. Just a round object that he slid out onto his hand. It was gold, around the size of a quarter, with several markings that Martin didn't recognize.

"It's a coin," he said. It had the character for the number "ten" on it.

"An old ten-yen coin?" Eiko took it from him and looked at it closely. "Wow, this thing is ancient. From the Meiji Era. Nineteenth century. But I don't get it. Why would the butler give you a ten-yen coin?"

Martin took it back in his hands and smiled. "I think I know."

He pressed the coin against his heart, then let it fall into his shirt pocket. On the canopy of his umbrella, the unseen artist painted the figure of one last person standing in front of the cave, an arm stretched above his head.

Martin tapped the coin in his pocket, then took Eiko's hand in his own. "Come on, Eiko," he said. "Let's go home."

Made in the USA
Middletown, DE
11 September 2020